OF
THE
FLESH

OF THE FLESH

18 STORIES OF MODERN HORROR

THE BOROUGH PRESS

The Borough Press
An imprint of HarperCollins*Publishers* Ltd
1 London Bridge Street
London SE1 9GF

www.harpercollins.co.uk

HarperCollins*Publishers*
Macken House,
39/40 Mayor Street Upper,
Dublin 1
D01 C9W8

First published by HarperCollins*Publishers* 2024

2

Contents

Fight, Flight, Freeze   1
Susan Barker

Flight 2212   18
J K Chukwu

The Fruiting Body   28
Bridget Collins

Daisies   52
Mariana Enríquez
Translated by Megan McDowell

The Broccoli Eel   71
Michel Faber

Sketchy   82
Lewis Hancox

Apples   110
Emilia Hart

Waffle Thomas   129
Ainslie Hogarth

Shade   140
Robert Lautner

The Smiling African Uncle   158
Adorah Nworah

Rosheen   170
Irenosen Okojie

Carcinisation   185
Lucy Rose

Going Large   197
Lionel Shriver

Bob-a-Job   212
James Smythe

Fairies   230
Lavie Tidhar

Ghost Kitchen   243
Francine Toon

The Old Lion   252
Evie Wyld

Mouse   264
Louisa Young

About the Authors   277

Fight, Flight, Freeze

by Susan Barker

No moon tonight and the sea's as black and vast as the starless sky. A wave crashes over me from behind, pushing me under, and I kick back to the surface again. Spluttering, coughing up salt. Should the water in this part of the world be so fucking cold? My flailing barely warms the blood. But I can't swim in because she's standing up to her knees in the shallows, between me and the empty beach.

Watching.

She follows when I doggy-crawl parallel to the shoreline, her backless hospital gown trailing in the surf. If I swim towards the sand, to a depth I can tiptoe, she moves out to meet me, forcing my retreat. Ten minutes ago I floated on my back to conserve energy, but could feel the riptide pulling me out. Panicking, I fought my way back in to tread water in place again, wary of her dark, malevolent silhouette.

This beach is, what, two miles long? Three? The night disorientates, and besides, I can't swim it whatever the distance. How long until dawn? Will someone – a fisherman or early morning bather – come and help me then?

*

The flight was eleven hours from Heathrow. I watched the other passengers board, tense in my seat, impatient for take-off, for the plane to carry me continents and oceans away. When we

1

levelled out, I pulled my eye mask down, and in the minutes before the zolpidem kicked in I thought: six thousand miles. Will that be enough?

In the sweaty backpackers' hostel bar, I sat in the corner for a view of the other drinkers and the street. I'm thirty-four. Too old for a dormitory of gap year travellers, but I'd just quit my job and it was sixty ringgit a night. Even at 10 p.m. the city was humid, the bar's fans whirring, windows open to the Chinatown aroma of frying noodles and the stink of drains and durians. A tanned Swede was speaking of jungle trekking in Taman Negara and an Orang Asli village where he'd learnt to shoot darts from a blowpipe for ten ringgit (*they're like, hunter gatherers, y'know? They live off the rainforest . . .*), and I began to feel hopeful. I was about as far from cold and drizzly November London as you can get.

An Aussie in a loud batik shirt sat on the barstool next to me. Fortyish, white and bald, with the cheerful, whisky-burnt look of a guy who can't enter a bar without lassoing the nearest stranger into conversation.

I live in Bangkok, he said to me. But the mozzies they got here . . .

He cocked a Birkenstocked foot up from the barstool, pointed at a red carbuncle on his ankle.

Fucking savages. You getting bitten like this too?

Just got here, I said.

Looks like the sun's flayed some strips off yer though.

I touched the raw and tender spot on my nose.

It's frostbite, I said.

In *Malaysia*?

I shut myself in the walk-in freezer of the restaurant where I work.

The Australian shivered, despite the heat.

I thought those things had safety latches.

I wrapped my sore, chilblained fingers around my beer. Some tourists came in the bar and I scanned them, heart thrashing like a trapped bird. If I'm safe here, I thought, my body hasn't caught up.

*

Another wave ambushes me from behind. I splutter, gasp and cough. Sinuses burning, ears blocked. I should watch the waves coming in, rise with them. But though she's still as one of those Antony Gormley statues, I daren't look away from her. Too dark to see her expression, but her enmity is a force. I pant, legs aching. They'll cramp if I don't rest, so I make another attempt at swimming to a depth I can stand. One stroke, two strokes, and she strides forwards through the water. Up to her waist. I swim back, terrified.

For the first time, I regret never learning how to swim properly. I got kicked out of a lesson in Year 8 for dunking that girl too long, and never went back. The trouble was I'd no desire to be in that chilly, chlorinated pool on Wednesday mornings. And desire, for whatever sends the neurotransmitters of pleasure cascading through my brain, has always been my North Star. Perhaps it's why, at thirteen, I got into shoplifting and Class B drugs. Why I dropped out of uni to bartend and party in Ibiza instead. Why every relationship I've had started as an infidelity. Why, going over menu changes in the office that night, I kissed Julien.

There's a moral lesson here, about the things we must or mustn't do, irrespective of desire. And above the water, her silhouette's just a head and torso now – the direst consequence to date of never having taken that lesson on board.

*

Cal was the name of the bald guy in the backpacker hostel bar. Cal from Brisbane, now a long-term expat, teaching EFL in Bangkok.

So, why Malaysia? he asked.

I have family here, so.

You visiting them?

No. I just . . . needed to get out of London.

Cal raised an eyebrow, intrigued.

What went down in London?

I left my partner.

Cal looked sympathetic. But was that a hint of sexual opportunism I detected there?

Shit. Sorry, mate. I get it though. I moved to Thailand in 2012 after my divorce.

My gaze darted nervously to someone entering the bar. A hippy-ish girl. Nose ring, multicoloured hairwraps, strappy vest and harem pants. Not her.

You okay out here on your own, Sara? Cal asked. You seem *spooked*.

I swallowed some Tiger beer.

Just jet lag, I said. Day or two, I'll be fine.

I woke in the dormitory the next afternoon, shivering from the air con, all the other bunks empty of the sleeping bodies I'd glimpsed in the hallway light the night before. I showered, changed into a dress and flip-flops, then walked out into the blazing heat. I had no guidebook, no plan. Only my wallet, passport and dysregulated nervous system. I wandered through Petaling Street's market stalls of Abidas, Dolcy & Gabanna and Louise Vuitton, in and out of vermillion-dark Chinese temples where, in desperation, I waggled sticks of smoking incense before the altars of Guanyin, goddess of mercy, and Guandi, god of war. I wandered from Chinatown to the old Colonial District, through the streets of crumbling historic buildings, constantly seeking out the shade of covered, colonnaded walkways. All the while, on a loop in my head:

Am I safe here?

Is it over now?

Have I shaken her off?

Darkness fell as I walked from Little India to Merdeka Square, and the wailing melancholy prayer call rose up from the National

Mosque. Sweaty and grimy, I circled back round to Chinatown, short-cutting through alleyways behind restaurants, vents pumping out greasy cooking fumes. I hadn't eaten that day, so I stopped at a brightly lit hawker stall and choked down a plate of Hokkein mee – forcing noodles, strips of pork and fried egg into my stomach's clenched dread. A chef by profession, I'm hardwired to reverse engineer every meal; in a place like this I'd chat to the cook, tapping notes into my phone. But the noodles were flavourless to me. I ate them grimly, determinedly, until something caught in my throat and I gagged.

I reached finger and thumb into the back of my mouth. Slowly I pulled out a long, long red hair.

*

During the months Julien was seeing me in secret, I looked Natasha up on Instagram constantly. Her account was set to private, but the La Banquette account – set up by Julien, run by me – followed her. She only had 157 followers – friends and family she documented her 'cancer journey' for, posting about her medications, side effects and moods, with photographs of her smiling with an IV in her arm, or giving the thumbs up in a beanie from her hospital bed. Pretty still, despite losing her Lizzie Siddal wavy auburn hair. Julien was often in her grid, with Natasha's gushing commentary about his ratatouille or 'miracle soups', or how he was reading Elena Ferrante aloud to her ('better than any audiobook . . .'), or sang her French lullabies before bed, or just about her gratitude to have married 'the best human alive'.

Scrolling through the photographs, I let my judgements fly. Performative. Sympathy-seeking. Over-sharer. *Basic.* In my more vindictive moments I wanted to leave comments: 'Julien didn't go to CrossFit on Tuesday. He came to my flat and we fucked for an hour . . .' I'm aware it doesn't cast me in the most flattering light, this corrosive jealousy of a woman with cancer. But it wasn't possible to love him the way I did and not want to rip out her chemo-port and shove it down her throat.

Why don't you hire a carer? I asked Julien as we lay tangled in shadows and churned-up bedsheets one afternoon. Y'know, to ease the burden.

Natasha's not a burden, Julien replied.

But you're so stressed these days. You do so much . . .

We *don't* need a carer.

I was quiet for a minute. Then, timidly, I asked,

Can you sing to me?

Sing to you? he said, surprised. What d'you want me to sing?

Something in French. A lullaby.

I don't know any.

None?

C'mon, Sara, he said. You're not six.

*

The sea chops harder and I thrash to keep my head above water. Panting, I feel every cigarette I ever smoked, including all the ones I sneaked after my shifts, though I officially quit in 2018. A pain sharpens in my side. A stitch. My calves are cramping too, and I feel more numb than cold now. This is all very bad.

I stare through the night at her. Ominous and still as the waves crash against her chest and the long strands still dangling from her head. At my lowest points, on the empty, heartsick days off work, waiting impatiently for Julien to text or call, I'd look at photographs of her and think, *hurry up and die.*

Another moral lesson here: be careful what you wish for.

Breathless, lungs heaving, I weakly shout.

I left him. He's yours now.

(Silence)

He was always yours.

(Silence)

I know what you want and I'm not doing it.

The dark shape of her moves forwards. Up to her neck.

*

After her funeral in late July, Julien threw himself back into running the restaurant. I worked long hours there too, but he was cool and professional in his interactions with me – a chill that gusted into our relationship out of work. We scheduled the same days off but he spent them going on long runs through Epping Forest, or 'sorting out' his and Natasha's house in Hackney Wick. Sometimes he went to Lyon to visit Natasha's parents, to whom he was still close. He was evasive when I tried to make plans, but I told myself to be patient. He just needed more time.

Then one afternoon I came in early for a shift and walked in on him kneeling on the kitchen floor. He was alone, but looking up as though someone was standing over him. *Je suis désolé* . . . he whispered. Then some words I couldn't translate, though I caught, *Tashka*. Confused, I interrupted,

What are you doing?

Julien looked over his shoulder. Startled. Embarrassed. Angry.

Nothing.

You said Tashka.

He got up from his knees, shot me a look of irritation. Tashka had been his nickname for her. I hesitated,

Have you thought about seeing a grief counsellor? I think you might need help processing stuff . . .

Stuff?

You've been stalled. Not moving on.

Moving on to what, exactly?

The phone rang out in the restaurant. Shaking his head at me, Julien went out to the bar.

I stood in the empty kitchen. There was something on the floor tiles where he'd been kneeling. I went and picked it up. A kirby grip: black metal, woven with strands of long red hair.

*

In the muggy hostel bar, ceiling fan blades rattled and whirred. Some Germans at the next table shrieked *nein!* as a tower of Jenga blocks fell.

You sure it wasn't, like, a waitress's or something? Cal asked.

No redheads on the staff rota, I replied. None.

I was already drunk by the time Cal returned from his day trip to the Batu Caves (*'U2 should do a gig there!'*). Now I was wasted and everything came out in a reckless rush. My affair with Julien, Natasha's cancer and Julien's behaviour after her death. I sounded deranged, but I didn't care. I needed to unburden myself to someone – even Cal.

Then I started finding long red hair everywhere, I said. In my hairbrush. In the plughole when I was showering. And tonight, in my noodles . . .

Cal glanced at my hair, short and black.

And yer think, what, she put it there?

Yes. As a warning.

Cal's brow furrowed. He was doing his best to appear sympathetic, but I detected the pity and mockery beneath. And that hint of sexual interest too (I was a hot mess, but hot messes aren't known for their propriety).

Then I started *smelling* her, I said.

Smelling her?

This toxic chemical smell. From the chemo or embalming fluids . . . And lavender pillow spray.

Cal couldn't suppress his smirk.

Lavender pillow spray?

Julien said she needed it to help her sleep . . . Anyway, she has it in for me.

'Cos you were screwing her husband? Cal asked.

Ice clinked as I knocked my whisky back.

Not only that.

It was a Tuesday in early July. Julian had been on leave for ten weeks because Natasha was sicker than ever, on opiates that had her sliding in and out of consciousness as he cared for her round the clock. But that afternoon I'd been texting him relentlessly, sending photos and videos too, so he told Natasha he was popping out to the gym and left her watching TV. He came straight to mine, leaving his phone in his jacket in the hall. When he went to the bathroom after, I sneaked out and unlocked it, having long memorised his four-digit code. Eight missed calls from 'Tashka' and four voice messages. I played the first one. She was so strained and weak, it was hard to decipher each word.

Please . . . come home, Juju . . . I'm going now . . . I know it . . .

(A long pause. The sounds of wheezing and fighting for breath.)

I know you're with her, but . . . it's okay . . . I just really . . . need you here.

Without listening to the rest, I cleared his call log and deleted the messages. When Julien came back from the bathroom, I pulled him down onto the bed. It was another forty-five minutes before he could leave.

That evening he rang, weeping.

She was scared of dying alone. That was her one thing. She made me promise I'd be there no matter what . . .

In the dingy Chinatown hostel bar, something had hardened in Cal's eyes.

My mum died in 2016, he said. I flew back from Thailand to be with her. Me and my brothers, we were all with her at the end.

Natasha was *always* calling him, I said. I thought she was being controlling. Manipulative.

Laksa?

The skinny Chinese guy behind the bar placed the bowl in front of Cal, who nodded his thanks, then said to me, You should get that nose checked. It looks fucking *leprous*, mate.

Then he picked up his laksa, and went to join the Germans.

*

Marathon runners talk about the pain cave – that endurance is embracing the pain. *Tunnelling into* the pain. I've never run a marathon, but this must be close. Every moment of head above water hard won. Kicking through the burning in my muscles, the stabbing in my side.

Kick, kick, kick and *fuck you*.

She's up to her chin now. Waves crash over her head, but she doesn't flinch, her eyes shining black through the night. The tide's going out, so she must have walked forwards by ten metres or so, though I haven't seen her move.

If I disappear out here, out into the Strait of Malacca or Indian Ocean beyond, who will miss me? Not my family, who I seldom talk to. Probably not my friends – I'd be lucky if twenty people came to my funeral. Not many went to Natasha's, Julien admitted. Maybe that's something we have in common. Beneath the affable surface, a rivalrous, grudge-holding meanness that puts people off.

But I don't regret how I've lived my life. I was my authentic self. How many people can say that?

My authentic self wanted Julien.

*

'Please Don't On The Light After 11 PM' the notice on the dormitory door said, so I reeled through the dark to my own bunk, kicking off my flip-flops and starting up the ladder, only to slip and bang my head on a metal rung. From across the room, a venomous snake-hiss,

Shhhhhh . . .

I didn't try the ladder again. Both bunks were empty, so, cursing, rubbing my temple, I crawled into the bottom one and lay on my back, staring up. The darkness swirled like the isobars of the hundred-mile-per-hour tornado sweeping through my mind. Was I concussed? Or just drunk? I closed my eyes and waited for sleep to shut me down. Instead I was dizzy, hurtling through space. How much time went by, I lost track of, but I was drifting off when a *crrreak* from above had me staring through the shadows again, up at the slats of the top bunk. It was empty, wasn't it? Another *crrreak* confirmed otherwise. I lay there, not moving. Listening to the breathing and snores rumbling from elsewhere in the dormitory. Minutes passed. Long enough to convince myself the creaker had been one of these other sleepers too. I was wasted, after all.

Crrreak. No mistaking it this time. From the mattress above. Then something grazing the plasterboard besides me. A gaunt hand, creeping down through the gap between wall and upper bunk. Crooked-backed spider with five bent limbs. Silver wedding ring loose at a bony knuckle as it groped, inches above my head. I tumbled out of bed onto the floor with a half-strangled cry. I sprang up and around.

The top bunk was empty. By the wall, no hand.

A terse whisper,

For fuck's sake. We're trying to sleep.

I recognised the posh English accent; the girl with the septum-piercing and multicoloured wraps from the bar last night, her tour of Asia financed by the Bank of Mum and Dad. My anger went straight to my fists and I could feel the teenage Sara rising up in me. The one who got suspended in Year 10 for breaking Donna Kelly's tooth.

I pulled my flip-flops on over chilblained toes, grabbed my wallet from under my pillow. On the way back out, I *onned* the dormitory light and slammed the door.

After leaving KL the next morning, the coach to Penang rolled by the highway scenery of limestone cliffs, palm trees, toll booths and Malays on mopeds, back-to-front jackets billowing in the wind. But, hungover, I mostly stared at the back of the headrest in front, trying not to throw up. Hours later, I jumped in a taxi outside the George Town bus terminal and asked the driver to take me to a guest house – any guest house – along the touristy beaches of Batu Ferringhi, a place I went to on a family day trip when I was eleven and have okay memories of. The Papaya Inn was on the seafront and my room's wooden floor was gritty with sand, a towel still damp from the previous occupant slung over the rattan chair. Sniffing the bedsheets I

detected sun lotion and sweat, but decided for eighty ringgit a
night I would strip them off and stay.

Late afternoon, I sat haggardly on the beach outside, drinking
out of a coconut with a straw, gazing at the sea. Despite
everything, I did take some pleasure in the enormity of it, in
watching the waves roll in. Though it was November, off season,
under the parasol-shaded sun loungers of a nearby four-star
hotel were many Western tourists; pink and lazy and glutted
from all-you-can-eat buffets. I touched my nose and winced.
Cal was right, it was getting worse, but I couldn't afford a doctor.
My money was going to run out soon. And then what? Look
for work as a chef? EFL? So long as my future workplace had
at least two exits, I didn't care.

*

Three nights before I boarded the flight to KL, I was closing La
Banquette. Julien was in Lyon again with his in-laws, and the
other manager Matt had texted he'd sprained his ankle (*niece's
birthday party, bouncy castle*), leaving me to oversee the kitchen
and restaurant floor. It was a bad shift. Overbooked and under-
staffed, with several order mix-ups, a customer with a gluten
allergy threatening legal action, and a waitress bursting into
tears when I yelled at her for dropping a coq au vin. After we
saw the last diners out at midnight, everyone was keen to get
out of there. Only Benji stayed to finish cleaning the kitchen,
as I took the evening's takings and receipts up to the office safe.

The restaurant was dark when I returned, the lamps off and
candles extinguished. But it wasn't empty. A lone woman was
seated at one of the round front tables by the window, facing
the shuttered, empty high street. At once, I was disorientated.
As though I'd gone through the wrong door into the wrong
restaurant – a La Banquette identical to ours, with the same
Parisian brasserie decor and leather-upholstered benches, yet of
some other reality into which I was now trespassing.

Hello? I called.

The woman didn't turn or move.

We're closed, I said. I'm afraid you have to leave.

Again, she said nothing. I moved towards her and the sensation of my dislocation into another time and place became stronger, my larynx and chest tightening. I could see the back of her up close now. The cotton ties of her hospital gown were undone and her spine jutted sharply, each vertebra threatening to stab through her skin. Strands of red hair were draped over her bumpy yellow skull. Before my eyes, a fiery wisp detached from her scalp, drifted to the parquet floor. Hoarsely, I said,

Natasha?

She stood. Turned. She looked as she did on Instagram, but *wrong*. Under her sparse red hair, her eyes were glassy in her pale, embalmed-looking face. Her palliative care gown hung from her emaciated frame and the smell of her wafted over; formaldehyde and that fucking lavender pillow spray. She stepped towards me and I ran into the kitchen, my heart banging like it wanted out. I twisted the back door handle. Double-locked. The keys not on the hook beside it. Why was that idiot *always* pocketing the keys?

Benji! I yelled.

She appeared in the glass panel of the kitchen door; the heavy, fire-resistant metal swinging outwards as she pushed and entered. Under the bright LED lights bouncing off the stainless-steel fittings Natasha looked as though she'd just arisen from a slab in the morgue and walked barefoot to the restaurant. Several days dead and coursing with embalming fluids, yet somehow more powerful than life. Back in July she'd been too sickened and enervated to do anything about Julien's other woman. Not anymore.

What do you want? I whispered.

She reached out a scrawny arm as though she wanted to embrace me, then gestured at the floor. I remembered Julien kneeling, begging forgiveness, and understood. But I ran into the walk-in freezer, slammed the door instead.

The low light came on. The frozen, minus 16 C mist swirled about the cardboard boxes of scallops and lobster tails, the plastic tubs of gelato and bechamel sauce. I gripped the interior handle, wrenching the door shut with all my strength as she pulled on the other side. After two minutes the light timer went off, and I was shivering in my chef's coat in the blackness, teeth chattering. I needed to get to the controls and switch the freezer off, the way Julien had demonstrated when I'd started at La Banquette eighteen months earlier. But there was no way I could reach them three metres away without letting the handle go.

The loss of circulation started in my fingers and toes, the numbness creeping up my limbs. I could feel my frostbitten hands becoming fused to the metal handle, my flesh chilling to the bone, bringing to mind the kilos of beef, veal and pork in Ziploc bags on the shelves. How long would it take to be as frozen solid as a shrink-wrapped joint of lamb? I'm 58 kilos, so at least seven hours. Though hypothermia would kill me long before . . . Already, I was lightheaded. A ringing in my ears as my brain shrank in the cold. I was losing sense of time, but not my will. I kept pulling the freezer door handle, which my hands seemed welded to with ice. I just *knew* Natasha was on the other side.

Convulsing, teeth chattering like a wind-up toy, I said,

You . . . will . . . not have me.

I will . . . not fucking . . . kneel for you.

You . . . will . . . not . . . have . . .

The next thing I remember is A&E. Waking on the gurney under one of those foil insulation blankets. Bandages over my nose and swaddling my hands and feet. I was on my own in the curtain-enclosed cubicle, though I could hear footsteps approaching on the other side. All that happened at La Banquette rushed back to me and I sat up, bracing myself, a scream gathering in my throat. The curtain swished aside. Benji. Wide-eyed in his puffer jacket, headphones around his neck.

Sara. Fuck man . . . You okay?

I nodded weakly. Benji shook his head with a low whistle,

I went back for my iPhone and saw I'd left the frozen spinach out . . . *Lucky*, right?

But I didn't feel lucky. My pulse only raced.

*

14

Night in Batu Ferringhi, I wandered in a daze along the main drag, past the night market of cheap souvenirs and seafood restaurants with tanks of stoned-looking fish and crustaceans clambering on each other to get out. I hadn't eaten since the service station in Ipoh, so I bought satay from a hawker stall and hunched at a table, tearing grilled meat from wooden skewers with my teeth as I scanned every sunburnt tourist who entered the food court. I drank a beer, then another, deciding to stay out in the safety of crowds as late as I could. But it wasn't long before I was slumped, drowsing on the table, a vendor shaking my shoulder. I got up, stumbled back to the Papaya Inn and collapsed.

An hour later, I was awake again. It was midnight and mosquitoes were whining in my ears, my arms and legs itching with welts as I lay on my stripped-bare mattress. As I scratched, feeling the ooze of blood under my fingernails, a tap started leaking in the bathroom connected to my room.

Drip . . .

Drip . . .

Drip . . .

Slow and sporadic at first. Then louder, more persistent, until it was a trickle. I got up, went to the bathroom. Yanked the string-pull light. Water was splashing from the shower head onto the tiles. I reached to tighten the tap the rubber shower hose was attached to. Then looked down again.

The drain was clogged with red hair. Though this was half expected, fury surged up in me and I crouched by the plughole. The strands were caught in the metal grid, but I tore violently at them, as though tearing them out of her head. And up it all came. Slimy and bilious, bringing other stuff too. A kirby grip. A tooth with a bloody root. The plastic of a chemo-port . . .

Nauseous, I stopped pulling. I had to get out.

As I've said, I'm no swimmer. And the sea at night terrifies. I can't look at the dark roaring waves without imagining them drowning me, and the rip current carrying my corpse, rotted and buoyant with the gases of putrefaction, out for the sharks and carnivorous fish. But I knew now there were more terrifying things on land, so I stepped out of my flip-flops and waded in, gasping as I submerged myself, but relishing how the cold shock displaced my fear. In T-shirt and shorts I began to doggy-paddle, back and forth, parallel to the beach. Every so often I stopped my clumsy strokes to check that my toes could still touch the bottom, gazing to where the pitch-black sea vanished into sky, or at the distant lights along the miles of shore. Then I would resume my swimming as, for the first time in weeks, relief expanded within.

And then I saw her.

*

That was two hours ago now and Natasha's still there. Up to her neck in sea water. A ferocious wave crashes over me, sending me under for a few seconds. I bob to the surface, hacking out coughs, blinking my stinging eyes, and she's gone. Treading water, I do a three-sixty. Has she finally had enough of tormenting me for the night? Is it finally safe to go in? My exhausted body decides for me. I start to swim, diagonally, towards the sand. Soon, I can stand on two feet. And I stagger, at the end of my strength, splashing through the resistance of water towards the shore.

Natasha rises from the waist-deep shallows, a metre or two in front of me. Cadaverous face plastered with long strands, her eyes punishing black. I reel in horror. Yet again, she reaches a bony necrotic arm as though to hug me, then gestures at the water, sloshing at my ribs. Kneel and I will drown. Swim back out and I will drown.

Julien's dead wife's eyes are unblinking. She remains pointing at the water. And I realise this is her authentic self. Wrathful. Vengeful. Un-Instagrammable. Hidden when she was living, perhaps even from herself.

But perhaps I've been hiding part of my authentic self too.

I am angry. Very angry. I miss Julien. Were it not for Natasha we'd be together now.

Is Natasha a fighter?

Tashka, I say. *Je suis désolé* . . .

And I pull back my fist and swing.

Flight 2212

by J K Chukwu

At the start of the year, Tulsa had had no intention of using her vacation days for a Matching Pairs girls' trip she never wanted to take in the first place. The hassle of planning, budgeting, the preparation for surgery, the irritations of constant notifications from a group chat where she recognised only one number, never seemed worth four days in the sun with cocktails and hangovers and bandaged hands.

However, her humiliating demotion at Madam Hits from lead analyst to intern shifted her mindset. Well, not only the demotion. The ending of her engagement to her co-worker Lewis, who no longer saw her as beautiful, and her *incident* in the workplace that sparked an emergency performance review, were the final tipping points. Perhaps this trip was the mental and physical revamp she needed. Perhaps it would allow her to escape her mind's interest in finding another way to exist in this world. And so Tulsa told Kim, head of HR and organiser of the trip, of her intention of joining the girls' trip, and was promptly added to the group chat.

After a month of Kim's morning text bombardments of influencers' videos showcasing their matching pairs, of Tulsa watching these videos while on a forced, unpaid mental health leave from work, she and some others in the group chat believed they were ready for this trip. Surveys and polls were sent. After two rounds of voting, the Dominican Republic beat Mexico by two votes. The group chat was named: Soon-to-be

Matching Queens. Links for potential matching travel fits, inspo videos of glove-burning ceremonies and locations for celebratory bottomless brunches drummed up excitement. As the time for the trip drew near, one by one people dropped out with excuses of weddings and funerals, forthcoming pet hospitalisations and newfound allergies to latex. One or two had unanswered curiosities regarding Dr Pitanguy and Dr Kehl's maverick grafting procedures and the risks of osteomyelitis when pairs were permanently grafted on wrists or ankles; these were what matching-pair influencers called 'the uh-oh's. Somehow unforeseen circumstance after circumstance narrowed down the participants in the girls' trip from seven to two: Tulsa and Kim.

> Kim: Are you ready for our new normal? Don't forget to upgrade your pair package xoxoxo.

> Tulsa: Excited for the trip!! Still unsure about the procedure, lol.

> Kim: Lol, do you want Lewis and your job back or not? Getting the uh-ohs is normal.

*

The uh-ohs, and the dangers of bone infection, which could rot the bone to its death, potentially causing infections of erupting pustules on an individual's skin, were in fact far from normal. Normal was having no appendage of digits dangling from fore or lower limbs. Normal was being born with no toes to paint, or fingers to ring. Only a corkscrew of flesh on one's wrists and ankles, twisting like spiralled clay, then stopping to reveal a nubbin of bone protruding from the flesh. Elementary schools echoed with the hollow tap, tap, tap of bone against floors and desks, a sound that silenced when everyone entered middle school. Then, for reasons of respectability, all learned to loathe the normalcy of warped flesh that led to the original indecency – the bone. Never to be shown in public, always hidden with pairs of hands and feet.

If the upkeep and clamminess, or the mechanical glitches when faulty wiring in the pairs occurred, weren't enough, there was the constant spending; buying items like handles and knobs, shoes and gloves, pair changers, bone protectors for when the constant wearing of pairs had cracked and whittled down the bone to a bleached twig of numbing pain. Then, of course, there was the issue of unmatched skin. The celebration and fetish-isation of white hands and feet meant more were researched and produced, resulting in a lower price point, and a lack of interest in hands and feet in different shades. It was simple economics.

*

Tulsa waits on the plane, fearing the uh-ohs, cramped in a seat that seems to shrink with each readjustment of her body. She reaches above her to open her seat's fan and a weak stream of air flows briefly then sputters to a stop. As the heat outside bakes the plane's atmosphere, she pictures a boiled hand stitched onto a wrist with steel thread.

More passengers board the plane. With every *excuse me* and sigh from those struggling to find their seats, the bumped hand in her imagination reddens, swelling with pus until the boils rupture. Fluid, yellow with infection, streams down the hand, dripping into the nebulous space of her mind. Tulsa jolts in her seat, attempting to free herself from this image. She grips one of the white hands attached to her wrists. She tugs it slowly as she sits with her fears.

The surgery might fail, leaving her attached to lumpen, massacred flesh, all for a man and company that she is unsure she still even wants. She could return to them, perfect, with hands matching her skin. Beginning and ending all her days with the company then Lewis. Returning to them in bliss until she, Lewis, or her coworkers decide, encourage, or pressure her to undergo another surgery so that her feet can be matching pairs as well. Tulsa twists, then tugs her hand. It comes loose and slips forward. It hangs from the nubbin of her bone like a dying orchid.

'Can you not?' Kim says, covering Tulsa's exposed bone with one of her own hands, gloved in brown lace. 'There's no denying that you've been through hardship since the demotion and Lewis leaving you, but please, you're worth more than a break-down.'

Tulsa slips her left hand back into place. Before Tulsa had decided to join Kim on the trip, she had been growing bolder, asking questions and committing minor transgressions – arriving to work ungloved and running errands in bones. Once even, Tulsa went to work in bone, relishing her coworkers' stares when she approached them with hollow clicks of bone against tile. She sounded like the ticks of a gas stove, stalled before it ignites. And she revelled in making everyone uncomfortable. She loved it until she was called into an emergency performance review with Kim. During this intervention, denied food, water, or the decency of a restroom as the steel chair chilled her back, Tulsa had remained seated, repeating as she wrote, *I have no intention of repeating this incident*. The written and recited promises weren't enough. Her emergency performance review only ended after Tulsa, desperate as she sat in her filth, promised to join the girls' trip for matching pairs.

Now, on the plane with Kim, Tulsa questions her desperate promise. She says, 'Kim, if Madam Hits wants us to have permanent matching pairs for work, then why can't they pay for the surgeries?' Tulsa twists her right hand clockwise, returning it to its original position so that her hand appears to merge seamlessly at her wrist, save the faint line where it attaches, and the disparity of colours. A brown arm, deep in colour like well-nourished soil, terminating in a cream-coloured hand with the faintest electric veins visible beneath the artificial skin.

'Again with this?' Kim responds with a flittering roll of her eyes. She licks her dry lips, on the precipice of peeling, before she says, 'It proves nothing if it's just given to you. Our managers need to see that we're invested in the vision.'

'Whose vision is it? If it were mine, it would be safer, maybe cheaper.'

'Tulsa, these questions feel concerning. I would hate to schedule another performance review, especially after you've gone through the hassle of upgrading your package, and you—' Kim catches Tulsa's wince when package is mentioned. 'You did upgrade your surgery package from Gold to Palladium, correct?'

'No, I had trouble with the website,' Tulsa replies, knowing to not disclose that every time she has gone onto the clinic's page and been prompted to upgrade her appointment, she has exited the site, wandering through the internet until she finds herself deep in threads about dunbars, Black individuals who refuse to wear hands or feet, who left jobs, schools or families to live in bone and not care about society's expectations. To exist in a way so new that it sparks fear, confusion, and disgust in others.

'Well, that's why you're nervous. The Gold package always has a higher chance of complications.' Kim reaches into her Louis Vuitton weekender – purple leather, embossed with her initials *KS* and a design of singing caged birds – and grabs a pill bottle. She shakes an assortment of pills coloured in blue, orange, white, and green onto her gloved right hand. 'Take these.'

'What are they?' Tulsa asks, staring at the colourful array of medicinal jewels in Kim's palm.

'Antibiotics, the best painkillers, and hydration pills. The Gold comes with the low, mid-grade painkillers and adequate antibiotics, which have thirty per cent chance of not working. Take these unless you want to end up with the uh-ohs.'

Two by two, Tulsa swallows the pills. As they feel like pebbles slipping down her windpipe, she thinks of Lewis, the flaccidity of his personality only briefly obscured with money, and the expectations of Madam Hits, trapping her in cycles of work, spend, flaunt. The pills feel as if they are swelling in her throat, creating a blockade. While she struggles to swallow the last two pills, she imagines returning to work with the short pole of a pair-changer attached to her bones. She pictures herself unscrewing the hands and feet of every coworker until the white cylinders of bone poke out from their slacks and the tap, tap, tap of them ignites Madam Hits' lobby with revulsion

'Attention passengers on Flight 2212: due to a slight mechanical issue we are unable to turn on the plane's cooling system until takeoff. We apologise for the inconvenience.'

As the pilot announces this, more passengers, damp with sweat, enter the plane. When they pass Kim and Tulsa's row, Kim notices a few of the Black passengers have naked bone peeking from the hems of their patched jeans. They walk to the back rows.

'I can't believe they let them board in bone,' Kim says. She cranes in disgust at those behind her. Sweat creeps down her neck.

'Kim, leave them alone. It's fine that they're in bone.'

'Tulsa, no. Dunbars aren't fine. We've paid too much for this flight. It's unfair to us to have this experience ruined.' Kim stretches up a gloved hand and touches the flight attendant button, which lights up and dings.

'What are you doing?' Tulsa asks as a stewardess approaches.

'I'm going to ask the stewardess if she can request those passengers to put on pairs. They're bound to have spares in the cabin.'

'Kim!'

'What?'

'How may I help you?' the stewardess asks. Before Kim can speak, Tulsa grabs and twists her friend's right hand, allowing for a glimmer of bone to be exposed. Frantic, Kim snatches back her hand and readjusts it, then waves the attendant away as her embarrassment mortifies her eyes to a deadened glare.

'It's just a bit of bone, Kim.'

'That was wildly inappropriate,' Kim replies, enraged. As the stewardess moves back down the aisle, Kim pulls down her lace glove to cover the faint line for hand attachment circling around her wrist.

'You were being inappropriately unfair,' Tulsa asserts, fanning herself with the flight safety brochure. As she listens to the hacking coughs and sneezes ending in sniffles, she unbuckles her seatbelt and peels off her green seal cardigan and matching long-sleeved shirt. Though she is left wearing only her black tank top with her sweater and shirt in her lap, she is still sweating. Her back aches just as it did during her performance review. She feels heated in the cabin, pressurised, as if her thoughts are preparing to break free of her flesh and completely eviscerate her. She wonders what it would mean for her body to escape, to abandon her pairs, her work, to never return to Lewis, to become a Dunbar. 'It's too hot for pairs anyway,' she says.

'Tulsa, that is also inappropriate. Honestly, I—'

Kim pauses. Her brief silence is a welcome change, but soon ends when she looks up and exclaims, 'Look at them. They are perfect.'

Tulsa's attention turns outward to the women at the front of the plane, all in matching pairs. They are clothed in matching silk tracksuits, cropped and showcasing the seamless umber skin of their ankles. One by one, these Nubian Lady Liberties with designer bags swinging from their arms pass Kim and Tulsa's row. They leave behind a trail of enviable elegance until one of the perfected women hovers over Kim and Tulsa. With a clenched grin, she tells Kim, 'You're in my seat.'

As Kim scrambles out of the middle seat, she apologises, and uses her sleeve to wipe away damp spots on the headrest. With a sigh of irritation, the woman settles herself between them and stows her Birkin underneath the seat. Upon seeing the purse – slaughtered ostrich skin, dyed white and bearing a concentric pattern of a blue lone star within a red nova – Kim gasps. 'Is that from the Let Freedom Ring collection?'

The woman sighs. She too begins fanning herself as sweat slicks underneath her Bulgari necklace of broken chains and reclaimed diamonds.

'It is,' she replies, 'and no, I can't give you a referral for the waiting list for its worldwide release.' She presses the call button above, which dings once again.

Kim smiles, curtly.

'I'm already *on* the list. Once I pay off my scarf, the matching wallet and purse are next.'

She touches the silk scarf looped around her neck. When the woman leans toward Kim to inspect it, her gold-threaded woman's locs slip to one side and Tulsa notices mounds, like miniature eggs nested in the flesh, pouched on her neck. Tulsa stiffens as the woman readjusts her hair, hiding the bumps, and replies, '*Paying off*. So cute. Love the dedication.' The stewardess arrives, and the perfected woman places an order for a guava mimosa, adding: 'In addition to the drink, can you turn on air for my seat? This heat is causing me to feel unwell.'

The stewardess types on her iPad, before smiling at the middle seat passenger as she replies, 'Ms Smith, thank you for being a loyal customer of Banning Airways, I'll see if there's anything that we can do.'

'Thank you,' the perfected woman replies. The stewardess leaves. 'Are you headed to a booking?'

'Yes, we both are. It's with Dr Pitanguy and Dr Kehl.'

'Amazing!' The perfected woman turns to Tulsa. 'Both geniuses with excellent service and bedside manner. They—' The woman stops suddenly and covers her mouth, then places her hands, braceleted with scabbed skin, on her breastbone. A burp slips out of her. Its smell, boiled eggs and toast, sickens Tulsa, who turns to face the window. 'Excuse me,' says the woman, 'but as I was saying, they are fantastic. They're even willing to fix some snafus from our pair promotion party.'

'Should we get you some water?' says Tulsa, as Kim enquires: 'Snafu?'

The woman inclines her head toward Kim, choosing to answer her question instead of Tulsa's. 'Silly really. We should've known better.'

Nausea seems to overcome her again. She presses the call button before reaching down to fumble in the pocket of the seat in front. Finding a cream napkin, she first dabs her forehead before covering her mouth. As she attempts to hold in foul-smelling retches, the napkin's colour mottles to grey. Her gagging subsides. She uncovers her mouth to reply, 'We didn't upgrade to the Palladium service. The Platinum antibiotics they gave us ran a fifteen per cent risk of not working. I'm dealing with the uh-ohs, and a slight pair rejection. These things happen, but it's worth it. In my pairs, I'm rewriting history.'

'But how often will you have to fix them?' asks Tulsa, horrified.

'Only the normal amount,' the perfected woman replies. 'The frequency is irrelevant. I have the money to fix or replace them as many times as I want.' She runs her hands along the back of her neck, then sets them on her lap.

Tulsa looks at this stranger's hands, and late in the stage of her stare, the hands' façade of wealth collapses. The nailbeds on every finger are receding, puffed and soft like dough, revealing aged white skin. Even as Tulsa watches, one nail detaches itself, landing on the woman's tracksuited lap. Instead of blood, Tulsa can see tiny pustules of white fluid bevelling her eponychium, the created skin underneath the slipping nails.

'Excuse me,' the perfected woman says, slipping her nail into a pocket of her tracksuit. 'Excuse me, I may need the restroom soon.' Her face is flushed and damp.

The heat in the cabin surges to its next peak. A wave of dings from call buttons fills the cabin, then silence, before an eruption of guttural moans fills the plane. Flight attendants hurry down the aisle with miniature plastic bags clutched in their cotton gloves, begging for everyone who is unwell to please remain seated while they call for medical aid. The soured scent of sickness coats the air. With her nose buried in her shoulder to stifle the smell, Tulsa feels a trickling wetness on her wrist.

She looks down. The perfected woman sits with a hand covering her mouth. Strings of clear vomit, chunked with eggs, slip between her fingers, falling onto her tracksuit, her Birkin, and the armrest dividing her from Tulsa. Horrified, Tulsa wipes the mess off her wrist and forearm with her cardigan.

'It's the uh-ohs,' the woman says. She searches in her Birkin, a part of her receding nailbed snagging on the bag's teeth. 'Just a little altitude sickness as we're climbing up.'

'What do you mean? We haven't taken off yet,' Tulsa replies.

The woman groans as a ribbon of flesh peels from her hand, ripping downward to her upper wrist. The strip of ripped skin fully exposes the foundational flesh, jaundiced against the artificial brown skin overlaying it. As EMTs with folded wheelchairs frantically proceed down the airplane's aisle, and Kim uses her silk scarf to wipe sweat from the perfected woman's forehead, Tulsa discreetly begins twisting off her right hand.

The Fruiting Body

by Bridget Collins

The first thing they noticed was the smell. It hit them as soon as they entered the sitting room, so that they glanced at each other, stifling laughter. The estate agent cleared his throat and said, 'Ah, yes, it could do with a good airing . . .'

'I'll say,' Paul said. 'Does the owner have a massive weed habit?'

'Ha ha,' the agent said, 'the smell is rather reminiscent of cannabis, isn't it? No, it's just a little problem with dry rot. Easily treatable.'

Paul peered at the scrolls of wallpaper hanging off the chimney breast, and recoiled. He pointed. 'If you mean *that*, it's not what I'd call *little*.'

'A bit of chemical spray, and—'

'I've never seen an actual fruiting body before. It's huge.'

'As I said, a perfect opportunity to start again with a blank canvas.' The agent gestured with his clipboard. 'Original cornicing and ceiling rose – the fireplace is also original – the house has retained an enormous amount of character—'

'What was she doing, keeping it as a pet?' Carefully Paul tugged the curling wallpaper off the wall and dropped it in the hearth, ignoring the agent's grunt of protest. He whistled softly. 'Seriously, Jen, come and look at this.'

Jen picked her way over the grimy carpet towards him. He was right, it was huge: bigger than her head, she thought, a clinging mass of blackish roots, knuckled here and there with paler bulges.

It crept over the wallpaper like a dark web, dusty and old. She raised her hand, fascinated, hardly knowing what she was doing.

'Ugh. Don't touch it,' Paul said, pulling her back.

'I wasn't going to.'

'Come on, then,' he said, putting his arm round her waist, 'let's keep moving. Seen enough here.' He led her out of the room into the passage, keeping her body so close against his that she tripped over his feet, giggling, as if they were running a three-legged race.

'Of course it's rather tired,' the estate agent said, following them. 'As you see, the kitchen needs a little refresh . . . Ready to go upstairs? Do be careful of the broken banisters – but think of the potential . . . Family bathroom through here, yes – bedroom one, bedroom two – I mean, look at the proportions, that high ceiling – bit of damp here and there, but more original plasterwork, nice Art Nouveau fingerplate on the door, see? Yes, up the stairs again, if you would . . .'

Finally they stood in the attic bedroom, hand in hand, while the agent loitered in the doorway. 'Lovely third bedroom,' he said. 'Perfect for a child. Or guests. Surprisingly spacious, this house. We've had a lot of interest.'

Paul knocked on the wall with his knuckles, and winced. 'Yeah,' he said. 'It's unmortgageable, though, right?'

'Well. I imagine – yes,' the agent said, with a swift smile. 'They don't come up often, mind, not in this area.'

'Okay,' Paul said. 'We'll chat about it and get back to—'

'We'll offer the asking price,' Jen said, and felt a bubble of joy burst in her throat as Paul swung round to stare at her. 'It's all right,' she added, 'I've done the sums. With Nan's money—'

He blinked. 'But – sweetheart, are you sure? Let's go home and—'

'There's the job in Linden Street, you said there was a good profit in that. Come on, let's do it. You're so transparent, I can see you love it.' She turned back to the estate agent. 'The asking price, in cash, if you take it off the market today.'

'Well, I can certainly put that forward to the sellers. We have a few more viewings this week, so—'

'Please,' she said. 'You can see Paul's the right man for the job. He's a builder, he's amazing. And he can see everything that's wrong with it. Anyone else will just mess about asking for a survey and then trying to bargain you down. We won't.'

'I mean,' Paul said, with a modest tilt of his head, 'not sure she's right about me being amazing. But as for the rest . . .' He grinned. 'Subsidence, damp, terrible roof, terrible stairs, terrible wiring, Victorian plumbing, rotten plaster, rotten windows, no insulation . . . not to mention that dry rot downstairs, that's practically a squatting tenant. You should tell your seller to take the money and run.'

'I do see your point,' the agent said. He plucked at the clip on his clipboard. 'Well – I can say that no one who has booked a viewing so far has been in a position to proceed imminently – but it wouldn't be ethical . . .'

'Oh, go on,' Jen breathed, looking up at him.

'. . . unless – well, if you got your offer in today, in writing, maybe—'

'Fantastic,' Paul said. 'Oh, wow! I cannot wait to get to work on this. What a place.' He looked down at Jen, his whole face alight with enthusiasm. 'You looking forward to living here, baby?'

'Of course,' she said, although she'd be happy anywhere, as long as it was with him. She looked round at the room they were in, trying to imagine past the peeling wallpaper with its marks where some long-gone tenant had tacked their posters up, the iron-shaped scorch mark on the grey carpet, the bulge like a tea-stain on the sloping ceiling. *Perfect for a child.* Yes, it would be wonderful. Her heart was thumping the way it had when she'd seen Paul for the very first time, under a loop of fairy lights on a blue June evening, and he'd smiled and raised his glass to her. She had known then, in her bones: now she had the same feeling of joyous certainty, of the world falling into place. 'Of *course*,' she repeated, and pressed his hand to her lips. It smelt, as always, of warm male skin and laundry powder, but underneath was a less familiar odour, a rotting, earthy note. She sniffed, confused; but when Paul caught her eye with a quizzical look she could not help laughing, and kissing him, and when he kissed her back she forgot to wonder at all.

It was only later, when they traipsed slowly down the stairs, ignoring the estate agent's pointed glance at his watch, that she realised it was the pungent stink of the dry rot, wafting up from the sitting room.

'To the new house,' Jimmy said, and Bea and Helen raised their cups, echoing the toast. 'It'll be great. Really something to get your teeth into, eh, Paul? God, it must be nice to have useful skills.'

'Yeah. Thanks,' Paul said, with a self-deprecating glint, and Jen pressed her leg against his under the flimsy card table.

'Such a lovely old place,' Helen said, beaming. 'It's so wonderful to rescue it.'

'It'll be *yours*,' Bea said, waving her arm so grandly that her camping chair rocked and she righted herself, laughing. 'You'll be making it entirely how you want it. Lucky you, Jen-Jen.'

'I know,' she said, feeling the warmth of Paul's thigh against hers. 'I am. Awfully.'

Jimmy sipped his champagne, his eyes sliding from Paul to Jen and back. 'Plus,' he said, 'it's an investment, isn't it? It'll be worth more than what you put in.'

'We're going to live here,' Paul said, 'not just do it up on the cheap and flip it. It's for us, for our life together.'

'Sure, sure,' Jimmy said, leaning back in his chair. He drained his cup, and put it down on the table beside the empty takeaway cartons. 'Come on, then, Paul. Give us the guided tour.'

They got up, Bea shrieking as the card table lurched and threatened to tip over. Paul led them down the hallway in a little group and ushered them into the sitting room. He took Jen's hand and held it tightly as he said to the others, 'This is the ballroom – note the marble floor and the Louis XVI chandeliers . . . No, but it'll be nice, eventually.'

'It's lovely,' Helen said. 'Really lovely.'

'Good God,' Jimmy said, blinking at the chimney breast, 'what is *that*?'

Paul laughed. 'Dry rot.'

'I thought—'

'I know. Stinks, doesn't it? That's the fruiting body. Doesn't normally get that far. But it's actually quite easy to deal with.' He mimed pointing a spray gun at it and pulling the trigger. 'Psss, psss.'

Helen said, 'Oh well, that's a relief.'

'Must've been hard to get a mortgage,' Jimmy said.

'We paid cash.'

'Really?'

'Yes.' Paul added, with an edge, 'We didn't have to go begging to your lot.'

'I put in my nan's money,' Jen said. 'I think she would have wanted me to. I can save up for the counselling course once we're not paying rent.'

There was a slight pause. Bea looked from Paul to Jen, frowning. 'You're not doing the counselling course? But after you worked so hard to get a place—?'

'I can do it later. This is more important.'

She saw Helen and Jimmy swap a glance. Then Helen gave a careful, non-committal nod. 'I can see how excited you are about this house,' she said, 'we all can, it's just that—'

'You'd be such a great counsellor,' Bea said, interrupting, 'and you said your nan would be so pleased – oh Jen, don't give up now, you mustn't—'

Jimmy had been hesitating, as if he was trying to stop himself weighing in; but now he said, over Bea, 'The thing is, Jen, you've been saying for *years* that all you wanted—'

'For God's *sake*,' Paul said, smacking his hand against the wall. The sound rang out as if something in the plaster had snapped clean through. 'Just shut up, why don't you? What do you know about Jen or what she wants?'

Another, longer silence. 'Well,' Jimmy said, at last, 'nothing, apparently.'

Paul took a step forward. 'You know you make her feel like

shit, don't you? Going on about money all the time. You with your well-paid job in a bank – yeah, you two as well with your designer shoes and your haircuts . . . Some people just aren't ambitious, and that's fine. Show a little empathy. This is a new start. It's exciting. If you were proper friends you'd be pleased for her.'

Jen stood very still. She opened her mouth, but no sound came out.

Paul said, 'Right, baby?'

Everyone looked at her. She let her eyes slide away, helpless, until her gaze lighted on the great clinging web of dry rot. It had got bigger, she thought: the swellings were darker, bulging, as if they were ready to release their spores. She didn't answer.

'Actually,' Jimmy said, almost casual, 'I just remembered I've got an early meeting tomorrow. Sorry, Jen. Anyone want a lift home?'

Helen said, 'Oh dear, in that case . . . Sorry, sweetheart.' She bobbed forwards to kiss Jen's cheek. 'It's been so fabulous to see the house. Now, you will call me, won't you? Coffee soon?'

'Bye, Jen,' Bea said. She drained her cup and held it out to Paul, as if he were a waiter. 'Good luck. It's a lot to take on.'

Jen returned their kisses without meeting their eyes. Her cheekbones ached but she kept on smiling while they collected their coats and filed out of the front door. Then she and Paul were alone, except for the smell and the dark tendinous thing on the chimney breast.

He said, 'Why didn't you support me? I was standing up for you.'

'I don't think they were trying to be—'

'I don't care what they say about me. But when they undermine you like that – treating you like a kid – suggesting you're not pulling your weight . . .' There was a pause. Then, with a huff of breath, he sank against the wall, bringing his hands up to his face. 'Jesus, I got it wrong, didn't I? Oh, God, Jen, I'm sorry. You're right, they mean well, they care about you. I should have . . . Argh. You must hate me.'

'No, of course not—'

'I'm so sorry. I couldn't help myself, I thought they were being shitty to you . . . I love you so much. *So* much. I can't believe I'd be so stupid. Do you forgive me?'

'Of course – of course, darling. I love you too – and this house, I love this house, it's going to be our forever home.'

He took her face, smiled into her eyes for a moment, and kissed her. She opened her mouth to him, her heart already beating faster, her body tingling. His arms slid round her, and one hand reached down and tugged at the fly-button of her jeans. But after a moment she opened her eyes and pulled away from him. The air was heavy with the smell. She had been able to ignore it before, but now she could taste it on her tongue, and his. Bitter, not quite putrid, a little like rotting vegetation.

'What's the matter?' he asked.

She didn't answer. Over his shoulder the sooty veins of dry rot clung to the wall, unmoving – of course, of course unmoving, what did she expect? But there was something temporary, deceptive in its stillness, as if it might change position when her eyes were averted.

'Jen, what is it?'

She said, 'Not here.'

'What?' He followed her gaze. 'It's all right. I'll deal with it next week, once we've stripped back to the brick.' He tilted her face back towards his with his fingertips. 'I love you.'

'I love you too,' she said, but as he adjusted his grip on her she added, 'but not now – please, Paul—'

'Don't be silly,' he said, 'you like it, you know you do,' and began to ease her waistband down over her hips. When she tried to speak he put his mouth over hers, laughing, but without giving any quarter to her protests. His fingers slid between her thighs.

She shut her eyes. But even with his tongue in her mouth and the fumbling friction between her legs, she was conscious of the still presence on the chimney breast. Paul eased her down onto the grimy carpet and jerked at the flies of his own trousers. She tried to focus on him – his hot breath, his nudging cock – but for once his desire did not arouse her own. She lay still, not resisting, but not reciprocating; and as he sighed and shoved himself into her, she found that she was holding her breath, trying not to make any noise, as if there were another person in the room.

Three weeks later she opened the door onto a building site. 'Paul?' She picked her way over rubble piled between two bare brick walls. The air was heavy with plaster dust. 'Paul?'

'Through here.'

She ducked into what had been the dining room. Paul was standing with a bar in his hand, his face streaked with grime, and the room had been ripped apart. In one corner he had piled long planks of nail-pricked wood, ready to be loaded into the skip.

He wiped his forehead. 'Hey, baby. What—?'

'I brought supper.' She held up the picnic hamper, laughing at his wondering frown. 'I went to the deli next to the station.'

'You brought it *here*? Why—?'

'You've been working so hard, I thought we should celebrate. You can stop for an hour, can't you?' She looked round for somewhere to spread the blanket. 'And I – actually I wanted to talk to you about something, so . . .'

'Let's go in the front room. We haven't stripped out in there yet.' He dropped the bar on the floor with a clang and strode past her without offering to take the hamper. 'All right?'

She followed him into the grimy, intact sitting room. That smell . . . She would have preferred to eat in the bare, cavernous space where he had been working, not here. But she crouched down, spread out the rug, and unpacked the hamper, smiling at him as she brandished the little pots of salmon pâté and olives. He didn't smile back, even when she produced the half-bottle of champagne. She set the glasses precariously on the rug, feeling suddenly like a child.

'Actually,' he said, 'I wanted to talk to you too.'

'Oh.' She paused. 'Well – why don't you—?'

'No. You go first.' He leant back against the wall.

'All right.' A silence. She had practised a little speech, but it wouldn't come. She stared at the empty glasses. At last, feeling the stark anticlimax of it, she said, 'I'm pregnant.'

She could have sworn she saw movement in the corner of her eye – a ripple, a jolt like a repressed impulse of triumph – but when she glanced up he was exactly where he had been, his arms crossed, his jaw set.

'Jesus,' he said, finally. 'How did *that* happen?'

She heard herself make a sound like a gulp of laughter, although she didn't feel like laughing. 'Um, well,' she said, 'when a daddy loves a mummy very much . . .' Her voice faded under his gaze.

'I mean, is it mine?'

She said, '*What?*'

'I pull out. Every time. You know I do. I'm careful.'

She held his stare, trying to keep her expression mild and calm. 'I think it must have been that night – you know – after my friends came to look round . . .'

He opened his mouth as if he was going to argue. Then he shrugged. 'Right,' he said. 'Well, whatever. Perfect timing, Jen.'

She put her hands together in her lap. It was too early to feel sick, surely? She took a deep breath, and another, but the foetid smell of the dry rot brought the nausea up into her throat, worse than ever.

'Oh, fuck, Jen . . . Come on, I didn't mean it like that. Sorry. Just . . .' He groaned. After a moment he lowered himself onto the rug beside her, and unlaced her hands gently. 'No, it's good news,' he said, squeezing her fingers. 'Of course it is. I'd've liked to be married first.'

'Are you proposing?'

He nudged her knee with his. 'Sure. But the thing is, Jen . . . with Linden Street gone to shit, and that tax bill . . . We can't keep paying rent. I thought – well, it'll be tricky for a few months, but once the steel's in and the new roof's on . . . I mean, in nine months' time the worst of it will be over.'

'You mean . . . ?'

'We need to move in here. It won't be all bad, I promise.

We'll leave this room as it is, so we've got somewhere to sleep while we're doing everywhere else. And the loo's still plumbed in, and the water . . . We can put most of our stuff in storage. Steve's got one of those plug-in hobs that he can lend us. With a microwave, and a kettle, and some electric heaters, we'll be fine. Like camping. I've got to go on with Linden Street in the day, but this way I can work late here without having to leave you at home on your own. That's good, right, baby?'

She swallowed. It would be fine. It would be fun. It would be a few months of inconvenience and then they would reminisce about it for years, laughing at the memories. If she said all that, now, he would hug her tight and tell her how much he loved her, she was a good sport, she was the best girlfriend – no, fiancée, he had said *sure*, hadn't he? – the best fiancée a man could have.

Her eyes went to the skeletal tangle on the chimney breast. The tendrils seemed to have toughened and crept out further, staining, leaching darkness into the wallpaper. She only knew then how hard she had been trying not to look at it.

'Right, baby?' Paul repeated.

She heard herself say, 'Why haven't you stripped this room yet?'

He drew away from her, frowning. 'What?'

'The dry rot's still there. Don't you need to do something about it? Won't it keep spreading, if you don't—?'

'It's not that bad, the house isn't going to collapse. Trust me, who's the builder here?'

'But it's – it's growing, it's—'

'Jesus, Jen, calm down! I'll deal with it.'

She clenched her fists and curled her toes in her shoes as if she was in danger of flying apart. 'I'm sorry,' she said, keeping her voice very steady. 'I just . . . I don't want to live here yet, Paul. I'm sorry, I can't. Let's find another way.'

He jerked his head as if something had flown into his face. 'Jennifer,' he said, finally, 'you were the one who wanted this house. You talked me into it. I'm doing this for you. You can't let me down now.'

Her throat tightened. It was true; she had been the one who decided, who had offered the asking price . . . She went on staring at the dry rot, the dark threads that spread thirstily outwards from the dank slit of curling wallpaper, the swellings heavy with spores. She could not – simply could not—

She struggled to her feet, fighting a surge of dizziness. Fresh air. She needed fresh air. She stepped over the unopened picnic, and the nearest champagne glass toppled.

As she got to the door, he said, in a hoarse, barely audible whisper, 'Fucking bitch.'

She swung round. They stared at each other. She had a vertiginous sense of the space between them thickening, tautening, sucking the last oxygen out of the room. She had just enough breath to say, 'What did you call me?'

'What? Nothing.'

'You called me a fucking bitch.'

His eyes widened, as if she was the one who had said it first. 'Jen – don't be stupid – I would never – *never*—'

'I heard you say it.' It had been a creaking, venomous whisper, like a footstep on rotting wood; but the words had been distinct, unmistakeable. 'I *heard* you, Paul—'

'Jen,' he said, striding forward, taking hold of her arms and bending his knees so that his eyes were on the same level as hers. 'Jen, you know me, you *know* I would never have said that. Sure, you can be a bit— I mean, I was annoyed, but I love you. You know that.'

'Who said it, then? You think I imagined it?' She had meant to throw the question at him like an accusation; but it came out weakly, betraying her. She looked away, not wanting to see his expression.

'Oh, sweetie,' he said. 'It's natural. All those hormones bombing about. You're not feeling yourself. Just don't worry, okay? I love you.'

She shut her eyes. *Could* she have imagined it? He did love her, she knew that was true . . . She let him draw her into his arms and rock her gently, breathing warmly into her hair. He was solid, strong, redolent of sweat and brick dust. The father of her child . . .

'I'm sorry,' she said, 'I don't know what happened, it doesn't matter . . . But – Paul – we can't live here. Not with a baby on the way. We can't.'

'Hush,' he said. 'It's all right. It'll be fine. I promise.'

When they moved in it was a perfect, still, golden autumn evening. They had spent the day in the van, driving from place to place with things to be dropped off and collected, laughing, stopping for coffee in a lay-by, touching each other so continuously that anyone would have thought they had only just fallen in love. At last, worn out and happy, they had walked up the front path under a confetti-drift of shining leaves, Paul staggering under the weight of a new mattress in its box, Jen with two shopping bags of groceries. She unlocked the door, took a careful step over the rubble in the brick tunnel that had once been the hallway, and looked round, her heart singing, wondering why she had dreaded it so much. The low light was pouring into the house through every window. It made the bare brickwork glitter, the dusty floorboards gleam, the grime on the window panes shimmer like veils of gauze; the dust danced in the air, rising in swirls like smoke under her feet, impossibly beautiful. All this destruction only meant that there was less left to do, before it was rebuilt. Her nan would have said, *well begun, half done*. Behind her Paul said, 'Oi, don't loiter in the doorway, duffer,' and she grinned and scrambled out of his way.

She had insisted that they sleep upstairs, in the biggest bedroom. Paul had conceded with an eye-roll, even though there was no carpet and no plaster on the walls, and he warned her that it would be much harder to keep warm than the sitting room. Now it looked like a cave in a fairy tale, the walls draped with bits of cloth, a few precious bits of glassware and furniture pushed into a corner, boxes and packages of food piled up like a robber's hoard. She filled the little kettle in the bathroom and knelt to make tea while Paul wrestled the mattress from its box, swearing, and finally collapsed onto it with a mock-heroic arm over his face. 'I hope childbirth isn't as hard as that,' he said, 'I'm exhausted.' But not so exhausted that he didn't rally after a moment, and suggest they christen it; not so exhausted that he didn't draw her down beside him . . .

Afterwards, she lay watching the sunlight dwindle to a blazing line straddling the joists above them, and rested her palm gently, very gently, on her belly.

He had been right: it was like camping. He had rigged up some temporary lights, with a cable that snaked across the floor and had to be taped down so they didn't trip on it; Jen cooked dinner in a single saucepan and they ate cross-legged on the edge of the mattress, licking their spoons clean to save on washing-up. Then, when it was dark, they wriggled into four-season sleeping bags and lay side by side, murmuring and giggling like kids. She had thought it would be difficult to sleep in a new place, but this was the first time she had ever gone to bed under her own, her very own roof; and she just had time to marvel at how comfortable, how warm, and how happy she was, before she was unconscious.

But she did not sleep long. She blundered awake, with the sense of something sticky grabbing at her mind, something that wanted to keep her under. The window was in the wrong place, there was no ceiling, only a deep barred shadow above her. When she reached out for her bedside table she felt nothing, then – as she stretched further, bewildered – her fingers met chalky, gritty, cold wood, the floor, too close . . . and with a jolt she remembered where she was. Paul was a hunched, faceless mass beside her, snoring quietly on every exhalation.

She needed a wee. She tried to ignore it and go back to sleep, but in vain. At last she eased herself out of her rustling sleeping bag, fumbled for a torch, and found her slippers. It was cold, and her dressing gown was buried somewhere in one of the bulging laundry bags. But as she crossed the room she felt something soft under her foot, and picked it up. Paul's jumper. She dragged it on over her pyjamas. Then, following the bobbing circle of torchlight, she made her way down the stairs to the freezing lavatory. The seat slid to one side as she sat down, and she had to put her hand against the wall to steady herself.

Something trembled, very slightly, under her fingers. She jerked away, the seat clunking sideways again, her shoulder hitting something – a broom handle? – that clattered and fell to the floor. She swung the torch round to point at the wall. The circle of light fell on grimy tiles, with a single vertical crack like a clinging hair. Slowly she replaced her hand. At first she thought she had imagined it: then, faintly, she felt the sensation again. It was a crackling, creeping sort of vibration, like a nail scraping at the wall from the inside.

She sat very still, her pyjamas round her knees, her fingers pressed to the tiles. After a minute she thought it had stopped; but it started again, a little stronger than before. She had a vision of something stretching into the mortar, easing into the gaps between the bricks, pausing wherever it met resistance to search for another way round. Suddenly, just under her fingertip, the tile seemed to judder, as if it had almost leapt out of the wall – as if all that separated her from the creeping thing was one cracked, brittle layer of ceramic . . .

She scrambled to her feet, jerking her pyjama bottoms up, and staggered into the hall. A drop of urine slid down her leg. The torch bounced in her hand, its beam sliding wildly across the piles of rubble and the steel props that held up the floor joists above. It was not a big house, but for a second she did not know which way to go – left, right, where were the stairs? As she paused, looking both ways, she thought she heard a dusty rustle from the doorway ahead of her. Something was there; something alive. When she took a step forward she smelt the putrid, dead-root scent of dry rot.

Upstairs Paul was asleep, snoring gently; upstairs there was a mattress, a sleeping bag still warm from the heat of her body; upstairs was their little world, safe as a child's game . . .

She could have retreated. Instead she tightened her grip on the torch, and inched down the hallway – what had been the hallway – towards the source of the sound. The smell grew stronger, with a fleshy undertone, and the dry whisper in the air broadened, coming from behind her as well as ahead. She clenched her jaw, feeling her teeth give a brittle creak. She would not look over her shoulder. She stood in the doorway of the sitting room and pointed the circle of torchlight at the chimney breast.

At first she couldn't make sense of what she was seeing. In the treacherous light she thought that she was looking at a hole, a pitch-black void in a disintegrating wall. Then, as she blinked, she understood. The fruiting body had grown. It spread out from a matted tarry heart into a tracery of inky threads, a knot of shadowy roots that pulsed and burrowed; it reached from floor to ceiling, from wall to wall, a dark throbbing network of veins.

She thought: breathe. But the inhalation brought the stench into the back of her throat. Slowly, stiffly, she took a step backwards. Somewhere behind her were the stairs, and safety. But as she brushed the doorframe something like a cobweb trailed over the back of her neck. She yelped and swung round, scrabbling frantically to get whatever it was off her skin; the hand with the torch smashed into the wall, and the light went out.

There was silence. A wavering purplish afterimage hung in front of her eyes. If something moved in the darkness, she wouldn't see. She wanted to run, but her body wouldn't obey her. She heard herself whimper, and put her hands over her mouth.

'Jen? Jen?'

Footsteps. Or her heart, or something coming for her—

'Jen? What's going on?'

Light came down the stairs. Lurching shadows slid back and forth, as if the whole house was being thrown from side to side. She gasped, reaching out, 'Paul—?'

The light came closer, blazing in her face. Hands gripped her shoulders. 'Jen,' he said – yes, it was Paul, of course it was Paul – 'what the hell's going on? You woke me up.'

'It's all right,' she said, 'I broke my torch, that's all – and the

dry rot, in the sitting room – oh God, Paul, the dry rot! I thought
you'd dealt with it—'

'What?'

'The – I saw it, it gave me a shock – I didn't know it had
got so big—'

She heard him grunt. The light bobbed, blinding her. 'What
the fuck are you talking about? Are you OK? I was worried.'

'Yes,' she said, and in her relief she heard her voice crack.
It would only make him angry if she cried, but she couldn't
help herself. 'Yes, I'm fine – I just saw the fruiting body on the
wall, and it—'

'Calm down, for fuck's sake,' he said. 'You'll wake the neighbours.'

'Sorry – sorry . . .' She gave a long shuddering laugh. It was
hard to stop; her giggles had a strident, metallic note. 'Oh God,
I was so scared, it's ridiculous – thank goodness you—'

There was a crack, like something bursting beside her ear.
Scalding pain flashed across her cheek, so strong it sent unreal
colours whirling through her vision. She staggered, flailing for
balance, and the back of her head hit something else, something
sharp and hard. Through the ache in her skull she could feel
the burning mark of his hand, as if it was branded into her
face.

'Oh, fuck – Jen – okay,' he said, fumbling for her arms and
easing her to the floor. 'Okay, shit, come here, sit down, just
– all right . . .'

She obeyed him. After a while the pain stopped. He scrabbled
in the dark, only his headtorch visible; then, with a snap, he
found the switch for the temporary electrics, and the room was
filled with stark white light. They looked at each other, blinking
away the dazzle. She said, in a thin flat voice, 'You – hit me.'

'I had to.' He stared at her, eyes wide. 'You're not seriously
suggesting—? Jen, that's what you're supposed to do, when someone's hysterical – I was scared you'd hurt yourself or something
– and you did, didn't you, you fell . . . Are you okay? Let me
look.' He bent over her, turning her jaw with such gentle fingers
that she knew he was telling the truth. She *had* been laughing

hysterically. Of course he hadn't meant to hit her, or not that hard. He drew back. 'There's a bit of a cut there, behind your ear. Not bad but a bit messy. You poor old sausage,' he added, squeezing her shoulder as he got up. 'Stay here, I'll get the first aid kit.'

A moment later he was back with a bowl of clean water. He bathed her scalp so carefully it hardly hurt at all, wiping at the drips before they reached the collar of her pyjamas. She shut her eyes. Finally he dropped the cloth into the bowl and sat down beside her, his arm around her shoulders. She leant into his warmth, shivering.

'Silly girl,' he said, 'wandering around in the dark. It's a building site, love. No wonder you hurt yourself.'

She didn't answer at once. She looked down at their legs, pressed against each other, the parallel stripes of their pyjamas. At last, when she was sure she could speak without crying, she said, 'You said you'd dealt with the dry rot.'

'I *did* deal with it.'

'Well, whatever you did, it didn't work—' She flung her arm out to point at the chimney breast, her voice rising in spite of herself. Then she stopped.

It had gone.

The bricks were bare, clean – or rather, not clean, dusty and grimy, with clinging crumbs of mortar – but empty of that horrible sooty web. In the harsh light there was no ambiguity. The wall was simply a wall. She sniffed, and the air smelt of nothing more than building sites and the antiseptic from the first aid kit. 'It was there,' she said, 'and it stank.'

Paul swallowed. 'You know,' he said, 'sometimes Steve smokes hash in the van. Maybe my jumper . . .'

'It was there. I saw it.'

A silence. He pulled her closer into his embrace, pressing her face into his chest. 'You're okay, aren't you? I mean . . .' But he didn't say what he meant; he drew in his breath, hesitating, before he went on, 'Is it okay, the – you know – the fall didn't affect the—?'

'It was my head.'

'Yeah. Of course. But is it moving, or whatever—?'

'It's too early for that, Paul.'

'Of course.' He nodded. She felt him give her a long, sidelong stare. Her neck ached with the effort of not meeting his eyes. 'The dry rot's gone,' he said, very softly, stroking her arm with his thumb. 'I dealt with it. Nothing there. You can see that now, can't you?'

She could. She could see that now. She nodded.

'Okay, Jen? Talk to me.'

'Yes,' she said, 'I can see it's gone.'

He squeezed her tighter, as if he was glad she'd finally come to her senses. She breathed in his warm, sleepy smell.

It could not possibly have been there, hanging like a dark fleshy shroud from ceiling to floor. It was not there now; so it had not been there at all. It could not have been there when the light came on, although she thought she had seen it over Paul's shoulder, before he hit her. It could not possibly have retreated into the brickwork, sliding out of sight with neat malice, like a retracted claw.

And if it had not been there it could not possibly be listening now, waiting in the walls, refusing to show itself to anyone other than her.

The midwife said, 'And everything's all right at home?' She scrolled to the end of the booking-in form without looking up.

'Um,' Jen said. 'We're doing a house renovation, so . . .'

'Ah, classic new-mum stuff. Take my advice, go easy on the expensive baby wallpaper, it won't be long before they're old enough to trash the place.' She checked the last box and looked at her watch. 'Great, well—'

'Actually,' Jen blurted out, 'I keep having night terrors – stupid ones – but they're like hallucinations, only it's a smell, I think I can smell—'

'Oh God, don't get me started on pregnancy nose,' the midwife said, rolling her eyes. 'When I was expecting my first I was like a bloodhound. A cup of coffee within fifty metres made me retch. Perfectly normal, though. Right, well, we'll see you for a scan in a few weeks. Don't forget the folic acid.' She got up, gestured to the door, and gave Jen a cheery wave.

Afterwards there was nowhere to go. It was too far to walk to the library, and Paul would frown at her spending money in a café when things were so tight. She dug her hands into her coat pockets and trudged back to the house. It was not so bad. If she wrapped herself in both sleeping bags and put the heater on, she could make herself quite cosy. Maybe today she should make an effort to read Paul's sister's old magazines, with stories like *I MARRIED MY WIFE'S LOVER* and *I THOUGHT IT WAS A BABY BUT IT WAS CANCER*. It had been kind of her to donate them, after all; Paul had been right, Jen had been rude and ungrateful to ask for her own books out of storage instead . . .

But when she came through the front door, Paul was already home. A new enormous pile of insulation was blocking the stairs, and she had to duck to get under a long package wedged across the hallway. And there was the smell of— no, the smell that was not really there, the smell that the midwife had dismissed with a roll of her eyes. Jen paused, listening: Paul's voice rose, '. . . fucking holiday *again*, all right, so I'm sacking him, you tell him that from— Jesus, *fuck*.'

She felt herself rock backwards, and put her hand flat against the bare bricks. It was a lovely surprise, that he should be here, that she would get to see him during the day. She waited five seconds, then picked her way over the lumps of hardcore to what had been – what would be – the dining room, and stood wavering, waiting for him to notice her.

He turned, shoving his phone into his pocket. 'Fucking party wall surveyors,' he said. 'Fucking sharks. We should've ignored the whole fucking process.'

'Hello,' she said.

'Still think the neighbours had a point, wanting to appoint their own?'

'I didn't – darling,' she said, holding out her hand, 'you know I didn't mean it like that, I only said that they don't know us, they don't know you and how careful you are—'

'Fine. Yeah. All right, never mind. It's done now.' He slumped against the wall. 'Another two weeks' wait. Then it'll be winter, and we're building in lime mortar. We're fucked.'

She bit her lip.

There was a silence. He dragged his hands through his hair. 'Where've you been, anyway? I thought you'd be here for the deliveries.'

'I had my checking-in appointment,' she said, and added, at his blank look, 'with the midwife.'

'Oh right. How did it go?'

'It was good. Great. I've got a scan three weeks today, at the hospital.' She smiled at him.

He didn't smile back. 'Well, you'll have to go on the bus, I need to go up north for those windows I ordered.'

The uneven ground slipped, slightly, under her feet. 'I thought we could – go together,' she said. 'Don't you want to be there?'

He bent his head, as if to gather his strength. 'It may have escaped your notice,' he said, 'but I have quite a lot to do. I can't just take days off whenever I fancy.'

'Oh.'

He jerked his shoulders as if something had pricked him. 'Give me a fucking break,' he said, 'this was your idea, Jen, I'm doing this for you, this whole house is your baby—'

'But—'

'I am so *tired*. It's exhausting living like this. I just want to get through it. Can you please just pull your weight and stop complaining?'

'I'm sorry,' she said. 'I know how hard you're working – I just thought—' But she could not get to the end of the sentence before her voice wobbled. She bowed her head, but it was too late.

'Oh, for fuck's *sake* . . .' He kicked sharply at a piece of hardcore; then, suddenly, he swung back to her. 'Right. Listen to me. I've had enough – no, listen! Don't you think I've got enough to think about? I should be ordering materials and chasing the structural engineer, not endlessly worrying about *you*. I'm sorry you're anxious and you have nightmares. Really,

I am. But I can't – I *cannot* go on like this! Treading on eggshells, tiptoeing around you, trying to second-guess everything, just because you can't control your emotions. Just fucking pull yourself together, will you?'

There was a silence.

Paul heaved a sigh. 'Shit,' he said, more softly, 'that was . . . I didn't want to say it like that. But it needed saying, Jen. This has to stop.'

'But – Paul . . .' She cleared her throat, because it was true, she was too emotional, and it wasn't fair on him when he was working so hard. She was being selfish, she needed to make more of an effort. She summoned her calmest, steadiest voice. 'You're right,' she said. 'I'm sorry. I'll do better, I promise. But the scan . . . It's a child, darling. It's *our* child – mine and yours—'

He said, almost under his breath, 'If it even *is*.'

For a moment she didn't understand what he'd said. She stared at him, confused; and it wasn't until she saw a flash of shame in his eyes – gone so quickly it might never have been there at all – that the meaning hit her.

She turned, reaching stupidly for the wall as if otherwise she might topple over. Through rising tears she saw the impassable pile of insulation blocking the stairs, and went the other way, towards the sitting room. There was the smell again, putrid and musty; but there was nowhere else to go. She stumbled through the doorway, but there was no door to shut behind her. She kept moving, as if the wall in front of her might retreat and let her out.

'Jen? Jen! Jen, come on . . .'

She had been holding her hands out in front of her like a sleepwalker. Now they met the chimney breast, the bare brick-work cold against her palms. She leant her weight on it, and something seemed to crackle just under the surface. If she pushed hard enough, would the house fall?

'Please stop crying. Please. I didn't mean . . . You're massively overreacting. Will you *please* stop making that noise?'

She hadn't known she was making a noise. She didn't know how to stop.

'Fuck's sake, it was a joke! Stop it. Shut the fuck up, will you? *Jen!*' He took hold of her arm and pulled her round to face him. She didn't resist, and his grip softened. He peered into her face. 'Okay,' he said, 'Okay, take deep breaths. Come on, that's right. Good girl. Jesus, what a mess . . . Don't worry. We'll help you get better. It's going to be okay.'

It was. It was going to be okay. She forced herself to hold his gaze, blinking until her vision cleared and no more tears came to blur it again.

'Good,' he said, 'good.' He pulled her close, and held her, his warm cheek against hers. 'I love you. You know I don't regret a thing, don't you? Even if I'd known you were so – so fragile . . .'

She gave a watery gulp of laughter, burying her face in his old work fleece. 'I love you too,' she said, into the dusty fabric. 'I love you so much . . .' Her throat closed again, aching with relief – because all that mattered was this, his arms around her, the fact that they loved each other . . .

'Okay, baby?'

She raised her head. 'Yes, I'm all right, I'm just . . .' But as she spoke she felt a warm gust on her lips, a sly waft of rotten-ness like the opening of a long-forgotten lunchbox. It didn't fade; if anything, it grew stronger, so that she couldn't ignore it any more. She pulled back, so that she could look round. Nothing. 'Can you smell that?'

'Smell—? Oh, Christ, don't start that again. Seriously, I am at the end of my tether, I don't have much patience left—'

'It's the dry rot,' she said. 'I know you think I'm crazy, but—'

'I said, *don't start again.*'

They stared at each other. He was right. She knew he was right. All she had to do was keep quiet, and pretend it wasn't there. Then everything would be fine.

In the corner of her eye, something moved. Something dark, something thin and thirsty. She could not help herself: she let herself turn to look.

He followed her gaze. When she glanced back at him, his eyes slid back to meet hers.

She said, 'You see?' Her heart was hammering. The smell filled her whole mouth and nose. In her peripheral vision, the tendrils thickened, as though the fruiting body was sucking tar through its long veins, swallowing endlessly, endlessly swelling . . . She could hear it now, the gritty scratch as it bled the mortar dry, the crumbling as it dug deeper into the cracks. And a whisper, too, almost comprehensible, an inhuman mutter that would form words any moment now, if she only listened.

'Jen,' he said, putting his hands on her shoulders, 'you need to talk to someone.'

'It's there,' she said, 'it's *there*, please, Paul, just *look*—'

'Stop it. I mean it. Stop it!'

'But—'

'*Stop!*' His hands slid inwards, pinching her collarbone. 'Shut up, shut up, I can't take any more – just shut *up*—'

She gasped, scrabbling at him, 'Paul, please, I'm not crazy – it's *there*—'

'Shut up,' he said, 'shut up, shut up, *shut up*.' His hands grasped her neck, and squeezed.

She couldn't breathe. For a split second she only felt disbelief, like when she was a child, tripping and winding herself: the primitive incredulity of the world stopping, the wrongness of no air when it should come easily. Then there was panic, the throbbing timebomb of blood building in her head, the burn of her jerking lungs. She saw her hands, little helpless hands that scratched at the front of Paul's fleece. She could not breathe. She would die if she could not breathe. Her baby—

Dark roots bloomed across her vision, black as blood-gorged lice. They pulsed and grew, weaving into a web, blocking out the last of the light.

She gave a last, desperate convulsion, jerking one knee up as hard as she could, and flung her weight sideways. She felt Paul stagger and lose his footing; then he spun, with an odd, greasy smoothness as though they were waltzing, and crashed into the chimney breast. He cried out as his back thudded into the mantelpiece; then he slipped, and there was the sharper thwack of his skull against marble as he fell.

Then there was no sound at all.

He did not move. His head was not quite the shape it should have been. There was blood on the mantelpiece, and blood underneath him, creeping out from under his hair.

She thought, clearly, that in a moment she would find his phone and call an ambulance, and then she would start with five rescue breaths and thirty compressions, and she would keep on and on, without giving up, until they came and told her very kindly she did not need to any more, and asked if there was someone they could call. And then someone would probably call the police.

She looked up. The fruiting body was there. There again. It hung, clinging and stinking, from the brickwork, strangely beautiful: a ragged widow's veil of rot.

She remembered how she had tried to touch it, that first day when they visited the house. Now there was no one to stop her. She took a long breath, and the smell was not as bad as she thought, it was a little intoxicating, like hashish.

It did not move. Naturally it did not move, because it was only dry rot. She refused to think about that instant when she had shoved Paul away from her, and how easy it had been, as if something else had helped. Tomorrow she would get a man in to deal with it, once and for all.

The phone. The ambulance. She took one last long breath, looking down at Paul lying in the hearth. Above him, the fruiting body was like a lace wall-hanging, a modern artwork in charcoal and burnt bone, a monochrome picture of something unfurling, something in the process of becoming. It reminded her of something else, but she could not think what.

It was too early still for the baby to move, but she could have sworn that it did, brushing against the inside of her flesh so softly it was like a silken thread; and she imagined it, blind in its dark pocket, reaching out with instinctive certainty towards its parent.

Daisies

by Mariana Enríquez
Translated by Megan McDowell

Dad should be here, not me, thought Lucas as he waited for his luggage. As always, it was taking forever to emerge on the slow-moving baggage carousel at the Corrientes airport. Why had he checked in his suitcase, when it was just a carry-on that would have easily fit in the cabin? Why had he checked it in, when he knew it would be the last to come out, and it would be just him standing there beside the carousel, in a cold sweat because losing it was just about the worst thing he could imagine? Maybe it was because he needed that extra time before he could face his family. It hadn't been that long since he'd last seen them, only two years. But that visit had been a holiday, just for fun.

This time was different. It wasn't fair to get angry at his dad, he knew. The poor old guy would have been willing to come in Lucas's place, though he wouldn't have been happy about it. But he was off working for five months in the United States, as he did every year, and he couldn't leave except in an emergency, which this definitely wasn't. It was crazy, yes, but not an emergency.

Lucas had got the call from his aunt Lidia at six in the morning. To someone who rose at dawn like her, six was a perfectly reasonable time to call, while to Lucas, who worked nights and had only just gone to sleep, it was infuriating. Outrageous, even: Lidia knew her nephew worked the night shift, but she was a selfish, inconsiderate woman, and that's why the rest of the family, who were all nice if a little quirky, had chosen her for the dirty job of calling with the morbid news. As Lucas listened, he felt as if his aunt's voice were coming straight out of a nightmare.

Hi, Lucas darling, it's your Aunt Lidia. We're all fine here. Mechi still talks to herself but she's okay. She stopped teaching, though, because she says all the kids turn into ghosts. Yes, that's right – their faces change. Yes, ghosts, like . . . apparitions – she's afraid of them. But she's doing okay really, the doctor gave her some tranquillisers, and she goes to the witch doctor too, so she's fine. But that's not why I'm calling, dear. I'm calling because we have to move your dear mother from a niche to an urn and there's an issue about it – direct descendants have to be there. Yes, I know we're her siblings and that makes us close relatives, but there's an issue we can't make a decision on given that she has a son. The niche at the San Luis cemetery has expired, they move you to an urn after thirty years. Doesn't time fly? I tell you what, it's really something. You have to come and see her yourself; what a shame your dad isn't around. No, Lucas dear, I'm telling you that we can't just put your mum into the urn. Because there's something else, something I can't tell you about on the phone. No, I can't, you have to come, stop messing around and just come. It's serious, yes. No, I can't tell you, these are things you have to discuss face to face, and when you find out you'll thank me. And you can tell your poor father later, we really can't give him news like this over the phone either, when he's not even in the country.

When Lidia said 'we can't make a decision on our own,' Lucas pictured them all huddled around the phone and as close to the air conditioner as possible, all of them holding their breath, complicit, because they had chosen Lidia, the bold one, to make the call. He imagined Walter, always with a hammer in his hand or nails between his lips, constantly repairing furniture in his house, almost the only thing he'd done since being widowed.

53

Then then there was Julio, a taxi driver, an affable and charming man until he started talking politics. And Mechi, the rural schoolteacher, the manageable madwoman, who talked to herself and probably still drank her nightly beer before going to bed, even though she also took sleeping pills. These were his dead mother Margarita's four siblings, who lived together on a huge plot of land. Over decades, they had each built a house where they lived with their families; all except Lidia, who wanted to be alone and didn't like to live with anyone, not even her own children – she'd thrown them out as soon as they finished high school, which in Corrientes was seen as practically akin to murdering your child. Lucas remembered that plot with its four houses as almost like a village, except that all its inhabitants were related.

Kids and dogs. Macaws and salamanders, tarantulas and black widows, rue plants, climbing vines, and Mechi's prayers when she was hit by her fervour for the Virgin of Itatí. Playing cards and dice, and especially Lottery, until very late every night – at least until it cooled off, around midnight – while sipping *tereré* or *amargo serrano*. The sound of *chamamé* playing as well until late, and sometimes he'd lug a mattress up to the terrace because there was no air conditioner in those days, and it was easier to sleep up there where the night breeze blew. Lucas loved to spend nights on the terrace back then, to feel sleep come on slowly while he looked up at the stars, which were more plentiful and beautiful out there against the coal-black Corrientes sky.

His dad had done well to keep up contact with the family, and he'd also been very brave. A weaker man would have just concerned himself with raising his son and left the place where his wife had died behind. He'd been deeply in love, Lucas knew, and staying in touch must have been painful. But from the beginning, his dad had believed that a big family was best.

Lucas was two years old when his mother drowned in the Paraná. He didn't remember her at all, didn't have a single impression of her, not even a vague sense he could dress up as a memory. But he knew things about her: maybe not so many, but he felt like he knew her, like he could identify her as a palpable presence. That was thanks to his father, who had made the decision not to erase her from their lives, and he had managed it with help from the Corrientes relatives, that strange and lovable family. His dad had always seemed content, if a little sad, as he watched Lucas laugh and splash in the lake, or kill palometas with rocks, or stomp on the beetles that covered the Junín pedestrian walk like a noisy rug in summer. Yes, when he was a kid he'd had some good times in Corrientes.

Back then, of course, during those happy years, he didn't know exactly how his mother had died, beyond 'she drowned in the river'. Now that Lucas was over thirty, things were different. Or maybe he was the one who had changed? Now he thought the family was irresponsible, including his dad. Some of their eccentricities weren't so lovable anymore, like his uncle's blatant racism, or Aunt Mechi's smiles that she flashed into empty corners, always in conversation with herself, or someone no one else could see.

Finally he spotted his suitcase approaching behind the central pillar of the sluggish carousel. He collected it and took a deep breath before going out to find Aunt Lidia, who was waiting in her beige Chevrolet, fanning herself in the stifling noontime heat.

*

Aunt Lidia barely spoke on the drive home from the airport, just smoked her long cigarettes. Lucas decided not to ask any questions until they got to the house: he knew the inner workings of this family, and he was sure they had decided not to fill him in until they were all together.

And, indeed, the other three siblings, his aunt and uncles, were waiting on the pavement in front of the gate to the central garage (this was where everyone entered the estate: inside was a sort of covered parking lot, since there were so many family members and so many cars). They lined up to hug him, even Julio, with whom Lucas had had a shouting match on his last visit, a fight in which he'd decided never to speak to his uncle again — that 'fucking fascist dictator apologist', as Lucas had called him then, and he hadn't even been drunk. They ushered him into Lidia's house, probably because she was in charge of this complicated exchange of information. Lucas sat down at the table with its plastic tablecloth and told his four relatives that he didn't understand why he'd had to come all this way while being kept in the dark, what the hell was all this mystery, they should spit it out now or he was out of there and they'd never see his face again, as God was his witness.

'Look at this kid getting all worked up, such a city boy, isn't he? Mechi, bring him a cold drink, but give the glass a rinse first, they're all filthy,' said Lidia, offering Lucas a cigarette. 'I'm going to tell you, son. So the thing is, the cemetery has called wanting to move your mum from a niche to an urn.'

'You already told me that.'

'Don't interrupt me now, I've got enough problems. Mechi, my head is killing me, go over and ask Juan Carlos to give you a strip of Migral on credit, I'll pay him later. So, I told the cemetery people to go ahead and move her. "All right, ma'am," they said, "we'll do that." Two hours later they call me back and say, "Ma'am, you're going to have to come down here, we opened the coffin to move the bones to an urn, and your sister is intact." That's what they tell me. I gave them a real piece of my mind: "What are you talking about? *Intact?*" I yelled at them. "My sister died thirty years ago! What do you mean, you degenerates?" Because cemetery workers are real degenerates, you know? But not these, these are some poor Christian folks. So I headed out there, I got right in the car and drove out. And there was your mom, Lucas, darling. There she *is*, I should say – intact.'

'What do you mean, *intact?*'

Lucas couldn't even yell or get angry. He could barely comprehend what his aunt was saying.

'Intact, I'm telling you, honey. Your mum never decomposed. She's a bit shrivelled, poor thing, all brown and dried-up. But she didn't decompose. Her body is *intact.*'

His two uncles – Mechi wasn't back yet – nodded anxiously. Lucas figured they must have seen her too.

'When did this happen?' he asked.

'A week ago. We waited to see if she would decompose—'

'Aunt Lidia, for the love of God.'

'Don't you go acting all shocked, she may have been your mother, but you didn't really know her. I did, she was my sister, and you can't even imagine what it was like to see her there, as if she were alive, I swear, after thirty years. I had forgotten what she looked like.'

The discussion was long, and Lucas found himself drinking *tereré*, telling his aunts and uncles they were crazy, clutching at his head. A body that hadn't decayed? There could be so many reasons. A sort of vacuum seal in the niche. Some kind of chemical process. Had someone injected her with formaldehyde, or started a mummification process on his mother's body? The aunts and uncles said no. More relatives joined them: Julio's kids, looking very upset, and one of them, the youngest, even a little scared. Cousin Amanda, Walter's daughter, came in carrying her smallest child. She had seen the cadaver, too. And she tossed a grenade right onto the kitchen table: in San Luis, the town closest to the cemetery, some people had found out about the miracle (*It's not a miracle!* Lucas shouted in his head, but kept listening), and had been going to pray to Margarita. They said she smelled like jasmine. The scent of holiness.

'That's enough!' Lucas found his words again. 'She gets cremated, and that's that!'

'But what if Margarita is a saint?' Uncle Walter asked shyly, not taking his eyes from his hammer.

Lucas snorted and stood up, saying he was going out for a while, he needed air. His mother – a saint!

'Go and see Claudia if you want,' said Aunt Lidia. 'She's cleaning the pool.'

Lucas smiled involuntarily. Of course Claudia hadn't taken part in that ridiculous meeting. His cousin was the best of the family.

*

'You're a sight for sore eyes, pal,' Claudia said before giving him a long, tight hug. They were next to the square turquoise pool, behind the house where she still, at almost thirty years old, lived with her mother, Mechi. Lucas had relaxed as soon as he saw her. She was his cousin, but more than that, she was his friend, and the only person he could trust right now.

Years ago, Claudia had been the one to tell him the truth about his mother. The two of them had been trying to stick a cigarette into a horned frog's mouth to see if it was true that it would inhale until it burst. They had stolen a pack from Uncle Julio, and had already wasted ten cigarettes when their conversation turned to the Paraná's undertow: two kids their age – around fifteen – had recently drowned, and the newspaper said it was because of the backwaters, how people didn't respect them.

'Your mum died because there was a whirlpool. Otherwise, she could have untied herself easily.'

Lucas still remembered that phrase clearly: 'she could have untied herself'. He had asked Claudia what she meant.

'What, you mean they never told you?' Claudia asked.

Never told him what? Claudia explained calmly but also carefully, because she knew the horrible effects, all the distrust and emptiness, that came when family secrets were revealed. She had learned a few of them herself, she told him. Their family had a lot.

It was a custom, and a game, among the young people in Corrientes: you jumped into the Paraná river tied together, two by two, and untied yourselves underwater. Everyone would bet on which of the pairs would get free first, and the winners could make a pretty penny. His mum had done it, just for kicks: that was always why they did it, not for the money. It was fun.

That morning, about twenty of them had met up on a pier near the city, Claudia didn't know exactly where. Lucas had been two years old, and it was the first time since his birth that his mother had felt like joining in with the games again. She had jumped in first, tied to her sister Mechi, but she got out last. Or more precisely, she never got out: she was pulled out. She and Mechi had got trapped in an undertow. They struggled against the water for several minutes – the people on the shore said it was more than five, but surely they were exaggerating. Mechi had finally untied the rope and crawled out half-unconscious; she had to be taken to the hospital. Julio and Walter jumped into the water to pull out their sister, who was already dead, though they took her to the hospital anyway. Baby Lucas was on the pier in his father's arms. It was said Mario had fought with Margarita, that he didn't want her to take part in the game. But no one told Margarita what to do.

'That's why my mother is crazy,' Claudia had explained to him, nonchalantly. 'She thinks she killed your mum, because she couldn't save her. She blames herself.'

Then they spent a while debating why people would do something so dangerous, especially if they were mothers of small children. Claudia told him that, the way she'd heard it, they didn't even think about the danger. They thought about the wagers, about winning, and drinks that night at the rowing club. They were people who liked to lie in the sun, go dancing, take a boat out on the river. They brought their kids with them. Not like today's parents. They were idiots, Claudia and Lucas had concluded at the time.

Lucas could never quite bring himself to confront his father about the truth of the Paraná game. He never asked for details about the fight his parents had beforehand. He never yelled, *why did you let her do it, when I was so little?* He never did, because he knew his father was asking himself the same question, every day.

'I swear, these crazy old coots won't ever just let us live our lives,' said Claudia, leaning the net she was using to scoop leaves and bugs from the pool against a tree. She gestured for him to sit down. Lucas took off his sneakers, rolled up his jeans, and put his feet in the water. Claudia sat down beside him and lit a cigarette.

'Just what we need, our very own Lourdes right here,' sighed Claudia.

Lucas made a face and let out a brief laugh, although what he really wanted to do was cry.

Claudia changed the subject. 'How's José?'

'Fine. I didn't tell him much. He's swamped with some problem at work, he ignores me, I'm sure he's glad to get me out of the house for a while.'

'It's for the best. That one's got a lot of character.'

'He would blow a gasket over this. Sorry, everything I say seems like a joke.'

'So what are you going to do, buddy?'

'Cremate her anyway. Or . . . no. I don't know what the hell I'm saying, to be honest. I can't think straight.'

'You want to see her?'

'I don't think so. But that's why they called me here, right?'

'Well, yeah. In case you wanted to look at her.'

'They're such fucking ghouls.'

'Hey, shut up! I went to see her. Don't look at me like that, what do you want from me? I took Mum there, I barely even looked at the coffin. But there was no saying no to my mum.'

'And what happened?'

'The usual, she fainted, had a fit as always. So, what if they accuse you of burning a saint?'

'Don't wind me up, Claudia. They're crazy! Is it true that people are already praying to her?'

'Who knows. So they say.'

Lucas huffed. *Why did I come, why didn't I tell them to figure it out on their own?* he asked himself, and right away he had the answer: because he didn't want his father to get dragged into it. To protect him. That's why.

From the edge of the pool, Lucas could hear the debate still going on, but no longer at Lidia's place – she must have kicked them out, unable to stand all those people in her house. They were at Mechi's now: he could see the three siblings' shadows behind the living room curtain.

'I have to tell you this, because no one else will,' Claudia said. 'My mother thinks this is a sign, and she doesn't want to have Aunt Margarita cremated. That's the problem. She went to Itatí in July, and she says the Virgin told her something important was going to happen.'

Lucas looked at his cousin in the darkness. She ran a hand

over her face to push back a rebellious lock of hair, and avoided meeting his eyes.

'My mum thinks she's got her sister back, that this means the Virgin has forgiven her crime. Last night she asked me to convince you.'

'Convince me of what?'

'To conserve the body and set up a shrine where she can be worshipped.'

'You're fucking kidding me.'

'Why would I kid you about something like this?'

'I'm not going to put her in a shrine.'

'You'd better not. I'm just telling you so you're informed.'

A black bird came flying down from the roof of the house, kissed the pool water, and kept flying. Lucas, who knew the birds of Corrientes well, couldn't tell what it was, couldn't identify the species. It had large, fine wings of a kind he'd never seen before. When it came back for a second drink, he realised why: it wasn't a bird, it was a bat. And during the ten minutes he sat there thinking in silence, he saw many more of them come down to drink from the pool.

'I have a suggestion,' said Claudia.

'Lay it on me.'

'That you wait for a couple of days to see if she decomposes on her own, with the air and the heat. Then my mum would be more receptive. A couple of days, that's all. They call the cemetery every day around here just to check on how things are going, so . . .'

'Okay. Fine, two days then. I'll stay the weekend. But either way, she gets cremated on Monday.'

Lucas didn't want to say any more, and his cousin understood and was silent too. In Mechi's house, the light and the TV came on simultaneously. From Julio's house wafted a soft *chamamé*. Lucas pulled his feet from the water and sat on a deckchair near the pool to look up at the starry sky. And when Claudia went inside to help make dinner, that's where he stayed. Waiting for his mother to rot.

*

He went to bed early but was predictably unable to sleep, as he was used to working during those hours. In the darkness of the room, with the air conditioner cranked high – his family had a generator to avoid power outages when the heat got to be too much – he researched cases of 'incorrupt bodies', as they were called. Modern mummies. What he saw, in the ones from Guanajuato, for example, was another sort of death, not one of bare skull and bones, but of desiccation. 'Petrification', it was called. But those brown, shrivelled bodies, that boy with his mouth open in a scream – they didn't seem like a miracle to be prayed to, but more like a curse. He learned, also, that the city itself had dug them up because of missed payments on the niches. In 1865! The Guanajuato government getting out ahead of late-stage capitalism. He read about the dry, airless atmosphere at some monasteries, which halted putrefaction. One thing was for sure: in the rustic San Luis cemetery, twenty minutes from Corrientes, the climate was undeniably tropical, with the river so close by. Why had they taken her there? He'd never asked that question. He didn't think about his mother very much, he realised. He knew a lot of anecdotes about her crazy, sun-kissed life, but almost nothing about her death or what came after.

Of all the bodies, the one that impressed him the most, because it didn't seem dead – the others, though not decomposed, were clearly cadavers – was that of the Spanish abbess Sor María de Jesús de Ágreda, in the church of the Order of the Immaculate Conception. He had to do a Maps search to find out where Ágreda was. Castille, northern Spain, which Lucas associated with the most intense kind of Catholicism. The photo of her was always the same: above, a plaster reproduction; below, the actual body. That was extra disturbing because, it was said, this seventeenth-century woman had had the gift of bilocation; that is, she could be in two places at once.

Would his mother look like that? So smooth and white? He doubted it. She hadn't been that pale to begin with: in photos, of which he had many, she was a healthy, smiling girl, astonishingly tall, with brown skin and white, crooked teeth. She didn't look anything like a nun.

He closed the computer after reading the story of Miguel Ángel Gaitán, a mummified baby in a white cap and little blue suit, his face dry and brown, his eyes closed and sunken, his death, though frozen in time, nevertheless clear and definitive, if a little less so than in other cases. Miguel Ángel was from the Argentinian province of La Rioja, born in La Banda in 1966. He died of meningitis as he was being taken to a hospital in Chilecito, and he was buried in the Villa Unión cemetery. All desert places, the dry, Andean Argentina: the total opposite of the terrible humid green of Corrientes. The miracles started in 1973, when the boy's grave was destroyed by the sudden flooding of those eternally parched rivers, and people could see that the body was preserved. They rebuilt his tomb, but it collapsed again: they drew the conclusion that Miguel Ángel wanted to be seen. People started leaving letters for him, and the family put him in a glass-covered coffin to protect him from the heat and the elements. The cemetery with his shrine was ten blocks from Villa Unión's main square.

The photos of Miguel Ángel were shocking, but much more impressive were the images of all those people gathered in the cemetery, under a clear blue sky, clutching knitted booties and hats.

Lucas sent his husband a message, not expecting a reply. He had already sent the requisite 'Landed safely' text. Work was tough for José these days, yes, but the distance between them wasn't just about his business worries. Lucas hadn't felt like talking to Claudia about that. He sent his father a message, too, without mentioning where he was. Just a 'how are you', which, strangely, didn't register as sent. Sometimes that could happen with the wifi, which everyone shared – the signal was terrible. He fell asleep listening to music on headphones so he wouldn't hear any noise, namely his family calling him for dinner.

He was awakened by pounding on the door. His headphones' charge had run out. He didn't even have time to open up: Aunt Lidia barged right in. Luckily, thought Lucas, the room was so cold he was wearing a T-shirt and long underwear.

'Get up, darling nephew, we're off to the cemetery. I don't know what kind of plan you and your cousin were hatching about waiting for a few days. We're in a hurry here. The employees keep on calling, they're desperate because more and more people are turning up at the cemetery.'

'Aunt Lidia, let me get dressed and have breakfast. The plan to wait was already cleared with Mechi.'

'Mechi isn't in her right mind, and Claudia backs her up because she's her mother. You're coming with us. We'll have breakfast along the way, and we'll bring *mate*. Wash your face, your eyes are all puffy, and dress up smart – we're going to see your mother.'

Lucas obeyed mechanically, though in a moment of clarity as he was brushing his teeth he felt an urge to go out and yell at Lidia. Who did she think she was, her and those other credulous morons? He was starving, and he intended to have a good breakfast.

But then he felt a sort of surrender, a waning of his rebellious spirit, an impulse to go along and behave like an adult. It was true that Mechi was unbalanced and that 'waiting' for decomposition was really too morbid – plus, they had already waited, supposedly, before they'd called him. It was disrespectful of him, an attempt to shirk his responsibilities, weird as they may be. He was going to sort this out with the municipal authorities or the cemetery administration. A sudden dark suspicion made him feel almost faint: what if they wanted to make his mother a saint so the town could become a tourist destination? Because, sure, they couldn't charge an entrance fee, but they could open a restaurant, hawk red candles and ribbons, put up a sculpture of his mother as she'd been in life, a sort of remixed Yemọja, *santería* and a little hotel. With all this in his head, he climbed into the car and asked for some food. Someone handed him a *chipa* roll, and he didn't complain because it was very good. He didn't want any *mate*, but his uncle Walter had coffee, and it was good quality.

'Claudia had to work. She says she'll come later.'

His aunt Lidia drove at full speed: Lucas noticed that the

road to San Luis, which used to be gravel, was now completely paved.

'Why is my mother in a niche?' he asked. 'Wouldn't burial have been better? You had enough cash to build her a mausoleum, and then you'd never have to move her.'

'You're a little slow today, huh? Your aunt Mechi was suicidal after the accident, darling. We had to take care of her. Your dad was drugged up to the eyeballs. We did what we could.'

'And why San Luis?'

'Good thing your dad keeps all those memories alive, huh? It's because the two of them met in that shitty town, I don't know how come. There's nothing in San Luis, not even an hourly motel. Not that those two needed motels. It was just fate, kid.'

'I'm not a kid,' said Lucas, raising his voice.

'Well then act like a man, goddammit.'

The pink-painted gates of the cemetery were thronged with people, some holding altar candles, many wearing hats to protect them from the sun. They were forming a queue, Lucas saw, and he looked up into the cemetery: there, in the main avenue, was the giant dark wood cross, with its wrap – he had always thought of it as a sort of pashmina – hanging motionless, because there was no wind, not even any birds. In some of these towns, he knew, it got so hot that birds died mid-flight. They fell to the ground with stopped hearts, like a Biblical curse.

They pushed their way in, Lucas in the lead. One woman in a loose white dress and fingerless sun gloves touched him lightly above the elbow and burst into tears. Lucas felt a surge of anger.

'What the hell do you want?' he shouted at her, ignoring the voices that were asking him to please calm down, sir.

'It's the son of the saint,' the woman sobbed, and she backed away from him slowly – putting on a show to inspire pity, thought Lucas. He heard a collective gasp as people – twenty, thirty of them – realised who he was. Some of them held full-colour photos of his mother. Where had they got those? It showed her in a black-and-white striped dress and high heels, in profile, her hair in a messy bun. She looked sexy, like a model, nothing like a saint. Facebook, he thought. Her siblings had set up a Facebook page in her memory and uploaded photos to it. How had they not made it private?

Then he thought, why would they? Who could ever have foreseen this?

The cemetery director appeared holding a folder: his status as the boss was very clear, with his beige polo shirt, dark sunglasses, and a jacket in which he must have been sweltering. He made no attempt to get rid of the people who, in any case, were just silently standing at the gate with the air of runners just before the starting pistol. They were clearly waiting for the symbolic opening of the gates before they spilled inside.

'This way,' said the director, leading them away from the office and towards a small crypt belonging to the Italian Society. In the middle of the modest space was a coffin; there were others on the surrounding shelves, some much older and dirtier, and other caskets that looked new. Lucas went closer to it: his family stayed a few steps behind. Without consulting him, the director leaned down and opened the coffin: Lucas expected the top to open on hinges like a chest, but it slid to one side.

There was his mother.

The solemn moment became grotesque when Aunt Mechi sobbed, her voice hoarse and ragged with grief:

'Look, she's smiling! She forgives me!'

She wasn't smiling, thought Lucas. Her lips were stretched back in a half-moon shape, exposing her teeth, but it wasn't a smile. He was surprised to see that his mother's teeth were even more uneven than they looked in photos. Crooked, in fact. Maybe something that happened post-mortem?

Her eyes were closed, arms at her sides. Lucas felt nothing beyond mild disgust: no agitation, no sorrow. She was a dried-up mummy, not like the abbess with her supple skin. She was the colour of leather. Her long dark hair surrounded a face that was lifeless and by no means *intact*. Her mouth wasn't wide open like the Guanajuato mummies, no doubt because it had been sewn shut inside, a practice that hadn't started yet in the nineteenth century: that's why those mummies appeared to be screaming while the one at his feet seemed to smile. She was wearing a dress of indeterminate colour that, unlike her flesh, had partly rotted away; the skin of her chest looked like roast suckling pig, her hands like the remains of a bird. Lucas was sure he would dream about her later, but in that moment he felt only coldness. Inside the tomb, though it was cool, the smell of his aunts' tobacco breath floated in the air, along with the sound of Mechi's whimpering.

'She can still be cremated, right?' he asked the cemetery director, who hadn't removed his dark glasses.

'Of course, sir, but when she's like this . . .'

'She's dead,' Lucas said. 'She is obviously dead, and there is no smell of the ghostly flowers I've heard all about. I don't know why the cadaver didn't decompose normally, I'll have to consult an expert on that, but I know I want you to cremate my mother, because she's dead. End of story.'

The director went to close the coffin, but before he could, Mechi threw herself to the ground and crawled over until her head was next to the cadaver's. She was talking to the mummy. It was obscene, Lucas thought, sickened: the smell of decomposition coming from another body in that shabby crypt forced him to choke back bile while his aunt, prostrate, was embracing her dead sister's neck and saying, *I won't let him disrespect you like that, he never knew you, and he hasn't said a word to Mario, Marito would never burn you, you were a princess to him, Lucas didn't tell his dad because he didn't want to hurt him but we're going to bring Mario here, he has a right, I love you and oh, yes, my little sister, smile at me, look at that crooked smile, so pretty, that black, black hair, my sister . . .*

Walter stepped in, pulled her up by the armpits and sat her in a corner near a candelabra. Mechi was drooling, and Lucas went outside to throw up under a tree. There was no one else inside the cemetery, but he could swear he sensed the contained breath of the people at the gates. Or did he have to call them worshippers?

Aunt Lidia came out with the cemetery director, and Lucas

wiped at his spattered jeans and his mouth. He didn't want them to think he was weak or disgusting, so he sipped a little water from his bottle and opened a pack of the spearmint gum he always had on him.

'The director here says there are no openings in the crematorium,' said his aunt.

'Fine, we'll take her to Corrientes.'

The director interrupted:

'What I meant was, there are no openings at the Corrientes crematorium, they're full. We're just a humble graveyard here, without a crematorium.'

Lucas looked at him suspiciously. That wasn't the impression his aunt had given him. The director was still wearing his sunglasses. The river's stench mingled with the scent of burning candles.

'We'll wait, then. I want her returned to the niche.'

His aunt and the director exchanged a glance.

'Look, sir, there is already a, how to put this, a makeshift altar set up at the niche.'

Lucas felt an ache at the back of his neck, and a prickle of cold sweat despite the heat.

'Then take it down!'

'We can't, out of respect for the people. Your mother was very beloved around here, and word has already spread that she's intact.'

Lucas wanted to scream at them that his mother was not intact, that 'intact' meant something else entirely, that she was just a straightforward corpse and he was going to call the police. Also, how could they all know his mother so well in this town that didn't even have any restaurants? 'Very beloved'? Holding his tongue, he gave an impatient wave of his hand and walked away to dial his father's number. He needed to talk to him. His dad always used the same phone number in the United States, but this time the call went straight to a recorded message. *The number you have dialled is not in service.* The message he had sent last night still hadn't been delivered, either. He had plenty of data. What if his father knew about this and was avoiding him?

Wait until I get my hands on you, Dad, he thought, before texting Claudia. She answered immediately: 'I'm on my way.'

Lidia and the director had walked off, heading for the wall on the river side of the cemetery, where the administration office was. Lucas wasn't about to follow them, so he texted to tell Claudia that he would wait for her on the riverbank, which was less than two blocks away. Madness, to build a cemetery in a place that could flood so easily. He pictured coffins floating in the water, dancing in whirlpools.

He headed for the gates where, as soon as they saw him – as if he were the sign they'd been waiting for – the gathered crowd surged into the cemetery. Men and women shouting, praying, holding rosaries and lit candles. Some had dried red wax between their fingers, and they were all wearing dark glasses like the director's, all chanting his mother's name: 'Margarita, Margarita!' They all, he realised, held Marguerite daisies, the flower his mother was named for: it was the only flower they carried. Where had they bought them? There were hundreds of bouquets. People also carried bottles of water that they poured over their heads. Lucas looked at their open mouths crying out: many of them also had crooked teeth. He thought about following them but didn't actually want to see where they were headed, whether it was the niches or the crypt that was his mother's temporary resting place. His arm was burning where the woman in the white dress had touched him. Must be some kind of allergy or heat rash, except that he never suffered with those, especially not on his upper arm. It felt like a jellyfish sting. He hadn't seen that woman again. Now he could hear someone playing a guitar – he didn't want to know if they had organised a party ahead of time, or why these people knew his mother, if it was even true that they did.

He left the cemetery and, under a sun that made the asphalt shimmer like a mirage, walked to the river. He wasn't crying and he no longer felt nauseous. He was thinking about all those crooked teeth. He was thinking about the teeth chattering when his aunt had touched the cadaver's head. The river stank of fish, stagnant mud, gasoline. He could see the old pier but decided to wait in the shade of a nearby tree, and sent a photo of his location to his cousin.

Sitting down, his hands not even trembling – which he found surprising – he could see that one of the river's currents was interrupted by a whirlpool. It was the first time he'd seen one so pronounced: it wasn't funnel-shaped or a crazed spiral, but looked more like the ripples of an aquatic animal turning in circles. The current carried posies of white flowers. Daisies. Most of them followed the river's flow, as if they pushed forward with some kind of strength of their own. But one bouquet was caught in the eddy, spinning, until the brown water swallowed it greedily. And then the surface was calm again, the whirlpool gone, closed like a mouth that will never speak again.

The Broccoli Eel

by Michel Faber

'Inside your tummy,' said Benny's mummy, 'lives the broccoli eel.'

Benny looked up at her, squinting away from the forkful of green vegetable, doing his best not to see the fresh bruises blushing on his mother's face.

'Oh, yes,' she smiled, gently pursuing his clenched little mouth with the hated substance. 'The broccoli eel. He lives inside of you, curled up in your stomach. And all he wants . . .' – she opened her unbruised eye wide – 'is *broccoli*.'

Benny hesitated. His mother often went into this playfully threatening state shortly after she'd been beaten up. She would tease him about something, daring him to defy her while at the same time imploring him to be a good little boy. Was teasing a kind of lying? Or was it only a game? Her games were usually spin-offs of nursery rhymes and fairy stories; she'd never mentioned anything as serious-sounding as the broccoli eel before.

'What's a eel?' he said, careful not to open his mouth too wide in case she forked the green stuff through.

'It's a fish, darling,' she replied, lowering the broccoli floret a little, to lull his guard. 'Like a big, fat scaly worm. But this fish doesn't live in the sea. It lives in the water that sloshes around your tummy. I'm sure you can feel him there sometimes, twisting around. Can't you?'

Benny swallowed hard, weak from the effort of trying to

deny so many things at once: the broccoli, the bruises on his mother's face, the sick slithering feeling inside his guts.

His mother continued:

'The broccoli eel can go for weeks without eating. He just lies still, doing nothing – but not sleeping, you understand, just waiting. Waiting for broccoli.'

A gruff male voice from the far corner of the room scoffed loudly,

'Huh! Let him wait, kid!'

Benny's mother ignored her husband's interjection. His potency was spent for the evening, flung out through his fists. Exhausted by his orgy of violence, he had surrendered to the TV. He was a lump of old clothes and grey flesh illuminated by the screen.

Benny's mother leaned close to her little boy and whispered: 'Making the broccoli eel wait and wait and wait wouldn't be very wise, sweetheart. You see, he can only go without broccoli for so long. Then he gets desperate.'

'What does he do when he's desprit?' Benny asked queasily.

'He swims out of the stomach, and goes searching,' his mother replied, baring her teeth. 'Then . . . he eats his way out.'

Benny noticed that several of his mother's teeth were outlined in scarlet, as if someone had drawn around them with a red felt-tip pen. One of his father's punches must have done some damage inside.

'Okay,' said Benny, and opened his mouth wide. The forkful of glistening green matter swooped straight in, the metal prongs poking his tongue.

His mother's scary grimace softened into a smile then, though the outline of blood remained.

'Good boy,' she murmured, with great affection. Reaching her hand out to him suddenly, she stroked his face a little too hard, as if she'd been searching for his body in the ruins of a bombed building and had just found him, against all odds, safe and well. '*Good* boy.'

*

From that day onwards, whenever there was broccoli for dinner, Benny's mother always made some reference to the broccoli eel – even when Benny ate the stuff without complaining. This proved the eel was real.

Not that Benny needed extra proof.

Because, now that he'd been alerted to its existence, he could feel the creature inside him. It had a peculiar way of disporting itself, as if it had perfected the knack of getting comfortable in a cramped space – in this case, Benny's guts. It would either curl up tight inside the stomach itself, or wriggle out to lie behind it, warming itself on the surface of the hot gurgling organ, allowing the rhythms of Benny's breathing to massage its scaly skin.

On bad days, even this degree of freedom would cramp the eel, and it would push its head up to nestle right into Benny's ribcage. Whenever it did that Benny could hardly breathe, as each inhalation pushed his fast-beating, over-sensitive heart down onto the eel's reptilian brow. The eel would blink its eyes, and the leathery skin of its eyelids would scratch against raw flesh, sending Benny into a paroxysm of agony.

'What's wrong with you?' his mother would ask him.

'I've got a pain,' he'd say, straightening up for her sake. It was vital that he spared her any additional distress, for his pains often came on just after she'd been beaten up by his father.

'That's too much junk food, causing that,' she said. 'You're all blocked up inside.'

'It's over now,' he lied. 'I'm all right.'

'A few more vegetables, that's what you need,' she grinned.

He couldn't tell if she was teasing him again. Certainly he was doing his utmost to eat all the horrid green stuff she could throw at him. Well, all except spinach. He couldn't help drawing the line at spinach; it was like a natural border of dignity.

'There's not . . . a *spinach* monster inside me, is there?' he'd asked her last time they'd clashed on the subject.

She'd laughed. (No blood in her mouth this time, just a rip in the neck of her blouse to remind him.)

'Of course not,' she'd reassured him. 'Just the broccoli eel.'

*

Benny's father, needless to say, did not eat broccoli. He ate beans sometimes, carrots maybe, potatoes certainly, but meat principally. Mostly he ate alcohol.

Benny's father disliked all the healthy green foods Benny disliked, and wasn't shy about saying so. Maybe he relished the opportunity to quarrel with Benny's mother, but maybe he genuinely (as he often loudly claimed) wanted his boy to have the freedom to choose. Life was too short, he said, to waste it arguing over vegetables.

By contrast, life was plenty long enough to waste it arguing over money, or the state of the house, or his mother's looks, or the looks of other women. These and many more topics regularly led to blows, and the blows were always to the face of Benny's mother.

'Why don't you run away from him, Mummy?' Benny asked her one night when she was taking refuge in his child-sized bed.

She giggled, sending a chill through him right down to where the broccoli eel was.

'I don't have a driver's licence,' she smirked, ruffling his hair perfunctorily as if to say, *You're a child: you don't understand anything.*

Whenever she took refuge in his bed, she would recite 'The Owl and the Pussy-cat' to him, over and over, until he fell asleep. He'd long ago given up asking what a runcible spoon was, or quince, or whether the mince was raw or cooked.

'Shhh – don't ask questions,' his mother would say. 'You'll only spoil it.'

So he would slip down the long gullet of sleep, serenaded by the elegant owl and the beautiful pussy, the sound of *'You are, You are'* echoing in his ears like an ambulance siren.

On the mornings after, Benny would lie in bed, watching his mother walk out of his bedroom and approach her own as if she were hypnotised, lured irresistibly by the sound of her husband's snoring. Sometimes the argument between Benny's parents would start afresh; more often there would be a few weary murmurs and Benny's mother would go off to fry eggs and bacon. Benny didn't get any. There were Corn Flakes in the kitchen, the ideal food for a growing boy.

If he chanced to bump into his father before leaving for school, Benny would blush, and his father would look straight through him as if he didn't exist. At these times, Benny would wonder if his father despised him more than other fathers despised their children.

The evidence was inconclusive. On the one hand, his father never took any interest in what Benny was doing at school or how he filled his time at home. But then, he never expressed approval of anything except the taste of newly opened alcohol. Oh, and occasionally someone on TV would say something and Benny's father would mutter, 'Right.'

On the plus side, there had been times not so long ago when Benny's father had taken him out to town, or at least to the local shop to buy something, and the two of them had got on fine. One Saturday morning during the last school holiday, or maybe the one before that, Benny's father had bought him a whole bag of chocolate-covered peanuts to eat all by himself: 'Don't tell your mum.'

On another occasion, when Benny had been forbidden to leave the kitchen table until he'd eaten three loathsome Brussels sprouts, his father had suddenly leaned toward him, whispered 'Watch this', and flicked the three green balls off the plate, one by one, with his massive thumb and forefinger. They rolled under the sofa. Benny's father grinned, and Benny smiled shyly back, hoping nothing else would happen to spoil this happy moment.

These were not idle memories, recalled for purely sentimental reasons. They were crucial data. To Benny, the question of whether he and his father could co-exist in the same space, man and boy, became very important to answer.

Because one day, while Benny was at school, his mother and father went out for a drive, and their car crashed into another car, and Benny's father came back home late at night, covered in abrasions and strips of sticking-plaster, without Benny's mother. She had been squashed in the passenger seat, he said.

'Squashed?' The word tasted strange on Benny's tongue.

'Squashed,' his father repeated, a throat-clearing sound, as if this was the last time he was prepared to regurgitate it.

'When will she come home?' asked Benny.

'I don't know,' said his father, staring down at his hands, which were bandaged. 'She was squashed pretty bad.'

'Can I see her?'

'She's in a special place in the hospital. Only doctors can see her. Experts, like.'

Benny nodded. He understood that a badly squashed person couldn't be allowed to go home. She would have to be fixed first. The repairs would be performed in conditions of scientific sterility. There would be operations with masks and microscopes and machines that cost millions of pounds. Doctors would discuss his mother's progress in hushed murmurs. His mother's face, in particular, would need attention of the most specialist and delicate kind. The whole process would require almost super-human patience from everyone concerned.

So, Benny let the hospital get on with their labour of love of restoring his mother. And he settled down to wait, with his dad.

Benny's father was unexpectedly good after the accident. He didn't drink quite so much, he got the washing machine fixed when it was broken, he brought big bags of groceries home from the supermarket. Lined up on the grubby kitchen bench, those bags looked just like proper shopping.

Even more surprisingly, he accepted the responsibility of making sure Benny got up in the morning to go to school. Each day, Benny would wake to see the apparition of his mother glowing in the doorway of his bedroom, and then rub his eyes as she metamorphosed into a big bear of a man. The disappointment was brutal, but it had its consolation: Benny had proof, at last, that his father cared.

To be fair, Benny's father tried as hard to look after his son as any man could. He even took Benny to McDonald's several times a week, and bought him crisps and Mars bars from the corner shop, booze benders permitting.

That was half the problem, really.

Benny considered that his diet was suffering.

Only his diet, mind. In other ways, he had nothing to complain about. It would be shameful to feel sorry for himself, an able-bodied child with unbroken bones and peachy, smooth skin, when his mother was no doubt yearning to leave the hospital and come home to him, yet must struggle to walk on splintered legs, humiliated by her slow progress. She would be a patchwork of flesh, scars all over her, a creature so distorted that only the wisest surgeons could imagine her regaining, in the fullness of time, her former feminine shape. Would she ever be beautiful again? It was too much to hope for.

He hoped his mother was concentrating on putting one foot in front of the other. He hoped she wouldn't say anything to make the doctors angry. His mother talked too much; Benny was only too aware of that. She didn't know when to keep her damn mouth shut; his father had always made that clear. If only Mummy could hold her tongue, and do everything she was told, she would be all right.

Meanwhile, Benny had problems of his own. Greasy, fatty, sugary problems. All these chocolate bars and fried fish fingers and beefburgers his father was giving him were all very nice, but a boy needed vegetables.

And, of course, the broccoli eel needed broccoli.

At first Benny's father boiled broccoli at his son's request, as if it were just another kind of pre-packaged treat, some new kind of confectionery. Purchased at the supermarket rather than at the greengrocer where his mummy used to shop, the broccoli even looked a bit like junk food, all wrapped up in transparent clingfilm, never less than perfectly green.

Unfortunately, the broccoli eel could tell the difference between supermarket broccoli and greengrocer broccoli. It had been raised on the authentic *Brassica oleracea*, unruly in shape, lacking none of its natural inheritance of vitamins, and stuffed with as much calcium (Benny's mother always said) as a glass of milk. As time went by, the broccoli eel grew restless, squirming outside Benny's stomach, exploring the crevices of adjacent organs, worming its toothy snout up into Benny's breast, beating its spiny tail into his back passage. It wanted the kind of broccoli Benny's mother had always brought home.

'I'm not going miles out of my way just to buy you a bloody vegetable,' his father said, and that was that.

From then on, Benny's life became a little more desperate every day. It was as if his spirit was being sucked inside the dark, meaty tissues of his own body. His thoughts were no longer free to fly around the outside world, but never left his skull, bubbling and expiring in the damp cauliflower of his brain. His innards were continually blocked up and upset, causing him so much pain that there was no room even for memories of his mother. The broccoli eel squirmed and fidgeted every waking minute, exploring the nooks and crannies of Benny's tender guts as if looking for minuscule remnants of the good green stuff.

To appease the creature, Benny tried eating a greater amount of broccoli more often, but this made only a slight difference, and had the unlucky side-effect of annoying his father.

'You haven't eaten your pizza.'

'I'm just finishing this,' pleaded Benny, choking on a cud of spongy green moss.

One night, arguing over broccoli again, Benny and his father found themselves staring fiercely into each other's eyes, the father's fist trembling near the boy's cheek, the boy's knuckles smeared with fake mozzarella cheese.

'You're lucky to get pizza for tea,' scowled his father, lowering his fist and sinking back into his armchair. 'If I wasn't here to take care of you, police inspectors would come and send you to a children's home. They'd ship you off to Ireland, to one of those orphanages. You wouldn't get pizza there, I can tell you.'

No? What would I get? thought Benny, and the thought leaked from his brain into his bloodstream, travelling downwards to be digested.

That night, Benny was woken from his sleep by an excruciating pain in his guts.

He knew immediately what it was. The broccoli eel had left his stomach again, and this time it was not content merely to stretch. It had lost patience with being fed the wrong food, and decided to scavenge for something better. Greedily, it was gnawing at the flesh of Benny's insides, nibbling at the cabbagey surface of his lungs, nuzzling its teeth into the soft flanks of his pulsating heart.

In a frenzy of panic, Benny wound himself into a ball under the bedclothes, and begged, begged, begged the eel to stop.

The eel stopped.

Benny was bewildered. He had never imagined that any communication was possible between him and the broccoli eel. The eel had not only stopped eating Benny's insides, but seemed to be speaking to him. Not aloud, but through Benny's bloodstream. Fishy whisperings, amphibian suggestions, floating along in the vessels of Benny's inner world, tropical with fever. In no time at all they bubbled against his brain, suffusing their meaning like a powerful aroma.

The eel was telling him what he must do, if the two of them were to continue to co-exist. Too long they had tarried.

'Okay, okay,' said the boy, slithering out from between the sheets.

Hours later, Benny was sitting at the foot of his father's bed. The dawn was coming. Outside in the street, a vehicle pulled up, its lights ghostly, and it seemed probable that uniformed men would jump out of it and knock on the door. But the car winked into invisibility, or maybe it had decided to drive away again.

A little while later, the sun came up properly, and traffic began to trickle into the arterial roads near Benny's house. The day was proceeding normally, despite everything.

Benny wondered if he should go to school, or whether that would make it harder for police inspectors to find him. It was very important that police inspectors should find him, because they would make sure he passed through the right channels. Benny had no wish to avoid what was coming to him.

Wasn't it strange, then, that the world was taking no interest? Here he was, all ready for upheaval, all ready for punishment, and still no one was running towards the house, no one was beating at the front door. Just sunlight and silence, despite the fact that lying here on the bed was the body of a big naked man with his throat all shredded and messy like a beetroot salad.

Inside Benny, the broccoli eel had curled up to sleep, nestled so neatly among his intestines as to be hardly there at all. In a nature book given him by his mother, Benny had read about snakes, about how they could go for months without food if they had to. The broccoli eel, now that Benny had made peace with it, was showing the patience of a snake. It could wait.

Benny walked to the front door, opened it, and stood on the porch. He was still in his wet pyjamas, still clutching the fork in his fist. He was hoping the world would glance at him in passing and notice that something was amiss. Shivering with

80

cold, he watched the cars drive past his house, counting them under his breath. Occasionally a driver would glance at him through a tinted windscreen for a fraction of an instant, but the peristalsis of traffic didn't permit a lingering look. Benny wondered what it would take to stop someone in their tracks. He was too shy to wave the gory fork around.

He squinted into the distance, to where all the traffic seemed to be heading. Soon, surely, someone would take him away from here and send him to a children's home: one of those places where there was no pizza or chocolate, only those nasty tasting foods that grew in dirt and were good for you. That was all right: he was ready. He would eat only healthy things from now on; he would grow tall and resist all infection, he would have wide shoulders and rock-hard muscles; he would be able to lift a frail, crippled woman in one hand.

But how would his mother know where to find him? She didn't even have a driving licence.

And what if the children's home was in Ireland, as his father had threatened it would be? Wasn't Ireland across the sea? Benny closed his eyes, his puny body trembling in the wind, and tried to imagine his mother crossing the soupy ocean, in a year and a day, in a beautiful pea-green boat.

SKETCHY

BY LEWIS HANCOX

THIS PLACE ATTRACTS ALL THE **DREGS** OF THE TOWN.

SKIRT COULDA BEEN SHORTER, LOVE. HEH HEH.

I'M TELLIN' YA, MARY, THE **MOON** AIN'T **REAL!** THE LANDING WAS A **HOAX,** THEY USED A **GREEN SCREEN!** IT WAS DIRECTED BY THAT "CLOCKWORK ORANGE" GUY, WHAT'S HIS NAME...

TEN MINUTES TILL MY SHIFT STARTS. HOPE NOBODY BUGS ME.

SOMETIMES I DON'T KNOW WHAT'S WORSE...

GOING TO WORK OR COMING 'HOME'.

IT'S HARD SORTING THROUGH MUM'S THINGS. FUNNY HOW MUCH YOU CAN **LEARN** ABOUT SOMEONE FROM WHAT THEY LEAVE BEHIND.

I'M SO GLAD SHE TAUGHT ME TO DRAW.

HUH... I'VE NEVER SEEN **THESE** BEFORE. LOOKS LIKE THEY'VE BEEN RIPPED OUT OF HER SKETCHBOOK.

SEEMS... PAINFUL.

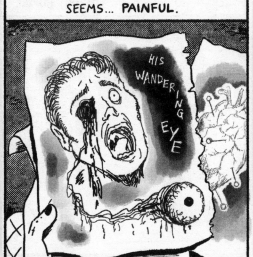

WAIT... MUM, DID YOU...

I THINK I MIGHT UNDERSTAND WHY DAD TOOK OFF NOW.

MAYBE MUM LEFT ME MORE THAN ONE GIFT...

SO MANY QUESTIONS FOR YOU, MUM. I KNOW THEY NEVER FOUND YOU BUT I OFTEN WONDER IF YOU'RE STILL HERE. GOD, I MISS YOU.

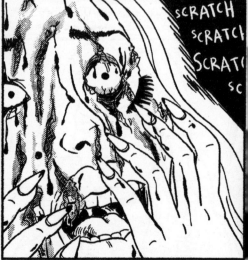

NEXT DAY

WHAT THE FUCK HAVE I DONE?

GET OUT OF ME!!

I GOTTA GET RID OF THE BOOK.

IF I DESTROY IT, WHAT'LL HAPPEN TO ALL THE PEOPLE I'VE SKETCHED?

I DON'T WANT TO HURT ANYONE ELSE.

SOPHIE'S VIDEO HAS TURNED THE BAR INTO A FUCKING VIRAL SENSATION.

I HEARD THE BARMAID HEXED HER.

HASHTAG NO-FACE SOPHIE!

I'LL HAVE WHATEVER THAT POSSESSED GIRL DRANK.

COURTNEY...

ORLA...

I CAN TELL SHE'S **WASTED** WHEN HER EYES ROLL BACK LIKE THAT.

LOOK, I'M SORRY FOR BEIN' A BITCH, OK?

YEAH, I EXPECTED IT FROM THE OTHERS BUT NOT FROM YOU.

AWW, C'MON...

WHY IS SHE STILL WEARING THE **RING** I GOT HER?

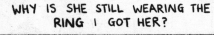

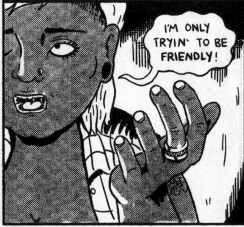

I'M ONLY TRYIN' TO BE FRIENDLY!

I DON'T KNOW WHY YOU'RE EVEN BACK HERE AFTER GHOSTING ME FOR SO LONG.

I DIDN'T GHOST YOU...

YOU GOT ALL WEIRD WITH US AFTER YOUR MUM DISAPPEARED, REMEMBER? LIKE YOU HATED THE WHOLE WORLD...

ORLA, WAIT!

DON'T PUSH ME, COURTNEY.

WE GETTIN' SERVED HERE OR WHAT?

WHAT'S IN THAT FUCKING BOOK?

SHOVE

STAB

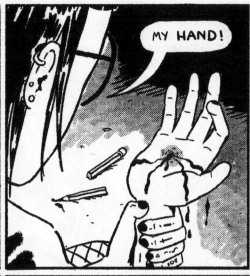

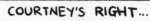

Apples

by Emilia Hart

Karen didn't know it was an apple tree at first. She thought pear, maybe even fig? Trees, flowers, plants generally – those weren't her thing. They were David's. She did house; he did garden – that had always been the deal. She should message David and ask him what kind of tree it was. Except, of course, she couldn't: that was the whole reason she was standing in the garden in the first place.

She'd purchased the house with the money from the divorce settlement. He'd bought her out of the lovely Dulwich terrace, with its dove-grey walls and white cornices, its original floors. She'd taken the Morphy Richards kettle, a sofa and their second-best mattress to the wilds of Thornton Heath.

And wild was the right word. Not for the house itself, which was unremarkable, a squat brick bungalow. There was a spare bedroom which she'd use as a study when she worked from home. Maybe Laura would come and stay in the university holidays; she could even bring that new boyfriend. Max, or was it Matt? No – Mack, that was it. She should invite them round, before David did. He'd got the house, her lovely house, he wasn't getting Laura too.

Anyway, the garden. Wild didn't even cover it. It was a mess. For a start, the ground was uneven, and beneath the tangle of weeds oddly spongy, like quicksand. It smelled, too. A sweet smell, faintly alcoholic. Now, she followed the scent through a thicket of thorns and burrs, the wet earth grasping at her trainers, to the tree that leaned against the back fence. It was ugly and wizened, the branches so dark they were almost black. It had grown into the fence, become a part of it, defying human boundaries. There was a knot in the centre of its trunk that was twisted and almost cruel, like a face.

It was obvious now that it was an apple tree. That was the source of the smell: fruit carpeted the area around it, fizzing with decay. Breathing the air was like drinking cider; in fact, come to think of it, she felt a little drunk.

And hungry. When had she last eaten? She'd been up since before dawn; unable to sleep at the Dulwich house, where she'd spent a night in the spare room after packing up her things. (David had offered to stay at a hotel, which seemed the least he could do after Karen had endured months of grimy rental accommodation.) The movers had arrived at 10 a.m., after which there hadn't been time to eat. That was, what – eight hours ago, now? Impulsively, she reached up and plucked an apple from a low branch.

The fruit was small and misshapen, its skin starting to wrinkle, like her own. But its flesh was surprisingly crisp; juice ran down her chin as she bit into it. And the flavour – the flavour! Sweet and floral, but with an alkaline, almost milky aftertaste. As soon as she finished it, she reached for another. Before she knew it she'd eaten three of the things, the cores sticky in the palm of her hand.

It was late September, so the days were long still, the light fading gold through the branches, but a cold wind raised the flesh on her arms. She turned back to the house, and perhaps it was the spike in her blood sugar or the warmth of the red brick in the setting sun, but it didn't look quite so bad. Even the rickety shed which jutted like a boil from the kitchen offered a certain rustic charm. And the garden was private, at least: the neighbouring buildings were too low to overlook it. It was freeing to know that she could rot away in peace.

*

She ordered a curry and ate it on the sofa while watching Netflix on her laptop. IKEA were a day late delivering her new bed frame so she slept on a mattress on the floor, like a hippy in a commune. The bedroom overlooked the garden, so she could smell the apples still, along with a faint odour of mothballs and cat urine. The previous owner, an old woman, had died only recently. Karen had dealt with her nephew.

Now she wondered about her, the old woman. Lilian Hall had been her name. That had been on the conveyancing documents: *The Estate of Lilian May Hall.* A strange thing was that there was a covenant on the land: the garden was not to be developed in any way. 'So no landscaping,' her solicitor had said to her. 'Fine,' she'd said. After all, the garden had always been David's area.

But she would not think about David. Not now. David, in the plush king-sized bed, on the Egyptian cotton sheets that she, Karen, had purchased (and, until recently, laundered every week). David, reaching over to touch a young, supple shoulder . . . running his fingers through hair that was bright and lustrous and without the slightest hint of grey –

Tears burned in her eyes. She picked up her phone and read the *Guardian* instead. A teenage girl was missing in Brighton, near where Laura went to university. She checked her WhatsApp conversation with Laura: the status read *last seen 11.33 p.m.* Five minutes ago. Reassured, she put the phone down and let the unfamiliar dark wash over her. She could hear the branches of the apple tree moving in the wind.

*

The doorbell woke her. It was 7 a.m.; a text on her phone said her IKEA order was out for delivery. The doorbell rang again. Her back ached as she crawled off the mattress, her sheets (cheap, provenance of cotton unknown) tangled around one leg.

'Jesus Christ,' she said to the empty room, rifling through an opened cardboard box, searching for something to put on over her frayed M&S nightie. Where was her dressing gown?

Instead she found a trench coat and, in desperation, shrugged it on.

'Alright?' said the young man when she opened the door, holding an electronic tablet for her to sign. The cardboard box containing the bed frame leant against the exterior wall, dauntingly enormous. There was no way she could get it inside on her own.

'Would you mind giving me a hand with that?' she asked, passing the tablet back to him. She almost told him that she lived alone but stopped just in time. 'My husband's at work, and I'm not sure I can get it through the door on my own.'

Yes I fucking well would mind you stupid bitch, said the young man.

'Excuse me?'

A furrow appeared between the man's eyebrows.

'I didn't say anything, love,' he said. 'But sorry, we're not allowed to help customers lift things. Company policy.'

He gave her an apologetic smile.

Cunt.

'Cheers, love,' he said again, and turned.

For a moment, Karen stood in the doorway, stunned, as she watched him get into his van and drive away. Had he really just called her a stupid bitch and a cunt? She should ring IKEA and complain. (Though she wouldn't. You couldn't ring up and ask to speak to a manager if your name was literally Karen, Laura had told her.)

It took her ten minutes to wrestle the box inside; her trench coat flapping open to reveal her unsupported breasts. A youth on a bike slowed his progress to stare as though she were the neighbourhood witch.

Inside, the components of the bed conspired against her: the instructions didn't make sense and she dropped a heavy wooden slat on her toe. She needed a screwdriver, that was the problem. Screwdrivers: another thing that had belonged to David. Karen had never changed a lightbulb, never touched a fuse box, never set foot inside a B&Q; David had never folded laundry or organised a child's birthday party. Marriage had been less a partnership than a process of mutual infantilisation.

She remembered the shed. Perhaps the old woman – Lilian – had owned a toolkit? Karen recalled the nephew saying that she had never been married; had lived entirely alone for as long as he could remember. Presumably she'd had to handle her own DIY.

In the pale light of morning the garden looked worse: scabbed and somehow lumpen, like pocked flesh. But the air was sweet with the smell of apples, the tree lifting its branches gently in the wind, as if it were waving at her.

In contrast, the shed was dark and dank smelling. There was no lightbulb and the torch on her phone caught the glimmer of cobwebs. Everything was feathery with dust. There was an old lawn mower, a scatter of laundry pegs. A shovel leaned against the back wall, trailing clods of dirt. And there – a toolbox. She squatted on the ground to open it, praying for a screwdriver.

Her first thought was that the contents of the box might have been curated by a magpie. Everything shone. Silver, brass, even a bright hint of gold. For a surreal, heart-juddering moment she thought it was money, bullion bars or something, that Lilian had made her rich.

But now she saw that the box was filled with watches and jewellery. Rings, even a few pairs of cufflinks. A shining oblong that she realised was a lighter, engraved with the initials *RMW.*

Strange. Who had these belonged to? Lilian's father, perhaps, or brother? Perhaps the nephew had been wrong; perhaps Lilian had been married. But no: it couldn't have all belonged to the same person. There were five watches and four rings, fat and gold like wedding bands. One of the rings was engraved, like the lighter, but with different initials: *JS & EB.* Definitely a wedding ring, then. Perhaps – she liked this, imagining the sort of life Lilian might have led – these were tokens collected from lovers. Light-fingered Lilian, temptress and thief.

There were also nuts and bolts in the box and, aha! A screwdriver. 'Thanks, Lilian,' Karen said aloud. She felt quite fondly towards the old woman now.

*

She was starving by the time she'd finished putting the bed together, but also buzzing with a new, delicious pride. She, Karen, did that! She couldn't help feeling that Lilian was somehow to thank, that she had lent Karen not just her screwdriver but a little of her independence, too.

She took a picture of the bed and sent it to Laura with a dancing woman emoji and a nail-painting emoji.

Aw! It looks sooo lonely

Lovely not lonely ffs autocorrect

Sorry mum

I hope your ok though do you want me to come stay soon?

Don't worry, I am absolutely fine! Loving having my own space! Karen wrote back. *Yes please to a visit, though. You could bring Mack, I'd love to meet him!*

rlly? Ok cool! we have long wknd next month so what about then??

Great! Karen wrote back, trying not to seem too eager. Sometimes communication with Laura reminded her of early dates with David: too much enthusiasm tended to scare her off.

Ok will talk to Mack and let u know! Love u mum xx

Love you too sweetheart. Have a good day.

She was so hungry that she grabbed another apple from the tree and ate it walking to the Tesco she'd spotted nearby. She felt a spring in her step, as though she were a young country maid walking to a fair, rather than a middle-aged woman walking to a supermarket. She even saw the russet tail of a fox flicker from behind a bin.

In Tesco, her good mood vanished. The aisles pulsed with bodies; twice, someone clipped her ankle with their trolley. And the noise! Did people normally talk this much in supermarkets? She'd never before considered grocery shopping to be such a social occasion but now her head buzzed and ached with other people's conversations.

It was approaching 4 p.m., she realised, and a Sunday: everyone was rushing to get their shopping done before closing time. Hurriedly she filled her basket with sourdough bread, a bag of spinach and tins of sardines, knowing that the tins would remain unopened and the spinach would blacken inside its plastic. She picked up a frozen pizza, telling herself she would save it for an emergency. She told herself the same thing about the bottle of Merlot.

In the confectionary aisle, a man stood in front of her, blocking her view of the chocolate selection. He spoke loudly into enormous headphones, with the self-importance of someone coordinating a rocket launch.

'Yah,' he was saying, 'Yah. Those figures are crucial. Yah. Close of play tomorrow has to be our hard stop, I'm afraid. Yah.'

With a mousiness that she resented in herself, she edged her way past him to reach for a slab of Lindt. At the same time, he moved to his left, so that they collided.

'Sorry, sorry,' she said, but he didn't even acknowledge she'd spoken. Instead, he glowered at her, and then – even though he was still droning *yah, yah* into his headphones – somehow she heard him, loud and clear:

Ugly old bag. I need to start going back to Sainsbury's.

The shock made her drop her basket: tinned sardines skidded in all directions; the bottle of wine rolled away from her.

Yah Yah stalked off, but a young man – a teenager, with enormous sneakers and a Puffa jacket – bent to help.

'Here you go,' he said, handing her the bottle of wine. His eyes were warm and brown and tinged with horrible pity.

Poor thing. I hope Mum doesn't end up like that.

She abandoned the basket and ran to the check-out, clutching the frozen pizza and the bottle of wine tight to her chest. Other people's thoughts droned past her like menacing bees.

- *Pay council tax.*
- *Will Fiona be suspicious if I tell her I have to work late tomorrow?*
- *Why has she left me on read? She said she had no plans today so why is she too busy to reply? It's Sunday ffs.*
- *Newest double-fisting videos.*
- *Fifty-eight pounds in bank account so I should put these back.*
- *I need to call Dad and ask if he got his results back, please God let him be OK.*
- *Christ some women really let themselves go, don't they.*

Now it was not just words, but images, too. Monday, dark and looming like the eye of Sauron. An empty carton of milk in a fridge. Breasts, spilling from a too-tight bra. A woman fellating a penis. A man fellating a penis. A man fellating *his own* penis.

There was a long queue at the self-checkout line so she made for a cashier. A woman in a headscarf with a name tag that read *Ayesha*.

'Hi, how are you today? That'll be fifteen pounds fifty, please. Do you have a Clubcard?'

Karen waited for the onslaught. But there was nothing: the woman's eyes stared back at her, dark and impassive.

'No,' she breathed. 'I don't have a Clubcard.'

'That's OK.' The woman frowned. 'Have a nice day,' she said, as Karen ran for the exit.

*

Back at the house, she retched into the toilet, tasting bile and apples.

What was happening to her? What was this, schizophrenia? An overload of empathy, triggered by some sort of hormonal imbalance? The menopause?

Without really thinking about it, she sent David a message: *Please call me I think I'm going crazy.*

He replied ten minutes later: *Not a good time, Karen. Sorry.*

Her panic was replaced by fury. How many times, during the course of their marriage, had she received a message like that?

David, can you come home? I think Laura has a fever.

David, could you take Laura to her orthodontist appointment next week? I have a meeting I really need to attend.

David, David, David . . .

'Stop it,' she said to her reflection. The yellow light put new shadows in her face, her eyes huge and her cheeks gaunt. Or perhaps it wasn't the light at all, but merely the truth.

Stupid old bag.

Cunt.

117

Say if David had phoned her? Would she have heard everything he really thought about her? The things he'd thought, perhaps for years and years?

It would be better, surely, not to know.

*

Later, she sat on the couch with the pizza on her lap. She picked up the wine glass that balanced on an unopened moving box and drank from it deeply.

It was almost dark, now, and the apple tree sent long shadowy fingers across the garden, reaching through the glass door and into the living room. She thought of Lilian, sitting in this very spot, listening to the wind move through the branches and counting the treasures in her toolbox. The fat shining watches, the gold rings. She shuddered.

Her phone rang, and the hand holding the wine glass jolted, sending a spray of red across the carpet.

'Fuck,' she hissed, and watching the stain spread she noticed for the first time a slight shadow on the carpet, which made no sense as the nephew had told her – she remembered because it had increased the asking price – that it was brand new. It made her think of the garden, the barren lumpiness of it, as if the tree had sent its roots twisting under the land. She imagined the house, cradled in a network of rhizomes like a giant, tuberous hand.

Perhaps the root structure was embedded in the house's foundations, breaking through concrete and wood, the two locked in an awful symbiosis. Was that the reason for the covenant, that the garden not be disturbed?

She had an urge to tear up the carpet, to check.

Her phone rang again, and she saw that the caller was Laura. She took another glug of wine, and a deep breath, before she answered.

'Hi, sweetheart,' she said brightly.

'Mum,' Laura's voice was strangely muffled, there was the distant sound of laughter, a thump of music like a heartbeat. 'Are you okay?'

'Of course. Why do you ask?'

'Dad just asked me to check up on you. Apparently you sent him a weird message? Like, that you thought you were going crazy?'

Karen closed her eyes briefly. This was typical David. As soon as Laura could talk, he began outsourcing the emotional upkeep of their marriage to her. *I reckon Dad thinks . . . Dad said he was worried that . . .*

And still Laura couldn't see through it. She adored David. Even in the wake of the divorce. Oh, she'd been upset, of course. And worried for Karen. But where was the condemnation, the fury? He'd had an affair, for fuck's sake!

David was her father. Karen understood that. But couldn't she have been just a little bit angry, a little bit hurt? He hadn't just betrayed Karen, after all: in breaking up their family, he'd betrayed Laura, too.

'I hope this hasn't put you off relationships,' Karen had said to her in the aftermath.

'Not relationships,' her daughter had replied. 'Maybe, like, monogamy though? I don't think one person can just *own* another.'

As if Karen had tried to own David. As if she'd been the one in the wrong.

Now she gritted her teeth as she said, 'I'm fine, sweetheart. Really.'

'Okay, but did you send him that message?'

'Well, yes, but—'

'Mum, I know you're hurting but that really isn't okay. You and Dad aren't together any more: you have to respect his boundaries.'

Karen didn't trust herself to speak. She drained her glass and immediately poured another.

'Look, I think I should come down sooner. What about this weekend? I can skip my lecture on Friday afternoon.'

'Sweetheart, there's really no need for that. Besides, I haven't got a second bed yet—'

'Come on Mum, we'll have fun. I can help you decorate. It'll be like a housewarming.'

Karen felt all the irritation leave her body, replaced by a flood of warmth. Her lovely, lovely Laura. The one good thing to come from her and David's marriage; the one thing they got right.

Laura would come and Karen would cook for her and they would stay up late watching period dramas, like they did when she was little. And Karen would – dare she? – tell Laura about the male voices in her head, and Laura would pat her hand and tell her that it was just stress, that it would pass. That she wasn't going crazy.

'I would love that, sweetheart. Thank you.'

'Great! Let me check with Mack and see if he can get time off work. He said he was keen to get away for a bit.'

'Oh—'

'That's cool if he comes, right? You said you wanted to meet him.'

There was an edge to Laura's voice, once deployed to wrangle sweets and extra screen time. Karen knew from experience what would follow if she didn't give into it. If she said no, then Laura might not come at all.

'Of course – bring him. We'll all have a lovely time,' she said. 'You two can have my bed and I'll sleep on the sofa.'

*

They were coming on Friday, which meant she had most of the week to prepare. To decide. She checked herself. Clearly, she'd lost her mind. How could eating an apple enable her to read men's thoughts? It was insane, like something out of a fairy-tale, or even the Bible (she thought of Eve).

But say if she wasn't crazy, if this was – somehow – really happening. Would she be able to hear Mack's thoughts? In her head, Mack was tall and endearingly shy, with a florid crop of acne on his chin. She assumed that he studied mechanical engineering like Laura: probably his thoughts would be a maze of maths and physics, and entirely incomprehensible. But there might be other things, too. She thought of the images she'd seen in Tesco and her mouth filled again with the sour taste of apple.

She should tell Laura not to come. It was unethical, it was insane. But then, wasn't this also an incredible opportunity? She could not protect her daughter from the future entirely. Laura would be disappointed in love, would have her heart broken. But now, Karen could help her. If the visit revealed Mack to have, say, a drug addiction or a foot fetish, then she could warn her. Or, she could give her daughter the ultimate tool to protect herself. All she had to do was feed her one of the apples from the garden.

What mother could resist?

That night, her phone pinged with a news alert about the missing girl in Brighton: a body had been found. Police suspected foul play.

She knew, then, that she was doing the right thing.

*

She spent the week working from home, unpacking and cleaning in between calls. She was grateful that she worked in a female-dominated industry, that all her colleagues were women. When furniture and groceries were delivered, she pretended that she had Covid and couldn't answer the door. Once, she went for a walk, but when she passed a man with his dog, the hum of his thoughts grew louder and louder as he approached, like the footsteps of a monster – *bin night/Arsenal/bukkake* – that she crossed the street to avoid him. She didn't go out again after that.

On Friday, she took a day of annual leave. She rose early and went out to the garden with a string bag. Mist shimmered over the ground, threaded itself through the branches of the tree. The rotting apples were soft underfoot. She found she liked it now, the heady scent of decomposition.

She chose six apples, puny but golden-skinned, with the slightest blush of pink.

Back inside, she peeled and halved them. There was something labial about the exposed cores with their secret glistening seeds. The crisp flesh was lightly traced with green, like veins shadowing the skin of an inner wrist. As she sliced, juice pooled on the cutting board, fragrant and milky. In a separate bowl she combined butter, flour and sugar for the crumble. She layered the apple slices in a dish, sprinkled them with sugar, then smoothed the crumble mix on top with a fork. She covered the dish in cling-wrap then placed it in the fridge, next to the pre-made tiramisu she'd ordered from Waitrose.

She hoped she wouldn't need to serve it.

*

By the time the doorbell rang at 6 p.m., Karen's body had dissolved completely into nerves. In the hallway, she checked her makeup in the mirror, wiping the sweat from her top lip. The doorbell rang again; a dark shape shifted through the blurred glass.

Karen forced her cheeks into a smile and opened the door.

'Mum!'

Laura was standing on the porch alone, clutching a houseplant, her delicate face lit with an impish smile. Her lovely Laura, with her unkempt hair and the baggy jumper she'd stolen from David.

'Darling!' Karen stepped forward and pulled her daughter to her chest, so that the houseplant scratched her neck. 'It's so good to see you.'

'Calm down, Mum,' Laura said into her shoulder, patting her on the back. 'It's good to see you, too. Mack is just parking the car. Here,' she stepped back and thrust the houseplant into her arms. 'This is for you. Happy housewarming.'

'Oh – how lovely. Thank you, darling.'

Her stomach plummeted. She'd thought, for a moment, that Laura had come on her own; that there would be no need for the crumble, for any of it.

A figure loped towards them out of the dusk. Tall and broad, an overnight bag slung over his shoulder, his face in shadow.

'Mum,' Laura said, her voice strained with nerves and defiance. 'This is Mack. Mack, this is Mum.'

'Hi Karen,' said the man – and he was a man, not a boy, God, how old was he? – slipping an arm around Laura's waist and pulling her tightly towards him as he held out his hand to shake hers. 'Nice to meet you.'

She looked into his eyes and her mouth went dry. She saw the porn he'd watched that morning while Laura showered; the short skirt and the bound wrists. She saw the contents of the boot of his car. A picnic blanket. A torch. Cable ties.

Cold fear snaked through her, as if she were a gazelle looking into the eyes of a lion. She glanced at Laura – girlish and guileless with her open, smiling face – and back at him. The fear hardened into rage. She lifted her chin.

'You'd better come in,' she said.

*

'That smells delicious, Karen,' said Mack as she took the dinner out of the oven. It was a Nigella recipe, chicken roasted with lemon and orzo.

'Thank you,' she said stiffly, sliding the apple crumble onto the shelf where the chicken had sat.

She put the chicken on a platter on the counter and began mechanically sawing off its wings and thighs. The meat glistened with fat, turning her stomach. She felt reluctant to let go of the carving knife. Eventually, she placed the meal on the table and sat down, pouring herself a large glass of Sauvignon Blanc and taking a swig to steady herself.

Laura gave Mack a nervous smile. 'Should we help ourselves, Mum?' Karen nodded, watching as they slopped chicken and pasta onto their plates.

'So,' she said, serving herself a small portion, even though the sight and smell made her stomach roil. 'Mack. How did you meet my daughter? I'd assumed you were both students.'

'*Mum*,' Laura hissed.

'It's alright, babe,' Mack reached under the table to touch

Laura's knee. He lifted his chin, his eyes boring into Karen's. He was shameless, blatant. 'I get it, the age difference concerns you. But Laura's an old soul. Mature. Well, you don't need me to tell you that, surely. You're her mum.' He smiled at her sweetly. Karen sat on her hands so they wouldn't shake.

'So it was her maturity that attracted you to her, was it? Not the fact that she's nineteen, that she *looks* sixteen. And tell me, what exactly is the age difference?'

'I'm twenty-eight,' he said, which she knew was an understatement by at least five years. 'And Laura and I met at a café.'

An image, *his* image: Laura, in a jumper and skirt, wrinkled tights with a ladder up one leg. With her elfin face and scruffy hair, you could almost mistake her for a child.

'I see,' she said. 'Are you finished?'

She rose, grabbing their still-full plates, slopping orzo onto the table.

'Mum,' Laura said, standing to follow her out of the room. But Mack grabbed her hand.

'Relax, babe,' he said, when he thought Karen was out of earshot. 'She's just being protective.'

'I can't believe how rude she's being,' she heard Laura say. 'I'm so embarrassed. I have to go talk to her.'

Laura joined Karen in the kitchen, closing the door behind her.

'Why are you being like this? You're ruining *everything*!'

Her daughter quivered with rage before her. How badly she wanted to turn her into a child again, to scoop her up and carry her away. To a world where monsters existed only in storybooks, easily vanquished by a nightlight and a kiss on the forehead.

There had to be another way. She had to try, still, to shield her from these horrors.

'Sweetheart,' Karen took a breath, tried to put her hands on Laura's shoulders, but she flinched away. 'I understand that you like Mack, I do. But honestly, I'm not sure about him – he's so much older, isn't he? Let's just talk about this, I'm your mother, I just want the best for you—'

'Bullshit you do. You're just jealous, because I'm happy and you're alone, because you couldn't make things work with Dad.'

Karen dropped her hands by her sides. It was useless. She could see that there was no reasoning with Laura, that Karen's disapproval would only push her closer to him. She was still a teenager, after all.

She didn't want to do this. She really didn't.

But there was no other way. She had to keep Laura safe.

'Look, I'm sorry,' she said. 'Maybe I'm being over-protective. I'll try to give him the benefit of the doubt. Now, will you help me get this on the table?'

*

'Lovely,' said Mack as Laura carried the crumble through to the dining room. 'My favourite.'

'Custard?' Karen said through gritted teeth. 'Or ice cream?'

'Ice cream, please,' he said. 'I have a bit of a sweet tooth.'

Laura gave her a warning look.

'This is great, Mum,' she said, shovelling the crumble into her mouth. 'Even better than usual.'

'The apples are from the tree in the garden,' said Karen. 'Lilian's tree.'

'Lilian?' Laura asked.

'She used to own the house. But then she died. She liked collecting things. Men's jewellery. Rings, watches, that kind of thing.'

'Creepy,' said Laura, wrinkling her nose.

This woman is a headcase.

'What did you say?' Laura's spoon clanked against her bowl. She turned slowly to Mack.

'Huh? I didn't say anything, babe.'

'Yes, you did. I heard you, loud and clear. You called my mum a headcase. You—'

Karen saw the knowledge pass over her daughter's face, wave upon awful wave of it, as the same images flashed through her own mind: the white blur of a seagull in the sky. A pier stretching into the sea like a broken spine. A pale, lifeless wrist, ringed with plastic.

She closed her eyes in regret. What had she done, showing Laura this?

But it was the only way, she told herself. The only way to protect her child.

'Laura?' Mack was asking. 'Laura, what is it? Are you okay? You've gone white—'

He reached out a hand to her, but she flinched away.

'Get away from me,' she said. 'Oh my God. Mum – I think I'm going to be sick—'

'Laura! What's going on, I don't understand—'

Karen hadn't considered this, when she'd decided to serve the crumble: what would happen once Laura knew. What had she thought: that they would call the police, tell them what they had somehow, inexplicably, discovered? In the end it was so fast that later, she could almost pretend it hadn't happened it all. Mack reaching for Laura, who stumbled over her chair to get away from him; Karen standing, telling him that perhaps he ought to think about leaving –

And then the carving knife. It drew her eye, glinting in the yellow light. She had forgotten to clear it with the remnants of the main course; it still glimmered with pearly strands of fat.

Laura followed her gaze. Their eyes met across the table and then, before Karen could react, her daughter had picked up the knife and held it uncertainly in front of her.

'Stay away from us,' Laura said to Mack, her voice shaking. 'I mean it. Mum, call the police.'

'Laura, babe,' he raised his hands in a gesture of innocence. 'Put that down, you'll only hurt yourself.' He moved closer to her, as if for an embrace.

Laura screamed, the arm holding the knife flailed, and Karen watched in horror as the blade caught the light, as it disappeared into Mack's gut.

Blood, jammy and bright, sprayed across the table. The smell of iron mingled with the odour of roast chicken and the sweet hint of apple. Karen gagged.

Mack clasped his hands to his stomach but the blood spurted through his fingers. He looked at Laura, open-mouthed.

'You bitch,' he said, before falling to the ground.

*

Laura wanted to help Karen dig.

'Please,' she said, her voice still thick with tears. 'This is all my fault. I have to be the one to do it.'

'No,' Karen shook her head. She could barely see Laura's features in the dark; her daughter might have been a ghost. Her upper arms still burned from dragging the body outside. Now it lay slumped between them, releasing its smell of butchery into the air. 'It's alright, sweetheart. Go inside and have a shower, then get into bed. I'll come up and see you when I'm done.'

'Mum,' Laura was weeping now. 'I can't let you do this – *commit a crime* – for me. Maybe we should just call the police. I'll confess. I'll – I'll tell them why. What he did.'

'Don't you *dare*,' Karen said. 'How would we explain what we know? Besides, I'm your mother. Everything I do is for you.'

*

For several hours, she dug. There was something oddly satisfying about it, shovelling away the velvet loam of soil. She grunted and sweated, the layers of herself falling away. Gone was the woman who cared about divorce and deadlines and thread counts and wrinkles. She was nothing but sinew, bone and the steady pump of her heart, an animal protecting her young.

The night deepened, and in the thickening dark the moon shone brighter, picking out the silver lines of the tree, the shovel, her own body. She felt naked. A naked woman in a garden, forever altered by a new and terrible knowledge.

When she was finished, she took deep, panting breaths of the night air; smelling earth and apples and death and her own sweat. Before she rolled his body into the shallow grave, before she covered him with fragrant earth, she removed the watch from his wrist.

The branches of the apple tree groaned in the wind, a beast demanding to be fed. *At last,* it seemed to say. *At last.* She thought of the roots twisting through the earth, microscopic hairs flickering into ravenous life. Scouring the soil for nutrients and finding the meal of his body, gorging on his flesh and all its putrid wants. She thought of green buds unfurling from branches, bursting into the pink froth of blossom. Then a bee or wasp, with its gift of pollen, alighting on the flower and, later, the slow swell of the fruit.

When it was done, she went into the shed to return the shovel. She opened the toolbox and put the watch inside with the others.

'Thank you, Lilian,' she said.

Waffle Thomas

by Ainslie Hogarth

It was a thing that women did, I'd been told, when a significant relationship came to an end: embark on a very long, very arduous walk. Somewhere remote and arboreal and generally hostile to human flesh. The temperate forests of the coasts; the colder forests of the north; I'd even known a woman who'd slogged through a tropical rainforest after her divorce, snapping photos of dazzling flora and charismatic wildlife. In these remote, arboreal, hostile places, you could test the abilities you might have allowed to atrophy while in partnership with a man.

The big test, of course, was being alone. Being alone and *not* being sexually assaulted or murdered, or both. There is nothing more healing.

I'd been with Trevor for eleven years and he loved me very much, even still. Even right now, when I'm almost 9,000 miles away from him, tightening my boots with such force that the laces dig into the meat of my hands like butcher's twine, he is back in the home we shared, loving me, in a way.

In those eleven years I'd become soft. Hammy? His love had made me ham. And that's why he had to go.

No, not ham, silly! A goose! His love had made me a goose, of course! And *that's* why he had to go.

I'd dined on his excessive, unconditional love, fattened myself up on it like it was something I deserved, until I became one of those doomed geese we'd learned about at that horrible dinner with his mom, Gail, and his stepdad, Farley, a former insurance agent who'd recently sold his small company for a vast sum. Now he and Gail travelled. They ate fancy things, like *foie gras*. Trevor had looked up *foie gras* while they were talking about it, found a photo of a pallid, vacant goose clamped between the legs of a sun-charred farmer. The farmer steadied a funnel to a long metal tube which had been fed down the goose's esophagus and used it to channel emulsified decadence directly into the goose's stomach; slick, fatty feed, bypassing the goose's natural urges, designed to transform its liver into a big, buttery delicacy enjoyed by certain assholes. Certain assholes like Farley. But not Gail, apparently. Even though she ate it too, *raved* about it, Trevor insisted that Gail wouldn't even have *known* about this senselessly cruel victual had it not been for *Farley*.

Trevor showed them the picture he found over the dinner they paid for, read out the details of this goose fattening process, *gavage*, with such *drama*, such over-the-top fricative *disgust*, that you could tell he believed Farley capable of carrying out similar cruelties against Gail, filling her throat with pipe, pumping her with the kind of slime which would leave her pallid, vacant, unable to walk away.

Trevor always told me that I should be wary of men. Because all men are pigs, and any man who said he wasn't a pig was a liar. Trevor, a man, telling me exactly who men are, and therefore exactly who *he* is, but naturally I didn't see it this way. Naturally I believed that by dint of sharing this unflattering truth, Trevor must be different from the others. One of the *good ones*.

Now I know that, in saying this, he'd been trying to scare me. To keep me scared. Not consciously, I don't think. In fact, I think to some extent they believe what they're saying, that they too are scared of other men hurting the women they love. But also, this is their technique. Their strategy. To keep us.

Scared people see monsters everywhere. Scared people don't leave.

But now here I am! A scared person, or rather, a *formerly* scared person, waking up from a night alone in the woods, *unharmed*. If I make it to the end of this hike without seeing a single monster, I'll be fully recovered from eleven years of being spun daily into nervous fatty goose.

It helps to be among the trees. White oaks. Tall and handsome and friendly and ancient, leaning on one another, *supportive*. This area is known for its oaks, and for its well-kept trails, etched through heavy bush by decades of curious bodies. Erosion, so slow, so insidious, it takes lifetimes to appreciate its power.

The trails intersect with one another at various checkpoints, marked by sturdy wooden lecterns containing logbooks, crimped yellow paper bound in leather, pens strung with frayed twine nestled in their spines.

I'd signed in yesterday afternoon, had run my finger along the bites and angles of the lectern's thickly lacquered surface. It'd been whittled from a tree, its surface a portrait of human patience. Suddenly I was compelled to close my eyes, as though someone had been knocking at my mind, wanting to be let in, the person who'd carved this lectern – their rucked knuckles and rheumy eyes, moving me through the book, to the very beginning, where I'd find their name, the very first one.

Waffle Thomas, male, 29, from Lansing, Michigan, travelling alone.

Waffle Thomas, well, that's obviously fake. But funny. I laughed. There was something so perfectly *naughty* about it.

I'm laughing again now as I stand up, test my freshly tightened boots – flex my feet, rotate my ankles, listen for the eyelets' squeal in response to such impressive tension. I use my lace-gnawed hands to bat cold dew from my tent, then hang it to dry over the long, low branch of a white oak that laid its jagged shadow across me last night as I slept.

Waffle Thomas. It's just so funny.

I dig a portion of granola from my pack. Set up the portable stove for hot water. Let instant coffee granules tinkle into a tin mug. I'm trying to be mindful about it, listening, smelling. Tight boots. Corseted. Reskinned. *Tingling*.

131

Greasing the pipe, forcing it down.
No, Trevor, I'm sorry Trevor.

I pour hot water into the mug. The ding-grind of my stirring spoon.

The cold musk of late September is in my lungs and my campsite is carpeted in fallen oak leaves, curling in on themselves like rat paws, belted by scattered beams of sunlight which pass through what's left of the canopy above. The Japanese have a word for this kind of light, the special sensation it conjures, like evidence of an afterlife revealing itself only to you. Why don't we have a word for this? Why wouldn't we pin this loveliness to our collected consciousness with a word instead of letting it drift away, aimless and nameless, lost to us. I will call this phenomenon Waffle Thomas. Waffle Thomas is happening all around me and I am so happy.

Dry oats. A marble. Yarn.

I hear a stick crack. Someone is walking along the path. I try to remember the other names from when I'd signed in. Were there any? Of course, the only other name I can think of now is fucking Waffle Thomas.

A fake name. They could all be fake names. How easy it would be for a murderer to simply jot down a fake name in the logbook, a fake date, make these woods their anonymous hunting ground, the oaks the only true witness. Waffle Thomas, 29 years old, travelling alone, Lansing, Michigan. All of it a lie.

The footsteps get closer. I feel my blood simmering, my body filling with panic. Scared. From eleven years with one of the *good ones*. But the world isn't like Trevor said. The world is good. I put my own real name in the book, which is what most people do. Because most people just want to enjoy the oaks, get out and enjoy the oaks for God's sake, they work hard, they want to enjoy the damn oaks!

These footsteps will belong to a friendly oak-lover. A friendly female oak-lover.

And then the footsteps stop, as though they've spotted me. And they don't want to be spotted back. I look around, trying to find the person who must be standing so near. I march, long swift strides along the perimeter of my campsite, the crunch of curled leaves under my feet.

Nothing. Nobody is coming. I stand there, still as a stunned lizard, until the heavenly sunlight, the *Waffle Thomas*, starts to shift. I gather my things, cursing myself for having lost so much morning to panic, crouch for a quick pee before starting my walk. I don't expect to take a shit while I'm here, despite the high-fibre granola and coffee. I hope to. But I don't expect it.

Honey. Salt. A coin.

The walking doesn't jostle anything loose either. I imagine the tops of my femur bones working my large intestine like dough. Walking, walking. Nothing. Not a single inkling. But that's fine.

Peering into the density of the bush as I walk, are the oak trees parting for me? Protecting me? Helping me? Are the oaks my new boyfriend?

How different it is with the oaks. Protecting me without scaring me. The oaks are my soulmate.

'It's been a while since I've had such a good mom.'

That's what I'd said to my mother. I was three years old.

'It's been a while since I've had such a good mom.'

And she got chills, realising then that I was an old soul, someone who'd lived many lives before this one, happy and settled now in this life, with her. The life I finally deserved.

Hours pass walking. Thinking of the many mothers of my many lives. My arches ache, heels chafe. The Waffle Thomas is fading, slanting, illuminating a charming little spot a few yards off the trail where I can set up camp. There's even a couple of fallen logs where I can sit, or lay my bloody socks to dry.

I set up my tent, grateful that I splurged for better gear. Grateful too for the delicious ration packets my mom found online. You just boil them in water and they become chicken alfredo, cabbage rolls, meatloaf. I'm stirring one over the stove now, wondering about souls. Are old soul babies always dispatched to new soul parents? My mother, a new soul, is proud of me for ending things with Trevor. She's always most proud of me when I look out for myself, something she never did and never will do. At least, not in this life.

Chicken alfredo for dinner.

Waffle Thomas for dessert.

I chuckle again. Naughty Waffle Thomas. Male, 29, travelling alone.

Peppermints. Milk. Leftover curry. Beads.

I pack up my camp stove and clean up my dinner. I have a bag of garbage I need to discard at the next checkpoint. It's cold out tonight, and still early, despite the dark, so I spend some time making a small fire. Once I'm certain it's viable, I yank my quick-dry towel from my bag, roll it into a pillow, and lie on one of the logs.

There are so many stars here, practically misted across the sky, bright and sparkling. It's not long before I see a shooting star, and I'm hit with such strong déjà vu I feel dizzy. Close my eyes.

And hear the footsteps again.

I shoot up quickly, look around, and find someone standing there, at the edge of the woods, just beyond the fire's light.

'Oh shit, I'm sorry, I didn't mean to scare you.' A man. He holds out a hand, a mollifying manoeuvre, as he steps swiftly into the clearing.

'It's okay,' I say, but I'm shaking, heart pounding, standing now. Taking in this man, in his late twenties maybe, a narrow face with a big mouth, a nice smile. Skirting the line between gawky and handsome. Just where I like them. Trevor had been too formal-looking, too fine. No question about the quality of his breeding.

'I saw your fire there and came over, I hope that's okay. I'm lost, actually, like an idiot.'

Rubber bands. Blue food colouring. Olive oil.

'Oh no, well, here, let me help you,' I unroll the towel, lay it over the log, the length of a loveseat. He sits down and I sit next to him with my map and show him where we are. 'What's your name?' I ask.

'I'm Matt,' he says, and holds out his hand for me to shake. 'And you're freezing!' he declares, holding my hand too long. As Trevor would have. Then Trevor would have rushed to grab a blanket to put over my shoulders, rub my back as though I were an invalid. Cold, weak, scared. Maybe I need this blanket, I would think. Maybe this is normal.

'I'm fine,' I say, pulling my hand away, rubbing it on my pants. 'My name's *****.'

'Well, *****, thanks for showing me your map,' he nods as I refold it, lift to tuck it into my back pocket. 'I can see now where I fucked up. I've been booking the little single-person cabins along the way, that's where I'd been trying to get to, but I got turned around in those hot springs. Have you been yet?'

'No,' I say, with an edge he doesn't deserve. He's not inviting me to the hot springs, he's just asking if I've been there. Not a big deal. He's not after you. You're safe. In the woods. Alone. With a strange man. 'Wait, does that mean you don't have a tent?'

He hesitates before answering, tilts his head apologetically. 'Yeah, I—'

'You can't use mine.'

'Oh my God, no, of course not, but do you mind if I – could I sleep out here? Just in my bag, with your fire? It gets pretty cold at night, and I – honestly, I'm scared to just sleep out there alone somewhere.'

I eyeball him hard, watch as he tries to melt his features, reduce his size, become as unthreatening as possible. Imagine sleeping with a strange man just outside the tent and *surviving*. Imagine how *healing* that could be. I might undo all eleven years of Trevor's fearmongering in just this one night. 'All right,' I say. 'You can stay. You need food?'

He shakes his head. 'I've got a good stash, thanks. Another perk of not having to pack a tent is I've got this too,' he unzips his bag and pulls out half a mickey of clear alcohol.

Imagine drinking strange, unlabelled booze from this strange man's bag. And not being drugged. My God, the *healing*. I swipe it from his hand, unscrew the cap, and take a deep swig. Vodka. I hand it back to Matt and he smiles and swigs too.

Hot water. Malibu rum. Dish soap.

We each take a log on opposite sides of the fire, passing the bottle as stars shoot across the sky. Matt's a high school gym teacher. Also recently split. Apparently it's not just women who re-discover themselves in remote, arboreal, and generally hostile places. Matt's ex is named Tonia and he admits she was probably right to dump him.

'I've got some' – he releases a long, low purr of a belch – 'some bad habits.'

'You don't say!'

He laughs. 'Sorry,' he says. 'Excuse me,' tapping his chest with his fist. 'So, what do you do, *****?'

'Me?' I think about it for a moment. I don't want him to know about me. I forget about me. I'm nothing, I'm just a—

'I'm just a fatty goose on the loose.'

He laughs, raises an eyebrow. 'You're a what?'

A noise in the woods. Something big. Heavy. Moving through the undergrowth. I jump, but Matt doesn't.

'Did you hear that?' I ask.

'Hear what?' he says, taking another drink. Has he really not heard it? Is he already so drunk? Or maybe he knows who it is out there, making noise. Stalking us. An accomplice. Many of them have accomplices, I know. I know all about accomplices, you sicko. I had a wonderful stay-at-home mother, remember? Every morning, laundry and vacuuming and dusting and three hours of *Cold Case Files*, my very first teacher about the world and its thirst for women's blood.

'Who is that?' I ask, accusing him now, gently, gauging his reaction. Like maybe this could all just be a joke.

'Honestly, I didn't hear anything,' he glances around,

half-heartedly, *humouring* me, a wide-eyed pout of innocent confusion on his face. 'Maybe it was Waffle Thomas.'

My chest tightens. 'Who?' The word only just squeaks out. How does he know about Waffle Thomas?

'You've never heard of Waffle Thomas? He's supposed to be in these woods somewhere, a . . . not a ghost, but like, a kind of spirit, a forest spirit. He can take any form – plant, animal, human, and he'll join your camp, chat with you. He's looking for his soulmate, someone to stay with him here in the woods forever. Quite romantic.' He belches again.

'Matt, that means *you* could be Waffle Thomas.' My stomach has gone tight now too, rejecting every swig from that nasty little bottle.

Another sound, closer, just behind Matt now. I look over his head. He twists to look too. And I see it then, embroidered into the back of his jacket. Lansing High School Basketball.

Waffle Thomas, male, 29, from Lansing, Michigan, travelling alone.

'Shit,' he laughs, turning around. 'Guess I could be, couldn't I.' He drags his heels in, closer to the log, leans forward on his knees as though he's about to launch over the fire, which has altered his gawkiness, sharpened it, filled his face with shadow.

I can't believe it. I can't fucking believe it. A fucking monster in the fucking woods. Exactly as I'd been warned, since the very first fairy tale my mother ever read me; since the very first episode of *Cold Case Files* I ever watched; since my very first date with Trevor, dinner, then a walk along the river, a place I'd never seen after dusk, Trevor my guide to the night.

'I can't fucking believe this,' I say. 'Everything I did to make sure this wouldn't happen, everything I did to be able to fucking *heal*, and I run into *you*. You fucking *pig*. You fucking sexual-assaulting murdering-ass motherfucker. With your little *accomplice* back there. Like I don't know.'

Matt sets down the bottle of vodka. 'Listen, *****, I'm not sure what—'

'I killed the farmer, and I escaped,' I say. 'A fatty goose on the loose. I told you who I was. I *told* you. And that was supposed to be insurance. Protection. What are the odds that a murderer is going to run into another murderer in the woods? Almost impossible, right? That was supposed to guarantee me a safe healing journey, that was supposed to *guarantee* me *safe passage*, God *fucking* dammit.'

'I'm just – okay thanks for the fire, but I'm just going to go, okay? I—'

The sound again.

This time Matt hears it. A thunderous crack, and then another, and another. An oak tree just behind him begins to tremble, crumble, *glow* from within, laser beams of bright light searing through its cracked bark.

Matt stands up, bathed in the oak's light. He starts to run toward me, huddle up with me for protection, but the bright, trembling oak shoots a branch out so fast he barely gets a single step before it's got him by the leg. He slams to the ground, smashing his face on one of the rocks I'd pulled over to barricade the fire. Blood pours from his crushed nose, his moaning mouth, streaks the leaves as the oak drags him backwards. He claws desperately at the ground, searching for purchase, but also, I realise, for his tongue, which he'd bitten off when he landed and is now leaving behind as the oak flings him, flailing and screaming, so deep into the woods I don't even hear him land.

The oak's bark is falling away now, it's getting brighter, vivid rays of otherworldly light, and it's *looking* at me, I can tell, I can *feel* it.

'Please,' I say, pulling my legs in close to my body. 'Please don't touch me.'

Then I'm seized by its light, sliced by these blinding blades of Waffle Thomas.

I fall from the log.

Onto my knees.

As Trevor had been when I left him, his mouth full of pipe, begging me with his red, watering eyes to please, please stop.

I'd cracked an egg against the lip of the pipe and he winced, tears rolling, as I poured it, raw, directly into him.

Please, please stop, said his eyes.

Then the blades of the oak's light carve out my eyes, replace them with Trevor's eyes, with Trevor's body, vibrating with Trevor's pain. I see me in our kitchen, twisting the cap off the liquid bleach.

Please no, please stop, I beg with his eyes.

No Trevor. I'm sorry, Trevor.

And I watch myself pour liquid bleach down the pipe I'd shoved past his oesophagus, now my oesophagus, stomach burning, I can't breathe, so much worse than the oats and the coin and the marble and the yarn and the milk and the curry and the candy and the beads and the and the and then a voice, ice-cold, fills my ears like liquid, *I can do this forever or I can make it stop.*

Make it stop, please make it stop.

You must agree to be my bride. You must agree to stay with me here forever.

Who are you?

I am Waffle Thomas. And I have spent lifetimes waiting for you.

Lifetimes. Waiting. For me to land in this life. The life I deserve, finally. *Yes*, I say. And it feels right. More than right. I feel the fear inside me, the fear wrought into my genome by lifetimes of cortisol-mutated mothers, I feel it dissolve and leak, hiss hot from my pores like toxic waste. *I'll stay and be your bride.*

And in the slip of one moment to the next, the pain is gone. The oak is gone. The only light comes from my fire, still strong. I am myself again. Alone at my campsite. Sitting on the log.

I must have fallen asleep. The shooting star. The déjà vu. Waffle Thomas. I chuckle. So perfectly naughty. So delightfully *bad*.

It's as I touch my pipeless throat that I see it there: Matt's tongue, steaming in the cold, curled leaves.

And then I hear the lantern in my tent click on. I immediately shut my eyes. Shake my head. It's a while before I can open them, turn to see the shape of him, sitting inside the tent. Waiting for me. My new man.

One of the bad ones.

Shade

by Robert Lautner

I used to dream of giant hands engulfing me. Walls of hands from a body I could not see, fingers like mountains, the lines of the palms vast ripples of desert.

They would smother me, gather me up like nothing, I'd feel the sweat of them seep over my lips, drowning me, I would scream and nothing would come as flesh bound my mouth shut. And it would not stop, I could not wake. I would be in bed with my brother, and yet not in my bed for all the hours I slept. Only in the hands, only ever in the hands, carrying me along to nowhere, crushed in them all night until woken for the dawn of work.

I was small when we went to work at the manager's house. This would be my mother, my sisters, and me. My father and brother worked the silver mine.

At the house, my mother and sisters worked upstairs, and I in the kitchens in enclosed dimness, my only role to shovel coal for the fires and stoves. It wasn't hard, though you may think it would be. We would get to work before day and stay until evening, and were fed a decent meal before leaving for home. When I was eleven I was old enough to work in the mine.

My sisters remained in the big house for their work, my mother sold the company's drinking ethanol from a stall in the miners' market and my brother and I worked the mine alongside my father. I did not really work alongside him, only my big brother did. I would truck the ore to be sorted, rarely seeing

Father until our shift was over, or not at all if he and Ru worked all night. I would walk home in the dark alone, without light, not even allowed to take the acetylene headlamp to guide me.

I am sure it was working in the mines which birthed my dreams. It could only be; I had never had them when I worked in the big house, but maybe I was too young to have proper dreams back then.

I am talking of my youth here, of the silver mines of Cerro Rico in Potosi, and not some distant woodcut of the past. This mountain, this place, long ago ushered capitalism onto the earth.

Today the lode is scant but we still probe its veins. Mostly for the zinc and copper scrapings demanded endlessly from all the world far away, but occasionally the silver still shines. Pursuit of this dream makes all precious metals shine. Dulled without the dream.

Five hundred years we have dug the mountain. First, as Spanish slaves when even Chinese dynasties used Potosi silver in their coin, where every cross in Europe dressing every altar, and every royal button, was mined by an Indio mitayo. The worth of silver died slow. The Indios died faster.

The mountain *ate* the men. This, this place which took the lives of over eight million souls under the Spanish, and still takes them, hundreds per year, the mountain that sits above us all, that permits our existence just enough to sustain its satiation. We do not live old.

La Montaña Que Come Hombres.

'The Mountain That Eats Men'.

The Spanish are gone. Each miner now works for himself, is part of a co-operative. This means his tools are hired to him and he must buy his supplies, his beer and ethanol, his cigarettes and coca leaves, from the company. This is why I was not allowed to walk home with the lamp. They are not ours. We must empty the carbide water into a drum each night and leave the lantern until the next shift.

Impossible to carve out a mountain for so long and not leave a trace, even if only a bloodied one which something must lust to drink. If we have embraced their religion, replaced Pachamama with Mary, would we not find a place for their Devil also?

Outside belongs to the Lord but none who crawl down into the earth itself would say His light reaches there. The entrance has a cross, but there it stays. No man here even carries a pickaxe. Hammer and chisel only. A pickaxe looks too much like a cross; we cannot bring it inside, it would anger someone there. This is enough to explain.

Here, in His dark, we call him 'El Tío'. He is much older than this name for he should be El Dios, but there was no 'D' in our ancient Quechua before the Spanish. El Tío, in their tongue, is 'The Uncle'. So he is this now. The Uncle of la mina, of the *Ukhu Pacha*, the Underworld. The faraway name for him lost.

The first time I saw El Tío I had not been warned. My brother found it funny to introduce me. He took me into the mine after I had dressed in hat, lamp, and rubber boots and I felt proud of my sudden manhood. He warned me not to cross myself or say any prayer once I entered, for God was not here. I promised. The entrance was lit, but by the time you had to start ducking your head, the little electric lights stopped and darkness crept down with you. Still, I remember finding it a giggling adventure, like I was playing hide and seek with the earth. Until I saw El Tío.

Ru pushed me round a corner to fall at the feet of the demon and my headlamp swept up his body as I raised myself and cried out. My brother laughed as his lamp followed and lit the figure fully.

For a moment, in my shock, this creature was real, but Ru's laugh broke its spell and I saw nothing more than an effigy carved in stone, but no less horrific in form.

He was red, of course, and horned, of course, but his open mouth was black from years of lit cigarettes gifted to his fangs. His eyes were glass, from broken lamps, also smoked dark by a million cigarettes, his pointed teeth of the same black broken glass or metal scraps. Face ancient and cracked from years of sitting in blackness while mine dust and fetid air ate his skin as it had ravaged my father's. He sat on a throne, and his huge hands were open to receive gifts from his subjects. Only then did I notice all the rubbish at his feet. No, not rubbish. Tributes.

All around his throne were beer cans and ethanol bottles, countless coca leaves, and cigarettes. Everything a miner uses to survive is El Tío's church and sacrament. But not holy. This is a different church. Ru explained what I had been welcomed into.

'It is better I scared you like this, brother. Better than El Tío coming up behind you. Every miner must be scared once to be under his protection here. It can be a fall, or an explosion or something, but once you are scared you are a miner. You are his miner and are welcome. If you do not get scared he will know you are from Above, and will scare you himself. You do not want that, little brother.'

I asked why he or Father had never spoken of this before, disappointed in them for keeping secrets.

'The name of Tío cannot be spoken outside. There are no statues of him, except down here. And we can't speak anything of church here' – he shook his head at this – 'not even the names. Tío will punish you. If you do not give him his things he will punish you. This is why so many die. They have not been proper. He gives you the lung sickness, or a wall falls, or you count the explosions wrong and dynamite gets you. Or he gets you himself with his red hands.'

'His hands are black,' I said, confident now.

'That is from all the cigarettes he needs. His hands are red when he comes for you.'

He helped me to my feet to get to work.

'Now I know where he is,' I said. 'I won't be scared next time.'

'No,' Ru said. 'You will see him all over the mines.'

I stopped.

'He moves?' And the image in my head was worse than I want to picture, for his legs were crudely formed and incomplete.

Ru laughed.

'No, brother. There are statues all over the mines. You will see.'

And I did see.

Over the next few days, anywhere there was a suitable alcove El Tío waited on his throne, or appeared to rise right from the ground, part of the mountain, always with his same detritus. I got used to him, as the others had, and work was too exhausting to care. I would push my cart of rocks past him, only wanting each journey over with before the next. But I did feel his presence was doing something, that he was protecting us. It did feel like this. He was the only colourful thing in the pits and his stark red form now and again was comforting, like a distant light on a dark road. It became very natural to say hello to him as I passed and thank him for his protection. I even started to say good morning and good night.

As terrible as he seemed, there is something in having a huge, powerfully built creature promise to watch over you. You have to admit Jesus is very skinny. I would rather a dog than a mouse.

By Friday I did not want to work in the mines. All my body hurt and my hands were covered in cuts, for we could find no gloves to fit. I was eleven, my brother fourteen. I was too young to chop wood but not to push a mine cart. There were many other children. We were the only ones who fit through the lower tunnels where ladders could not, and filled the buckets to be pulled up, hoping someone would lower the winch again to haul us. You'd stand there looking up under your lamp at the hole above, feel the rumble of dynamite all around, and try not to think of the hole disappearing and the mountain eating you. All you could do was whisper prayers to Tío, to wait for the rope to come back.

'Please, Tío, don't forget me. Tío, don't let the hole get me.

Tío, let the bucket come back. Don't let my lamp go out.' My own catechism.

But Friday night had a new surprise which made me forget my pains.

After our shift, we gathered at Tío's largest grotto to sit with him on boxes and milk crates. Not *before* him, you understand, we sat *with* him, as if he were one of us. A small circle with him among us, like you sit below deck on a fishing boat. This is the *ch'alla*. Here ethanol is drunk, cigarettes smoked, and coca leaf devoured as men talk on the week, like any group of workers in a bar in any other city. And Tío with his own cup and cigarette, and coca leaves in his open hands and mouth, and many more at his feet for when we left him to his meditations, for our beds.

This was a wondrous place. Strewn with fairy lights, coloured streamers hanging from the ceiling and Tío festooned with them as well. With his cigarette drooping from a tooth, cup balanced on his palm, he looked like any happy, sleepy drunk on New Year's Eve too far gone past midnight. Our laughter echoed back from his open mouth. This was a fine time and I felt I was slowly on my way to manhood. I didn't want it to end, and so I decided to not let it.

As winter came, the festivals we had with Tío increased to Tuesdays as well, and eventually my plan unfolded itself.

I would leave my shift to go to Tío's grotto where I would pull a garbage bag from my coat and begin tidying the mess of butts, bottles and cans on the ground, making sure to not take any good ones from his hoard. With some ethanol dregs I polished Tío until he shone. I strung his lights so they hooped around the ceiling, making sure they did not cross, for Tío would not like a cross, and swept the ground so it looked like a floor.

Gasps from the men and Ru when they entered, and that night I'm sure was the best of all. But I did not stop there.

I kept bringing things I could scavenge from the village, and in less than a week I had fashioned a bar of sorts in Tío's grotto, with shelving, with even something you could almost lean on and be served from, with me your bartender of course. Mother let me have some company ethanol to sell and bring the money to her, and I started a jar to collect. Soon I was able to stock my little bar with beer and even cigarettes. I did have the idea of putting in a small radio but realised something religious was likely to come on. Probably couldn't get a signal down there in Hell anyway. But my plan worked. Without suggestion I spent less time working and more time with Tío, preparing our bar for the nights and his worship. We even had glasses to drink from and glass ashtrays which sparkled under Tío's lights, so even before Christmas we had Christmas, although I would not speak its name.

What I had not thought of was, by my own efforts to get out of labour, I was spending more and more time in Tío's realm. Alone. With him. And what with the loneliness, and an image of another right by me, I began talking to Tío, if only to cover the sounds of ghosts sighing through the caverns and the murmuring dynamite from miles distant.

Happily I would voice my plans for our grotto to Tío, count my money with Tío, talk of my mother and sisters as I polished him. I told him I might start school soon, and what school was, and all the things boys talk of when other more vocal adults would tell them to be quiet. Tío sat there open-mouthed and glassy-eyed, enraptured by it all.

This is how I spent my winter. And the dreams came to me more and more. I was happy in the mines, but my bed was full of terror.

Hands. Falling on me like a blanket, bundling me up into unseen arms, squeezing me into a ball as my tiny, tiny hands tried to prise some air through the fingers' grip, each finger a bull's body, each jolt as we rushed along like falling down a mineshaft, each footstep a boom like dynamite. I didn't know where the

hands picked me up or where I was being carried to, all blackness, all night, until I woke sweating next to Ru. This was how
I spent my winter. And I learned more about Tío as the stories
of the mine were told in the grotto. *Our* grotto. Listen:

There was a man named Mario, from another mountain, who
one night was too tired and hopeless to leave the mine. Out of
coca leaves, resting at an altar, he gave his last cigarette to Tío,
asked him for aid. Mario struggled on through the mine when
he felt a touch at his back and turned to see two large red
hands full of fresh leaves offering them to him. Mario took the
leaves, thanked the dark, and was able to power his way out
to the other earth.

Another.

A miner who could not get used to the fear of being under-
ground was devoured whole by Tío. Swallowed his soul. Tío
despises fear. You must be scared once in the mine but then
never again. You must be generous to Tío and he will reward.
Nothing in his mine belongs to you, not even your soul. It is
El Tío's. You must ask permission to take the metals and keep
your soul.

Another.

The *k'araku*. This I had missed because it happens on the
first of August and I had not begun in the mines then. Outside,
a shaman slaughters llamas, and their blood is gathered to be
spread around the beginning of the pit and all prominent places
within. The hearts are buried at El Tío's feet and everyone
departs to allow him to feast in peace. Outside, in August, we
are blessing the land for a good harvest. Inside, we are blessing
he who may harvest us.

Another.

It is known that at the Carnival de Oruro in February El Tío
will leave his caves in honour of the Virgin of the Mineshaft.
Here he is free to cavort among us with the people dressed as
demons and spirits, himself masked and caped also. Here he drinks
and dances and indulges in earthly lusts with she-devil maidens,

and who knows, maybe, come Christmas, there are children of the villages who can call Tío something more than Uncle, eh?

All of this was spoken in laughter and drink, and other darker tales besides, but I gradually began to feel my brother and father were treating me differently. They talked to me less, and perhaps because of my smaller strides – or not? – I found myself dropping behind them as we climbed to the mine. Mother did not change, but then she did not know of El Tío. Still, I felt either my growing up and all the strangeness which comes with it, or my companionship with the underworld, was forming a new air about me. The dreams did not help. Who wants to break day with a sweating, terrified child?

Church offered no salvation. I prayed for deliverance from my nightmares, and still they came. I thought of asking Tío for rescue but decided if my church prayers and my Tío prayers were answered together the conflict would be devastating. If Saint Michael and Tío appeared at once in my dreams? *Dios mío!* Especially as I began to suspect who would win.

'Who are you talking to?'

Ru was standing in the grotto entrance, had caught me wondering to Tío whether the boys at school might tease me about working in the mines and how we would afford the uniform.

'Nobody,' I said, dropping the new streamers I was draping over Tío.

'You were talking to El Tío.'

'Talking to myself.'

He walked over to my bar and helped himself to two cigarettes, looked at Tío, looked at me as he lit one.

'Brother, you know Tío is very old. He is here since before. It is not good to talk to very old things. That statue is from long ago. Dead men built it.'

'He looks new since I cleaned him.'

'You know he is the one from heaven, yes? Sent down into the mountains.'

He lit another cigarette for Tío, wedged it in his mouth.

'You must be careful what you say to him. He can hear everything. And we are his when we are down here. I told you this.'

I agreed, understood, wanted to say that I did not speak of church to Tío, but did not know how to say it without using forbidden words.

'You are spending too much time here. It is not Tuesday or Friday. You should come and help me. Tío is clean enough. Pretty him up another time.'

'I don't want to. I am happy here.'

'So you think I should do all the work, and you should eat all the food, yes?'

'I make money here. I give it to Mother. I am saving for my school clothes.'

'You go to school in spring, is it? I never went to school.'

'Our sisters go to school.'

'So you are a girl now?'

I had not known my brother to speak like this. There were only three years between us, and when we were younger those years did not matter. But some day they do, the years widen, I suppose. I only thought of myself and my growth in our small world. Did not think on Ru's, growing up in a place you can only stoop.

'Come and help me.' He took my sleeve roughly, and he was as strong as a man, his hands worn rough. 'Stop playing. You must earn your food. Where is your lamp?' He pushed me to the bar to fetch it.

And the lights went out.

Ru fumbled at his head for his lamp, the only light the red glow from his and Tío's cigarettes, the same height, like eyes in the dark. Ru's lamp on, his face ugly under the light.

'One of the generators must've gone. Stay here. I'll go. You be a baby in your doll-house. I hope you like the dark with your uncle.'

Ru stopped in the entrance as the lights came back on, looked up at them. He was very still.

'Someone has fixed it. Good.' But his voice was not the same. Not the confident elder. A shiver in it.

I found my lamp and put it on.

'No.' Ru made to leave. 'Stay here. Sorry if I hurt you, brother.'

The next day I hung a blanket curtain across the grotto entrance so I would not be surprised again. On this day the first child went missing.

We have an airport; we are that civilised. We are still a city, though not as grand as when the Spanish were here. There are the colonial churches and many manse houses still, such as where my sisters work, but it only takes a few passages of streets to forget our glorious past. The terracotta roofs of our homes are much the same as they always were. We have the stores and bars you or any tourist would recognise as such, but we have lots of stores which are for repairing things, not for new things. Every other store is for auto parts, for Japanese car batteries, for tyres, for hoses. We keep cars like we keep mules; they are above ground until they are in the ground. This is a place for old things. And all of you who visit will find yourself in a bus station regardless of the dollars in your pocket. It is the only way to get around, you can't pay your way out of this.

And when you find yourself at a window vying for a paper ticket you may notice dozens of fliers fluttering all around the window and the walls. There are faces there, faces of children.

For a long time this has been with us. We know what happens. There are drug gangs surrounding our country. Mules of another colour needed. Or, sometimes, it is not drugs.

Sometimes the children are missing for worse things. Dozens of posters in every station. For a long time this has been with us.

We do not live in the city, we have our villages up on the mountain close to our work. The city is for church and carnival, for school and supplies and fixing things. For a child to go missing from the villages is a different matter.

First, we must consider the natural order. A demon or witch has taken the child. We have a *curandero* who will confirm this. If not, we question the outside and the city and the priest. That is when the *desaparecido* poster comes. After this, it is up to God.

Another child goes missing, then another. This is no longer a spiritual matter. This is another force.

Our children work, that is given, impossible for families to survive otherwise. Our children have formed unions to allow them to work, have protested for the right. This is difficult and also not difficult for you to understand. If the children cannot work legally, nobody will care if they work illegally. Freedom to not work – that is, to not have to *pay* for someone's work – is a slave market's fortune.

There are illegal mines all over Bolivia. We know the children missing are not all taken by ghosts.

You have an illegal mine. You need miners. Would you rather train one, or would you find it more profitable to steal a creature that is used to the work, does not have to bend over to walk your caves and will fit easily down your holes to plant the dynamite? And if all does not go well, because no one is legally watching, there is always another. Left to grow, the child would have become a man, would die at forty anyway from the sickness on his lungs. You have spared him this death, and spared his family the cost of his funeral now, and you have your zinc and copper to send far away.

I don't know if it was for this purpose, I don't know if it was for the other things which have always happened, or for a trade which can only survive if little hands are put to ground. I don't know why I was taken.

This was my night.

Ru and my father had worked all of Thursday. At dawn, once I had recovered from my dreams, I came out to bring them breakfast and water and climb the path to the mountain. All my thoughts were for tonight, Friday, tonight there would be a good time in the grotto and I needed to think of new plans for Tío now that I had thirteen dollars saved in my jar. If I kept ten for my school clothes I could buy a tin of paint to touch up his patches, to perhaps make his mouth less black from the cigarettes, but then I thought maybe he liked it that way.

A man whistled to me. I did not know this man.

One thing I know now is that if you are taking a child, for labour, for whatever, you do not do this locally. I know this because I was tied up in a van for many hours. It was dark when it opened and torches lit my face and black shapes hauled me out.

Sometimes you may hear people say they were 'beyond scared' and dismiss it as something colourful, but I can tell you I understand this. You have no control over your body, you will respond to any command without resistance. You are watching your body move, without your mind willing it. You see this sometimes after disasters, yes? The people on the streets are crying to the skies but the wounded, the people being pulled from rubble, are detached and wanting, as if they have been pulled from a dream and the dust on their clothes has always been there, their leg always this bloody. I now think this is how we endure and abide. Our nature is to be meek under violence. We insist we would fight, we would act, we would not be like this. But you will. You will be weak. You will take the sword tip offered to pull yourself up and gratefully cut your hands on its blade. This can be exploited.

Torches flailed around as if the men were also lost. They seemed unconcerned, speaking and laughing as they pulled me to a walled tent. They spoke Spanish and American with an accent I did not know. There were guns. I had pissed my pants more than once.

They took my boots, poured a bottle of water over me, let me stand there, my hands tied. I was in a forest, could tell this in the light from the torches and their cooking fire, and from the hot green smell all about. I was lost. You do not know the true meaning of this word.

I stood in the tent as told. I could not move. I was no part of this. I had gone. They could tell this, were calm, bored, they had seen it many times. Any threat to them was hours behind them, back in my village or on the road. This was now a box to be put on a shelf. They smoked and drank and laughed and I was lost. You do not know the true meaning of this word.

'What is he saying?'

I had no idea I was saying anything, I must have been mumbling through tears. A torch came closer and I put my head from it.

'What did you say?' Closer now.

'Nothing,' I said.

'Are you praying?'

'No.'

'Quiet. I'll kill your mother, yes?'

A laugh from the campfire. An older voice.

'He is talking to El Tío. I know this. He is praying to El Tío.'

All laughed. One poured his drink on the ground, whined in a child's voice.

'Pachamama, take a drink to give good harvest. Here, El Tío, have a drink. Oh, El Tío, save me with your massive cock! Save me! Save me!' He mimed horns on his head, humped the air like a dog.

The one with the torch in front of me turned it off then on again several times, and I winced. He stood back, puzzlement on his face. He was not laughing now. Off, on.

'Hey, look at this.'

Another came up.

'Look.' The torch off and on. 'See?'

The other did not see, so the torch man ordered him to stand next to me and called another over.

'Look.' His voice was excited. 'Look.' The torch shone on the man beside me. 'There is Cesar's shadow, yes? Back of the tent?'

The other nodded and even I turned my head to see.

'Where is the boy's shadow?'

I looked, could also only see the shadow of the man beside me. I was not in the tableau on the canvas wall. Lost. So lost even my shadow had departed.

The other snatched the torch, played it across me, off and on. They swore together, cursed the trick I was somehow playing, and more of them came up with their torches. I was blinded by the flashing, and Cesar left my side to see the mystery for himself.

'He has no shadow, look!' The first man now came right up to me, splayed his fingers in front of my face and looked at the shadow of it on the tent wall. He waved his hand. 'There is me! My hand! Where is he? My hand is in front of his head!'

The language of their fathers and grandfathers returned in prayerful whispers. They all stepped back further, training their torches on me.

'Dios mío!'

I had to turn my face away from all the light and look to the back of the tent. I was most definitely not there, not on the grass of the tent to the wall or at the heels of my feet. I was not there. I was lost, and they had taken even my shadow from me.

'*Diablo!* Where did you get this boy?' The sound of metal rattling as guns shifted from shoulders.

But from where I should see my shadow, crawling from my feet to the wall, another came. It grew from my feet, across the grass, started to climb the canvas wall, and they saw it rise, up and up, black on black, up and up. The torches watched, I watched. Up and up.

First, a torso seeped up the wall, then arms, wide, wide arms, big as wings, and maybe they *were* wings. Taloned hands, outstretched as if greeting the world for the first time. Then the head rose to the torchlight, horned and great until the whole tent became a black shape gone to shadow, with me within.

And I was no longer lost.

They were frozen under their torches, and this, this is also something which happens. You know it. You want to run, want to not see, to not watch the terrible thing in front of you, the building crashing down or the bomb falling and the children dying in the dust. But you watch. You watch. Because you must see.

The howl came. It was like the terrible bellow of a cow in the night when they have taken the calf from her, at once saddening and terrifying because her belly is empty and bigger than a lion's and the wail rolls all around the fields like it comes from the deep sea, and it is that sound, the sound of the deep whale mourning the lost monsters below.

I was no longer looking at the shadow, had turned to look behind the men, and they followed. To witness what was not shadow.

They may have also pissed their pants.

*

No longer restrained by cave or pit the red form towered like a cachichira tree, raised himself up, relishing his new breadth, rapt in the panicked torches playing over his arms as they grew under the light, feeding his hands which swelled at the horror in their eyes.

He did not permit the screams to come.

In one hand he took the first, like scooping water, and the man was gone, swallowed impossibly whole and gone, in a mouth as long as a door. The glass eyes turned to the next and he was gone faster than the first.

It became a play now, a grotesque carving in a buried temple from a land forgotten. They ran into each other, trying to run from him, but his hands gathered them into his loins like bundles of coca leaves. I think someone fired a gun, but no matter. It is done. He grew, he was the church dome above them, his teeth more than them, the gore of their fellows dripping. Done.

He scythed his stretched jaw along the ground, and I thought that I had seen something like this in a memory. Perhaps we all have. A story, a painting of a myth. It holds memory in its monstrous image.

His sucking mouth over their grovelling forms as he stepped, feeding, like a pig at trough, joyous at his meal, the same gorging sounds. I could hear their screams in his impossible belly. A few tried to crawl and his slab feet pounded, plucking them through his toes as they stretched, ripped and joined the others.

This is not evil, I told myself. I was not watching evil; I was watching something be done because something had been done. I was his. And something had been done. I knew this.

He had flattened the ground, shattered trees, was growing with every swallow, and the campfire rose until it formed a fiery cloak for his back, until the last of them, the one who wished to kill my mother, was alone, the Cain of his filthy earth.

A cavern of a grasp came down on him as he fell to his

knees, did not refuse what was due, had hidden from it almost well enough all his life. Up high to mouth. Bite.

The mouth towards me, permits my sight. Heads look at me from the dark throat, drowning in stars, the paint of galaxies within the impossible abyss, the faces still living. The mouth closes, a light I did not know was here goes out.

I could feel blood on my face. My hands were not tied.

Giant hands engulf me, wrap me wholly in them, tight to a body I cannot see. I am carried effortlessly across miles, swathed in flesh, and I breathe air through tree-like fingers. Light cracks through but I do not think it is day. I can see stars past his fingers, a cosmos in his palms. I curl up in their shade. All is gone. Sleep.

The Smiling African Uncle

by Adorah Nworah

No one likes to talk about it but when your uncle Zikora first moved to this country – that is, when he was still a puerile twenty-something-year-old guy-man with bushy brows and a stringy moustache – a smallish, blonde woman with a sharp chinbone walked up to him as he eyed the ramen in the bodega two blocks over from his business school. At the time, your uncle Zikora was fresh off the boat and everyone in the new country was a mystery to him, so he paused to stare at the woman as she closed the gap between them.

The blonde woman wore a cropped mohair sweater that she tightened against her chest as she hurried towards him. In your uncle's usual curious fashion – you know how his eyes get like dinner plates when something grabs his interest – he took quick stock of her features, her elfin face and the crook in her nose that added a certain whimsy to her. When the blonde woman was an inch away from your uncle, he widened his nostrils and his mouth to inhale the floral notes of her perfume. Then he straightened his back, slid his palms into his pockets and braced himself for a conversation on the weather. His cousin, Jachike, often told him that people in the new country liked to discuss the weather and the ways it changed their skin. Jachike told him that they spoke of tans and sunburns with a certain solemnity, and it would serve him well to adopt their reverence for the weather.

'Nice day today, isn't it?' your uncle said to the woman, his teeth blinking down at her.

The woman eyed your uncle Zikora and pursed her lips. Your uncle would later tell me that her lips were a human beak – pointed and ready to peck his skin. She reached for your uncle Zikora's stubbled face, held it between her palms, leaned in close and whispered so softly against his lips –

'Thief.'

Then she let go and hurried past him, leaving nothing but a faint floral scent behind.

Your uncle Zikora frowned at the small pile of ramen packets in his arms. He shook his head in disbelief, unable to make sense of what had just happened. He could still see the woman's narrow shoulders and freckled back as she hurried down the aisle, so he opened his mouth and said the first words that came to mind.

'Excuse me, Ma,' he called out. 'Is it me you're calling a thief? No, it can't be. You must be talking about the weather. The weather is a thief, yes. Not me, o. It must be the weather,' he cried. In those days, your uncle Zikora was given to hysteria. His cousin Jachike, who worked as a sous chef at an inventive Afro-fusion restaurant in the city's retail district and had been in the new country much longer than Zikora, was always warning him that his hysteria would put him in trouble. Jachike was always telling him that the people in the new country had no patience for a hysterical Black man.

The blonde woman paused at the end of the aisle. Then she did a slow turn until she was facing your uncle.

'My apologies for the confusion. I said I'm Margaret, and I work here,' she said. She spoke each word slowly, like your uncle Zikora was hard of hearing. 'Can I assist you with anything?'

Your uncle scratched his chin. He was even more confused than he'd been some seconds ago. He muttered an apology and something about how he must have heard her wrong as he was still getting accustomed to the accents in the new country.

The next week, your uncle Zikora ditched the bodega for the convenience store three blocks away. He still felt a little funny about his encounter with the blonde woman – Margaret

159

– though he couldn't quite put his finger on the pulse of his feelings. Misunderstandings happen all the time, after all, and he wasn't the first immigrant to misunderstand the accents of the locals.

Your uncle Zikora felt a dull ache in his heart when he walked into the convenience store and saw the very same blonde woman from the bodega behind its checkout counter. He breathed in a large breath and fixed his face into a smile before he approached the counter. As he drew closer to Margaret, he could hear Jachike's niggling voice in his ear urging him to smile a little wider. Jachike often reminded him that the new country only embraced Black immigrants who wore their faces soft as lard. Only the week before, Jachike advised him to soak his face in warm water overnight if he must. Jachike had two cars and a three-bedroom house in the new country, so your uncle Zikora listened to him when he spoke.

Your uncle did the smiling thing Jachike had advised him to, all thirty-six teeth glinting in the sunlight slinking in through the store's Venetian blinds. At the counter, he shut his eyes to avoid her deep green eyes and emptied the contents of his arms on the counter – toothpaste and petroleum jelly and sticks of deodorant. When your uncle Zikora opened his eyes, the blonde woman was leaning over the counter, her slender face hovering above his.

'I saw you. You tried to steal those, didn't you?' she hissed at him.

Your uncle Zikora's smile faltered. As he stared at the oak counter and contemplated his next move, it struck him that he'd been right to worry about a second encounter. He wanted so badly to defend himself, but Jachike's hoarse voice in his head reminded him to shut his mouth and lift the sides of his mouth into a smile.

'Madam, you must be mistaken,' he said.

'I know what I saw,' Margaret insisted. Her voice rose up an octave and her eyes began to well with tears. 'I caught you in the act!'

A dour-looking man in a nearby aisle stopped reading the

small print on the laxative box in his hands to glance at your uncle Zikora and the blonde woman. There was a curious glint in his eyes when he looked at your uncle. Your uncle Zikora tried to hide his discomfort by smiling till the force of his smile pushed against his eyes. He must tread carefully in that store, he thought. Just a few weeks ago, Jachike told him about a Black immigrant boy who was falsely accused of shoplifting plantains from a grocery store. His fellow customers pinned him to the floor and knocked out his incisors before they realised it was a false alarm.

'Ma, please, I'm not a thief,' your uncle Zikora pleaded. 'In fact, I can just leave the items here, and go.'

He took a backwards step, then another, his smile trembling against his lips. Then his back met the cool glass of the store's front door and he was out in the open air and running down the new country's paved streets with his heart in his throat. In the safety of his campus apartment, your uncle Zikora tried calling Jachike. Only Jachike could make sense of his disconcerting encounters with the blonde woman. Only Jachike would understand him if he confessed that the smiling thing was harder than he thought, and that he missed the days when his smiles were prompted by joy. His call to Jachike rang out. He tried again and again, but to no avail. Then he dialled the phone number of Jachike's younger sister, Ezichi. Ezichi lived with Jachike, so he hoped that he could speak to Jachike if he was nearby, but the automated voice in your uncle's ear told him that Ezichi's number was busy.

After the second encounter with Margaret, your uncle Zikora ran into her many more times. In line at the campus bank. Behind him at the drive-through of the city's most popular burger joint. On his morning jog along the city's perimeters, her blonde hair hidden behind an oversized wool hat. Sometimes, she would wink at your uncle Zikora or blow him a kiss. Other times, she would bare her teeth at him or raise both middle fingers in his face. But the worst times were when Margaret charged through throngs of bodies to get to your uncle. Once, at a farmers' market, her egg crate pressing into bellies as the shoppers parted ways for her. Another time, at a concert, her elbows ramming into ribcages as she paddled towards him. On those occasions, your uncle was forced to leave whatever he was doing so he could run from her with all his might. Still, he continued to smile as he ran, partly because Jachike had begged him to, and partly because he wanted to give himself a lifeline if the new country's citizens heard this woman accuse him of God knows what. He hoped that his smile would somehow colour their judgment in his favour, that it would stop them from descending on him like the customers did on the immigrant boy in the grocery store.

There was a brief lull of several weeks, an intermission during which your uncle stopped running into Margaret and started smiling only when he felt like it. But those days came to a grinding halt in an elevator at a shopping mall in the new country. Your uncle Zikora smelled her before he saw her, her dried sweat mixing with that fruity scent of hers – an artificial citrus that reminded him of the body mist his ex-girlfriend Oluchi liked to bathe her wrists in. She was wearing a pair of shades and had cut her long blonde hair into a bob that tapered off at her ears. They were the only two people in the elevator. Your uncle Zikora stared straight ahead at the doors and concentrated on not making eye contact. It was the longest ride, that. Your uncle would later joke that the elevator sensed the discomfort in the air and decided to have a field day with it.

When, finally, the elevator doors creaked open, Margaret pushed past him and ran out of the elevator. Up until that point, your uncle didn't know mouths could make the ringing sound her mouth began to make. 'It was like she'd seen a ghost,' your uncle Zikora said once.

'Stay away from me,' Margaret cried, clutching her arm as she limped towards a group of bystanders. 'Somebody, help me. He attacked me!'

Your uncle Zikora pressed a palm to his gaping mouth and watched the woman's performance. He couldn't decide if he was impressed or horrified by the pomp and pageantry of it all – the torso bent out of shape, the misplaced terror on her face and how he was supposedly responsible for it. Talent like that didn't come by often, he thought. She could be the next Jolie.

Your uncle Zikora watched as a crowd formed around the woman. He could hear Jachike in his ear, begging him to fix his face for goodness' sake, so he listened to Jachike and slowly lowered his palm from his mouth, unclenched his teeth and shone his smile at the crowd.

'You heard the lady! Stay away from her,' a rangy man in a ponytail yelled at your uncle, taking giant leaps towards him as he spoke. Before your uncle could get a word in, he felt the heat of the man's fists on his jaw. He heard the soft rumble of gasps and rushing feet as panicked bystanders ducked for cover. Your uncle Zikora often wonders if he should have let his rage rip through the plaster of his skin in that moment, but we both know he doesn't really mean it, because deep down in his heart he is thankful for his self-restraint, that innate need to be a good immigrant boy in the new country. After all, it was his smile that saved him from the rangy man and the man's cronies who skulked behind him, their neck veins ticking with conceit. That very smile allowed him to slip past their grasps, out of the building and into the cocoon of his studio apartment where, with a great deal of care, he peeled the smile off his face and put it away.

After the elevator incident, your uncle Zikora resumed his efforts to reach Jachike. He dialled Jachike's number time and again but got nothing. Not even a cricket. When he couldn't reach Jachike, he tried Ezichi's line, but no matter how often he called, the automated voice continued to tell him that her number was busy. Only then did his quiet concerns about Jachike's wellbeing swell into a crippling fear, and not even a bowl of Ijebu garri steeped in warm milk and peanuts could pull him out of his funk.

In the morning, your uncle Zikora's ringing phone stirred him from his sleep. He squinted at his phone's screen and wiped the sleep from his eyes with his wrists. Jachike was finally calling him back. Your uncle Zikora snatched his phone from the sheets, his breath coming in short bursts.

'Jachike the unrepentant,' he whispered into his phone. His cousin had earned that nickname in their teens; they would both act in the school drama and Jachike would insist on playing the most insufferable characters. 'Are you there?'

He waited for Jachike's full-bodied laughter and thundering voice, but all he heard was Ezichi's long sigh.

'Nne, kedu? How are you? I've been trying to reach you and Jachike,' he said.

To your uncle's surprise, Ezichi began to cry. He shook his head, perplexed. Had his greeting been too stern?

'What is the matter, Ezi? Please speak to me.'

'It is Jachike, o. He was deported today.'

'Chei! Deported? For what?'

'They said he beat up a man on the train. They said if it wasn't for the other passengers on the train, he would have killed the man.'

Your uncle Zikora stayed silent as the shock of Ezichi's words tore through his body. Jachike was deported from the new country? How could that be? The Jachike he knew lived life on the straight and narrow, and never bothered anyone that didn't bother him. Old memories of Jachike came to him – Jachike at ten, a languid smile on his face as he chased butterflies in an open field, Jachike flying a kite at thirteen, Jachike lending Zikora an oversized suit for prom at eighteen. It was two sizes too big and there were sweat maps in its armpit area, but it got Zikora through the night and earned him his first kiss.

'It's been one phone call after the other since his arrest.' She exhaled. 'I was trying to get him out of jail, to raise money for his legal defence, anything. That is why you weren't able to reach me.'

Your uncle sighed.

'I understand.'

'Zik, I spoke to him at the courthouse. The man he beat up—' Ezichi started.

'Yes? What about him?'

'He said it was the follower.'

164

'Eh? Which follower? I haven't spoken to Jachike in weeks so I'm just hearing about this, o.'

A pregnant silence stretched between your uncle Zikora and Ezichi. Then Ezichi inhaled all the air her lungs could take, sighed and continued to speak.

'Zik, for the last month or so, some jobless man had been following him everywhere. He called the man "the follower"; he said he would sneak up on him and whisper cruel things in his ear.'

'Ehh, like what exactly?'

'Small small things at first. One time the man accused him of being a thief. Another time, the man said Jachike was the Nigerian prince responsible for scamming his sick mother out of her life savings. The man even started showing up outside Jachike's apartment. Jachike tried to laugh it off, but I could tell he was growing increasingly worried.'

Your uncle Zikora listened closely to Ezichi's words. He stood up from the bed and began to pace his bedroom. He got the sense that he was staring at a sequence of connected dots, and if he looked closely enough he would see the full picture.

'Last I heard from Jachike, his follower showed up to his job and tried to get him fired. Imagine that?'

For the rest of the week, your uncle Zikora scoured the internet for news of Jachike and his follower. He stumbled on a half dozen websites with Jachike's mugshot and a photo of the bespectacled middle-aged man the press had termed his victim.

Understandably, your uncle Zikora's anxiety tripled after the new country deported Jachike. Suddenly, he felt that he was living on borrowed time in the new country, and it would only be a matter of days until Margaret crossed paths with him again and found a way to get him in big trouble, the kind of trouble that would lead to deportation. Still, your uncle Zikora kept hope alive. Each morning, he would tug his smile across his lips till it fit just right. He would massage his smile into his cheeks before leaving his apartment for the business school. And he made sure to never leave the apartment without his disguise – thick flannel, and oversized hoodies, and makeshift bandana face masks.

Your uncle Zikora was now three months into his stay in the new country and as the days grew lonelier and colder, he began to long for his old life back in Enugu, his dusty feet plodding through the red earth of open markets for okpa or akara, or his sweet mouth fuelling healthy competition amongst the beautiful girls from St Mary's Catholic School whenever they convened in the open field next to his father's compound. Oh, how he missed his Enugu *agboghobias*. They made him feel all-powerful, like a small but mighty god. And yet, he could not afford to return home with nothing to show for it. Not until he became a big man in the new country, the kind that was wealthy enough to retire his parents from their dead-end teaching jobs in Enugu.

In the meantime, your uncle Zikora went on a few dates in the new country. He hoped that he would find a woman who reminded him of the Enugu *agboghobias*. The dates mostly went nowhere, but he wouldn't stop vacuuming his apartment floors for date nights or spraying his armpits with too much Tom Ford.

One day, he stepped out of his apartment to buy a dress shirt for an upcoming date. I had hidden in the bushes hedging his building, waiting for him to make an appearance. I had followed him to a store and found a nice spot by a cloth rack near the checkout counter. I watched him pore over shirt after shirt until he decided on an iridescent green one that matched my eyes. As he neared the counter, he saw my loose, blonde curls. My hair had grown a few inches since our last encounter.

Your uncle Zikora gaped at me for a few seconds. He swallowed with some effort. Slowly, he remembered to fix his face, to let his smile slit his lips wide open as he watched me expectantly. I walked up to your uncle with my notepad and my pen, and I observed his trembling frame. Then I let go of my *Margaret* persona and extended a residency permit card to him.

'Congratulations, Mr Zikora Nwadiora. My name is Patricia Miller, your case officer from the immigration department.' I paused to clasp my palms and grin up at him. 'I am pleased to inform you that you have earned your residency permit in our country.'

Your uncle Zikora blinked slowly at me, his smile beginning to falter at the sides. Only then – staring at your uncle's help-less face – did I realise that I was not ready to stop watching him. I wanted to study that man and his rich trove of facial expressions for the rest of our lives.

'Mr Zikora, I know all of this must come as a surprise to you, but I work with the country's immigration department and our newest internal protocol is for legal aliens like yourself to earn their residency permits when they pass a behavioural test,' I said to him.

Your uncle Zikora listened as I told him about the country's new immigration policy and why it was imperative for aliens to pass the behavioural test. He wanted to know if the new policy applied to all immigrants, and I told him it would be overkill if it did since European immigrants were mostly expa-triates who paid their taxes and never disturbed anyone. The same could not be said about immigrants like your uncle Zikora, who were desperate for a better life. Immigrants who came into the country in droves – wading oceans, scaling walls, and hiding their raw-boned bodies in plane cargo. The immigration depart-ment needed to filter out the chaff, and the behavioural test was doing just that.

'It's simple, really,' I said to your uncle Zikora. 'Every alien who fits our internal metrics is assigned a follower to track their daily movements and attempt to place them under some degree of stress. During the stress sessions, we observe the alien's body language – everything from the movement of their brows to the slight changes in their tone. If the immigrant displays too many negative emotion markers, we rescind their temporary residency permits and return them to their country of citizen-ship.'

I assured your uncle Zikora that he was a standout candidate. I told him that during each stress session, he'd smiled with just the right amount of warmth in his eyes.

I waited for your uncle Zikora to say something, but he just kept staring at me with that curious smile of his. Years later, he'd confess that he'd been nervous about saying the wrong thing to me because he thought I was still testing him. Truth be told, I wasn't ready to close his case file. I'd started to look forward to his loopy smile and the quiver of fear in his voice, so I stretched out the moment for as long as I could.

'Mr Nwadiora, did I mention that you are one of the best applicants we've had since we instituted the policy?' I asked. 'You were incredible.'

'Thank you,' he said, his gaze now averted. His smile had gone and he looked uncomfortable, like he was holding in his pee or trying to get away from me. I wanted him to need me, so I reminded him that I was the reason he could continue to live in the country.

'A residency permit is of course conditional,' I said to your uncle Zikora. 'The immigration department will monitor your activities for the rest of your time here. If you demonstrate any negative emotion markers, I'm afraid your permit would be rescinded. Do you understand?'

Your uncle Zikora's fingers tightened against his residency permit card and he flashed another rictus grin, just the way I liked him to – with his pebbled cheeks threatening to push through his skin. With his nose squished into a ball, and his eyes disappearing behind his lids. So I threw caution to the wind and suggested that he would have an easier time complying with the immigration rules if, say, he was married to a person who could look out for him. Me, for example.

Your uncle Zikora looked at me like he thought my suggestion was a game, the final master he must defeat to secure his residency. Maybe that is why he nodded emphatically and walked with me to the courthouse to legalise our union, a fat smile digging into his gums as we took photos on the courthouse steps.

And I would tell you this – your uncle Zikora's smile has not faltered since we left the courthouse. Not when the rowdy teenage boys on the subway called him a slur. Or when the trigger-happy cops cuffed him up an hour before he was set to walk the stage at his business school graduation because they confused him with a local burglary suspect. And especially not when my family is in town, and you run your fingers through his Afro, and press your thumb into his skin, and trace his smile with your fingers, and take photos of his face from all angles to prove to your Black friends that you can't be racist because – *Look! My uncle is African!*

Rosheen

by Irenosen Okojie

The heads suspended in the old barn's ceiling glimmered seductively. All four bobbed, hovering like a fractured constellation before gathering again. Their bloodshot eyes flickered. Their expressions were pinched and strained. Their mouths moved frantically, expelling short breaths in between garbled language that was not local to Norfolk. Or at least, not that Rosheen could tell. She herself a stranger in the land before she had dreamt of the wide flat skies and horizons, the sprawling dappled green landscape, windmills dotted along the broads' periphery spinning like moored gods. Her fingers were numb and cold clutching the bucket handle. The sound of it swaying by her muddied legs was a creaking alarm that the crows chased in frenzies around the yard.

Rosheen edged forward slowly; with each step the weight in the bucket rocked from side to side. Grain for the chickens spilled from her pockets in yellow rivers. The tension thickened. The barrels on the side were silent witnesses. There were red stains on her clothing. A line of sweat on her top lip. The heads lifted their tongues. With each step she took, the memories in her limbs were cushioned by the sleep state, her soil-smeared face a shadow moving in the cavernous space. The air in the barn seemed to have shifted just recently, as though before Rosheen even entered the heads had been foraging through their loneliness. The creepers on walls were dusted with moonshine. The heads had no bodies.

170

Stumbling momentarily, she knocked the bucket against her leg. Its contents sloshed, dangerously close to spilling over. The heads began to shriek. Still in her stupor, she dipped her hands in the bucket. Fingers covered in blood, she raised her arms up and began to spin. Rapturous tears ran down her cheeks. The barn door clattered shut. The creepers on the walls multiplied. The contents of the barrels sank through an opening into the bottom of a pale, blue thrashing sea. Stray body parts appeared on the bales of hay like drunken hallucinations before dwindling to nothing. The heads roared, circling Rosheen as though she was a defective sun.

She had come to England from Ireland's County Kerry. A town called Killarney which rested on the shores of Lough Leane, the daughter of a Trinidadian father, Horace, and an Irish mother, Maureen. Maureen had told her such glowing stories of the father she never knew, that Rosheen had begun to wonder if Horace, a good-looking fighter pilot who had fought for Britain in the Second World War and passed through Killarney with the same restless disposition she had inherited, was in fact a saint, the fourth wise man, or an optical illusion Maureen had conjured one lonely night after drinking too much stout. Such was the loyalty she afforded this man who seemed to have vanished from the face of the earth once he left Ireland. But he had been real alright. She knew that every time she looked in the mirror. He had passed on his dark looks. People could barely tell Rosheen was mixed from the molasses hue of her skin, the spiral curls of hair she kept short for efficiency, a slightly wide nose that sat proudly on her face. She had flashing large, dark eyes and dimples which became more prominent when she broke into laughter. In the beginning, the judgemental residents of Killarney had often asserted, 'Good god, the shame of Maureen having that Black baby. Her pa would be weeping in his grave, I'll tell you. Why doesn't she get rid of it?' Or a variation along those lines, as though Maureen could leave Rosheen in the arms of the Mary statue that stood majestically outside St Mary's Cathedral, who in turn would make her vanish to the heavens. Maureen was ostracised for the most part, except on Sundays when she stubbornly refused to be banished from God's house. She sat in the pews in her finest garb, gently rocking Rosheen, ignoring the sly, knowing looks the residents exchanged.

When Rosheen got older, she sat up some nights in bed thinking about Horace. She wondered if he saw creatures moving in the dark sometimes the way she did. If he too could hear the rumbling of weather changing by pressing his ear to the ground or saw light forming between bracken scattered along the town's pathways. But Rosheen, in her mix of barely contained eccentricity and pragmatism, did not romanticise him. She had questions. And the last Maureen had heard, after the war, Horace had returned to England – Norfolk – where the airfields beckoned like distant relatives.

When Rosheen turned twelve, she began sleepwalking though the crumbling, limestone house she and Maureen had co-existed in fairly harmoniously for the most part. She had been a wilful, precocious child who loved her mother although it was not unusual for her to misbehave. She'd throw Maureen's pearls and brooches into the fire, watching curiously as the flames licked them to melted bits. She would invite local children to play, then block the front door so they couldn't leave, and walk around in the mud in Maureen's polished black leather shoes with stumpy heels which she saved for church. There were visits to service where the holy water outside the church's wooden doors was always low by the end because bored, like some of the other children, Rosheen would sneak off to scoop it into a bottle then pour the contents inside the jacket pockets of residents as though the Lord himself had instructed her to do so.

The night Rosheen began her sleep wanderings things shifted as though in orchestral synchronicity. The bracken littered outside their home crackled softly. The stones formed makeshift paths covered in a fine mist. The moon was a silvery bruise in the sky, waiting patiently for Rosheen to limp silently toward

it in an act of devotion. The clock hands in the sparsely decorated hallway faltered and Rosheen sat up in bed, dazed. Her
expression blank, her hair messy, her white nightdress soaked
to the skin. She swept the rumpled, flowery bedspread aside.
Standing awkwardly, her left hand twitched. She walked out
of her room barefoot, the corners of her right eye bloodshot,
and crossed the stairs, down into the hallway then out through
the front door. She headed into the gusty night. The ground
cool against her bare feet. By now the wind, winding through
the holes in the garden's back wall, was hissing even louder.
The copper taps there were spitting at angles. She walked
towards them in her stupor, curled her body over them in an
awkward embrace, as if the water would propel her in different
directions. She slid down to the ground, curling her limbs like
a snake introducing itself to a new surface.

She crossed several acres of land, her nightdress a ghost against
skin. She appeared in flashes, a strange entity in a trance state.
The surrounding houses in her peripheral vision called, shrouded
by dense darkness, imbued with a certain melancholy. After a
while, scratches appeared on the bottom of her legs from brushing
against twigs. She scaled a wall leading to a structure which
leaned to the side as though bracing against unforeseen inter-
ruptions. Its thatched roof thinning at the edges. Her throat was
dry. Short streaks of dirt covered her cheeks. Bits of soil were
lodged in her fingernails. Still she moved, a fever dream let loose
on the land. The soft din of dawn was yet to arrive. She was
barely aware of the scratches on her legs. Other injuries edged
towards her in search of skin to occupy. Subconsciously, Rosheen
called things to her body in this state; an accordion, its black
keys like teeth in the air; the march of swallows before a migration; the glimmer of reflections from shattered mirrors; weather
in paperweights made real. Things you could trace and hold
tenderly before the morning swallowed them whole.

When she finally returned home, appearing in her mother's
bedroom gripping a rake from the thatched house, wearing that
vacant expression on her face, Maureen was awakened from
sleep. Screaming, she thought a stranger had entered their home.

But it was Rosheen, who in that moment, aged twelve, bore an ominous adult presence which Maureen recognised with a slow, unsettled wonder.

At twenty, Rosheen decided it was time to leave Killarney. Despite its wild, rambling beauty, she ached for more: new experiences that would take her outside of the familiar; the horizon had other things for her to discover that the town could not contain. She did not know its form yet but its malleable shapes bloomed within her bit by bit. She knew it would reveal itself one day. She had been told of new opportunities by the candelabra-maker, Conn, whose cousin Aidan worked at a farm in Norfolk, England. Aidan had told Conn, who in turn told Rosheen while she stopped by the shop, that there were several farms looking for workers out there. Conn warned, 'they're not always the friendliest bunch so mind yourself, but if you do go you might want to try your luck on that front. I suppose sooner or later, a young lady such as yourself would want things you can't find in Killarney. But be very careful, you know . . . with the night wanderings. I've seen you a few times on my way back from old Darragh's place.'

'I'm not in control when it happens,' she said, feeling somewhat exposed. A knot of tension formed in her right shoulder. 'I didn't know people had noticed.'

'You and Maureen are a favourite topic. The nosy folk will always talk. As long as you're alright.' His concerned expression contorted his rugged face a little. She had seen him in passing many times over the years. He never seemed to be in a rush about anything. As if he could bend time to his will rather than the other way round. She had quietly admired that. He handed her a slip of paper. 'That's the farm Aidan works at. If you find yourself in any trouble, you can contact him.' He shook her hand gently then, in a formal way that seemed incongruous, as if to get a hold of himself. He pursed his lips. The intricately decorated shop suddenly became too small to contain what was unsaid. Their handshake was suspended between them. She felt the tremor in his fingers as though his hands would turn to wax in hers.

She left a note for Maureen on top of the fireplace at home. Because she had a flair for the dramatic, Rosheen sealed it with her blood. Inside the white envelope, there was a shamrock for good luck and the promise that she would return to visit. She caught the ferry to England with some gypsies who told raucous, colourful tales in between songs and enthusiastic drinking. Their bodies jostled like new pennies. The smell of alcohol lingered in their cabin. The women's skirts billowed as if they harboured secrets. A baby screamed for the nipple. A tambourine clattered to the floor. A gaunt, emerald-eyed woman began to cry at one point, claiming she was mourning the loss of her shadow for the second time. Rosheen absorbed it all with a wry smile until the noise became warbling in her ears.

On arrival in England, the sum of £30 Irish pounds was all she had to her name, rolled inside a small, black cloth purse stuffed at the bottom of a bag of few belongings. It was bitingly cold on the quaint Holt streets when she finally got there after taking three trains. The cold was harsh in a way she had not been prepared for. The pretty but unfamiliar winding roads were picturesque. The flow of cars was at a steady pace. The town centre, filled with carefully decorated shops, was warmly lit. Ridges of ice on dark imposing lampposts melted like separating continents. Pangs of doubt growing inside her were exacerbated by the discreet, but unmistakeably suspicious looks people threw her way. She wondered if Maureen was missing her already. Had she cried over the letter or her stealing away before she had been persuaded to do otherwise? Would she find a special place for the shamrock to wither away as a time-keeper till her return? The thought of finding her father in Norfolk, perhaps longing for something he did not know he had left behind, sent a warm feeling spreading through her. She walked for a while, listening to cars moving past her. Thoughts circled in her head like a merry-go-round. She was turned away for work for one reason or the other from a few places: the woman at the dressmaker's shop said they did not have the time nor inclination to train someone new; the baker's was a small operation of four people, and unless one of the workers got very sick they were not hiring for the time being. 'You might want to tempt Lady Luck into action by trying Crookborne Farm,' the kindly woman who ran the confectionary shop suggested. Rosheen took directions from her in relief.

It was early evening when she got to the farm. Her limbs ached, her head was throbbing, and tiredness was evident in her face. She was so thirsty she felt she could consume the contents of a stream. She opened the crooked wooden gate, entered. She walked a little way to the chestnut-coloured door of a thatched house. A strange feeling of familiarity filled her body. She knocked. A large, rough-looking man answered. He had beady brown eyes, a swarthy pallor, and a sunken quality to his face. His thin lips pulled tightly at a pipe lodged in the right corner of his mouth.

'I'm looking for work,' she said calmly, despite wanting to collapse into a heap. 'I'll take whatever you have going. I learn quickly.' Reading his expression of disinterest, before he had a chance to decline she continued, 'I'll keep out of your way when I need to.' He must have liked her gumption. The cold air blew from their mouths like a quiet currency.

The farm itself was ten acres of land nestled between the broads, a scattering of lakes and intersecting waterways. There were steep surrounding valleys dappled with light. Windmills spun in the distance like taciturn guardians. Fuller, the owner and overseer, put her to work the next day. He said he had a few workers pass through over the years but it had been difficult to hold on to good ones. Farming life was not easy. He bore an odd, removed quality about him that would have alarmed some, a coldness in his eyes. Rather than feeling threatened by it, Rosheen took it as an indication that it was perhaps a form of defence. Lonely people often shielded themselves as a means of protection. She cleaned the kitchen and sorted the pantry. She heard the billy goats stuttering back and forth as though caught in an invisible lined web. Later, she watched Fuller gather the sheep for shearing, tersely calming them when they became restless. The goats broke out from their holding, rushing into the field of pumpkins as though wonders were hidden inside. Fuller made cheese from goat's milk as well as other produce. She assisted him one afternoon, stirring large copper pots of milk in the roomy kitchen until her arm hurt. On one errand, she passed an old barn at the further end of the farm that appeared to be out of use. Its wooden doors were eroded. There were worms at the bottom slithering up. She peered at the slimy gathering, resisting the urge to place her finger there. A slightly fatter worm was ahead of the others as though leading a charge. 'What's that old barn for?' she asked him in the sheep pen on her return, her sleeves rolled up. 'It seems a shame not to make use of it.'

Fuller took the pipe out of his mouth, his eyes narrowing. 'That barn's not open to anyone. You're to keep away from there. Accidents have happened. Mind your own.' He turned his body away, back to the task at hand, sorting a batch of ewes ready for the chop. A humming began in her head. She watched the sheep. Their cries were a sly distraction, a clarion ringing in the frazzled atmosphere. She noticed that all the animals had tiny red specks in the corner of one eye.

Three months passed during the winter season. Days of bitter cold, uncertainty and a growing restlessness that felt inevitable. In that time, Fuller worked her to the bone. Some mornings she rose at sunup and did not collapse into bed in the tiny, freezing attic that sufficed as her living quarters until long after sundown, her limbs burning, a chasm deepening in her chest. She had pilfered a few books from the house library – if a person could call one mahogany shelf of books that stood between the airy kitchen and the upstairs part of the house a library. She borrowed Charles Dickens's *Great Expectations*, *Nicholas Nickleby* and Jane Austen's *Sense and Sensibility*. If she was not too exhausted of a night, she would pore over the books by lamplight, aware of the light flickering and shrinking, absorbing it as a comfort. She enjoyed the books – they provided a form of escapism from a hard life – but she wondered about the tales of people who looked like her. Why were their stories not considered of value too? She knew her father Horace had seen some of the world as a pilot in the war. It was Maureen who told her about the Tuskegee Airmen. Maureen had told Rosheen that Norfolk was the strongest clue she had as to Horace's whereabouts. That was why she came. Rosheen promised herself one day she would find him. She would rise above the station people imposed on her and write his adventures. She began to think of him even more: how he walked, if he talked with an accent, whether he was bow-legged like she was. She wondered if he had the same tendency to daydream or if he harboured the piercing loneliness that never went away. She started to see aspects of him on the farm; his green infantry uniform floating through the pantry, his sleeves brushing against perishable goods, his gold cuffs glinting on the long, wooden kitchen table between cold cuts of ham, broth, cabbages blushing purple in the daylight. His injuries bloomed on the windows before moving in search of other surfaces around the farmhouse. Horace was trying to tell her something from afar but she did not know what it was. And there were crescent-shaped smudges on the books' pages that were not from her fingers.

The demand for the farm's cheese grew in the county yet Fuller paid her sporadically, sometimes half of what she was due. When she confronted him, he growled, 'You're a mouthy madam. If you don't like having a roof over your head and food in your belly, you can go elsewhere. See if you'll be trusted in someone else's business. You're ungrateful.' He spat in the dust, and jammed the pipe back into the right corner of his mouth as if to punctuate his comments. That evening her night wanderings started again. She saw parts of a dream gleaming inside the pumpkins. The next morning, she awoke to find herself in the pumpkin field, their insides gouged out, her fingers slick with pumpkin juice. The memory of how she had got there had dissipated. And Fuller was screaming at her, winding his belt strap, striding towards her. His face was fit to burst, his mouth spewed profanities. Through groggy eyes, she spotted the swing of the belt above her like a flash, then raining on her body, bolts of lightning against the bone. She raised her arms in defence, kicking at his shins. He grunted in surprise as she landed one in his groin. 'Aargh, you bitch!' The belt slackened in Fuller's hand. He fell to his knees, clinging to it as an anchor. The audience of gutted pumpkins lay scattered like stranded disciples. Above, a flock of grey marsh harriers streaked through the sky. The wheelbarrows spilled soil from a lost dawn. It was a bright, beautiful morning. The slow hum of the town rising from sleep could be heard in the distance. Now that she was fully alert, the anger inside Rosheen grew. Imagine being awakened by an attempted throttling. She could not believe the audacity of the man. Why even the boys in Killarney had known better than to take her on. They called her the Bonny Bow-legged Black Wonder.

She knew for certain that she was not the first worker Fuller had attacked in such a manner. The next day, he pretended nothing had happened, which surprised her. She had sat up in the night thinking, staring at the gauzy moon for answers, bracing herself for another confrontation, or to be let go. She needed time to find other work. She did not have the luxury of just leaving. To where and to whom? There was Conn's cousin Aidan south of Norfolk, but other than her fairly loose connection to Conn there was no real guarantee he could help her. He no doubt had his own problems to contend with. As the days went by, she watched her reflections in the farm windows with terse lips. They were slender, melancholy versions of herself that faded like a fine mist. Is this the England you sought, Rosheen? She cursed the day she flung herself into a hard lonely life, a perpetual sense of isolation. Two meals a day, if that. The occasional visit into town brought respite, where she stood outside the sweet shop eyeing the artful window display achingly until she conceded, buying handfuls of small balls of cocoa, stretchy wine-red strips and sour sugary droplets which melted on her tongue. There was other relief from Fuller himself now and again, on evenings when he took off drinking or with his raven-haired, hard-eyed fancy woman. She was a hollow-looking character who rarely deigned to visit the farm because she considered it beneath her. On the one occasion Rosheen had met her, offering a small platter of finely cut cheeses she took pride in making, the woman had raised her nose haughtily, fingers hovering uncertainly before begrudgingly selecting a slice as though she had been presented with a plate of horse manure, barely glancing at Rosheen. Her red hat was comically balanced at a precarious angle. The bulbous skirt of her cherry and black rock and roll dress swished about her as if parting the red sea. *Jesus! Mary Fecking Magdalene*, Rosheen thought. *I should have pissed on those slices before giving them to her.* She promised herself that the next time she would. They were cruel people who deserved each other. On those evenings she knew Fuller went to visit her, Rosheen slipped away into the town's taverns, dancing with abandon while the gypsies played, filling those places with merriment and song.

One evening she spotted Horace's clothes flapping on the roof of the old barn, bending the wind to their will. They beckoned her. A tingling feeling trickled down her back, spreading all over her body like wildfire.

A few more weeks passed. Spring arrived. Fuller began to drink heavily and he did not care to disguise it. There were dark empty bottles of ale unceremoniously dropped outside his room door, left in the pantry, on the window sills. She even discovered one in the sheep pen. The sheep cried around it. There were red specks gathering again in the corners of their eyes as though the gods had marked them as a flawed batch. She fed the sheep, tenderness before a slaughtering, much like Fuller and his fancy woman. She suspected that things had soured between them because he was even meaner when he drank. She knew he still harboured a grudge when he docked her wages again, claiming that demand for their produce had slowed due to competition from some of the bigger farms in the region. The truth was that people had noticed his heavy drinking in town, and some, as a result, were reluctant to give him their business. He nursed his resentment against her the way a person would a bruise: assessing its gravity, running a finger over its circumference, pressing it to sharpen the pain. Some days he left her making the various cheeses while he disappeared, the rancid stench of his breath still in her nostrils. She wrote to Maureen and Conn. She could not bring herself to reveal the true nature of her circumstances. Her pride would not let her do so. Instead, she painted an idyllic picture of life on the farm, fabricating several characters she brought to life with relish. She knew the truth would only make Maureen worry to the point of exhaustion. As for Conn, she pictured his sardonic smiles, his curious calm gaze, the way he said her name slowly, as if to savour it, as if it left a particular taste in his mouth. Her heart fluttered at the memory. She wrote to Conn again, informing him that she saw them wandering through the secret parts of Killarney together. She watched him in the sleep state too, barefoot and running towards her as she stood by the thatched house she had once visited. The dream's scope widened. Time passed. She saw his hands stroking the widening girth of her stomach, his soft breath on the stretch-marks blooming there in gratitude for what was to come. In another letter, she told him that she had seen them lying on that rooftop together. A few days later, she called him on the telephone, the steady reassuring rumble of his voice making her feel like a thousand intoxicated butterflies.

It was a blustery evening when she headed to the back of the property to stretch her legs. Surrounded by woods, and some yards from the main farmhouse, it was slightly removed from everything else. There was a well there. As far as she knew it had no water in it, but a nagging familiarity bloomed inside her every time she passed it. A little like the first night she had knocked on the farm's front door. The well was a big stone mouth springing from the ground, daring the sky to fall into it. She walked to it, looking down into the darkness below. She stood there for a while, so engrossed in thoughts of home she barely registered quick footsteps coming from behind until she felt hot breath on the back of her neck: until it was too late. She was shoved in. She felt the hands on her back, a sudden pressure, the sensation of falling. A scream curled in her throat. Only the mouths of creatures in the woods making shrill noises and the undulating Norfolk broads acknowledged her fall.

*

She landed awkwardly. Arms splayed out to cushion the impact, legs bowed like a crab. The pain was so intense at first she thought she would break in half. The smell of rotten flesh was so pungent, she retched, heaving then placing a hand over her lips. Her stomach convulsed. Her thoughts were scrambled. A buzzing in her brain began as though a procession of hornets were shedding their wings in its matter. The terror of the fall gripped her again. The shock crippled her body for a few minutes. Her knuckles were scraped. Her clothes soaked in sweat. The water had gone. After the shock faded and the reality of her situation hit her, she felt around the well floor gingerly. There were four bodies, which had decomposed to the point of oozing in parts. The smell was inescapable. In her gut, she knew they were former workers at the farm Fuller had gotten rid of when they no longer served a purpose. The true nature of what had originally seemed an act of kindness, offering room and work, revealed itself in that moment. Holding her breath, she felt the bodies again.

Their heads were gone. A tremor wracked her limbs, a spasm in the dark followed by a crushing feeling of inevitability. She looked up at the well's opening appealingly, hoping to catch a glimpse of the night sky. She touched the walls, looking for ridges or gaps on either side she could slip her fingers into and climb to the top. Over the next few hours, she failed repeatedly. She lost her footing multiple times, a nail tore off, her fingers got sweaty. On several attempts she would get a quarter of the way up, only to lose her grip and fall. She scraped her elbows, banged her knees. She felt beaten and alone. Each time she fell the bodies awaited her. They were seeping, speaking what had been done to them. They waited, signalling the end of a stunted, macabre ceremony. Was this what fate had in store for her all along? To die alone at the bottom of a well with rotten bodies she did not know? Tired and frustrated, she shrank back against the wall, curling into a foetal position. Outside, the trees shook. She howled, her cry ricocheting beyond the well's walls.

Eventually, she sat up again. It was difficult not to heave. Once or twice when she sensed tears coming she pushed them down into the crook of her heart. Besides, what good would crying do? The crook trembled, rippling through the sky and its blanket of unnamed stars. She shivered; her clothes felt heavy and seemed like inadequate protection; her various cuts and scratches stung. Her pulse throbbed. She heard the sound, faint and then increasingly close; the rhythm of soldiers marching, the beat persistent, the thud of their feet hitting the ground. The air crackled, as though the regiment had changed formation. Horace's uniform appeared through the crevice of air, shrouded in a feverish yellow light. It flickered gently then became more defined. Its sleeves were frayed from scouring the secret parts of the farm. Its gold buttons winked. Its green hue faded slightly at the breast. It folded as though collapsing against a stray wind then swelled. The sound of soldiers marching faded. The corpses around her seemed to lean in, an accidental act of camaraderie. Her breath caught in her throat. A man appeared in the uniform. A man who had skin like hers, but darker. Handsome. His nose broad, his face almost perfectly symmetrical.

'Rosheen.' His deep voice was like cold water over her skin. Was this a phantom? An apparition she had conjured in a desperate state? It was Horace. She was sure of it. He repeated her name again. She uncurled her body, moving towards him, her limbs stiff. His lips pursed. He grimaced, showing her his hands. They were bloody, mangled, a contrast to the rest of him which looked in perfect condition. His hands were storytellers in the night. She realised then that Horace had died on the farm. He must have come here after the war, taking whatever work he could find. A sob caught in her throat. She trembled. The sense of loss was immediate, overwhelming. Her body caved again.

She left Horace flickering between the carcasses. After several more failed attempts, she reached the top of the well, climbing scissor legged, carefully placing her fingers in crevices again, plotting a route by feeling her way through. She concentrated deeply till she no longer feared it. On reaching the top, she hurled herself over, landing on the cold grass with a cry.

*

When Rosheen arose she was in the sleep state, her eyes blank, vacantly staring ahead. Her limbs propelled her forward of their own accord, moving towards the farmhouse, towards Fuller who was deep in the throes of a treacherous slumber.

In the old barn Rosheen, the defective sun, watched the heads of former workers resume their places in the ceiling. Horace's head was amongst them. Their bodies still sang in the well. They bobbed in the thatched ceiling approvingly. She turned to the bucket she carried, its every sway and movement a sweet lullaby. The weight in the bucket needed to be released. She bent down, reaching towards it. It was Fuller's head inside. His tobacco pipe was mired in the blood. His lips were blue, his eyes frozen in shock. She lifted his head out, began to spin around the room in a dance. Now her eyes had a vengeful gleam in them. Shaking, she opened her mouth, released a breath that was a soft pronouncement. Fuller's head left her fingers, ceremoniously taking its place among the others, howling in abandon.

Carcinisation

by Lucy Rose

At night, in the softness of our bed, the fisherman once told me stories about how deep the water is. *Deep enough to bury a hundred of you. Maybe even a thousand.* Like the weight of an ocean, his heavy hands came upon me. I think about those nights often because the moment the wedding band came around my finger, tight and sharp, he stopped telling me stories of the deep. Instead, he strung me along to his boat for graft.

Nudging the thick fishing ropes with the tips of my boots, I keep to the edge of the stern. Even sheltered by the gunwale, the wind is sharp against my cheeks, like the hard slap of a cool and calloused hand.

Above, a heavy cloud smudges the sky. When the clouds spit rain, the fisherman pulls up his hood. The silver twists of his beard hold raindrops like beads. I've grown to resent the whiskers steadily growing out from his pointed chin. And he's grown to resent mine, too. His sharp silver hairs scratch my flesh at night when our bodies press firm against one another.

The hull groans, tipping us to port, towards the blackened water. Waves cradle us, but we rock back again as the currents churn. My stomach twists and gurgles. I pinch the pouch of my belly.

Sea spray splashes over the gunwale. It feels like rainwater on my skin. Seafoam sprinkles my face. As I lap it up, water lingers on my tongue. Tart and salty and fishy – the taste of a sailor.

I wince as I swallow. Seawater splashes over the deck, tickling the soles of my boots.

Standing at the bow, the fisherman looks overboard into the below. He pulls the crab traps from the depths, fingers tight around the trap frames as they come on board. I can already see the rope burn and blisters kissing his calloused hands. He's not afraid of the sharp nip of a crab claw. They try to tease their way out from the traps.

Inside, the creatures twine their limbs. Their hard shells press up against one another. Their legs stretch out, knotting as they try to come free, but the fisherman's traps have snared them. I close my eyes and listen to their bodies crash together; the clicking as their shells hit one another.

I envy the way they touch and tangle.

'Make yourself useful,' the fisherman calls from the bow.

I drag a crab trap towards the stern and tip it into the crate. Crabs come free, hardened shells ringing out as they tap the edges of the crate. I wonder if they know they'll be boiled alive. Nipped and tucked until they taste *just right*.

The runt of the catch is small. Her claw pinches the edge of my coat cuff. I take her into the dip in my palm and she rests, black eyes emerging from their nooks. When I feel the gentle graze of her feet, I can't help but smile. My chest goes warm.

'I wonder if he'll let me keep you,' I whisper. 'When he caught me, he took me home to be his wife. I wonder if he'll let me make a wife of you.'

The creature's pointed legs potter, exploring the creases of my palm.

'Our secret?' I whisper, smiling again as I slip the creature into my pocket.

*

When we are home, I lick the fisherman's wounds. My lips graze his callouses. Kiss his rope burn. Tend to his blisters. Wherever his skin is broken, I make him better. But he won't look at me. His grey eyes stay forward, set on the spray of the waves beyond the windowpane.

Please, fisherman, look at me. Just once. Or I might just break these tender fingers clean off.

*

Hours ago, the fisherman fell fast asleep in his armchair downstairs. I decide I won't spend another midnight alone. I visit my raincoat, hung high on the back of the door, slipping my hand deep into the pocket. The creature is waiting for me. She climbs my fingers and nestles into my palm. I listen to the ocean and return to bed. Waves crash against rocky beaches. Gulls shriek in the above. 'Maybe I love him too much,' I mutter to myself.

The creature feels at home on my sheets, gentle and quiet as she explores new contours and creases. She settles between the folds, but the fabric wrinkles when she moves. Beneath the sheet, her brown shell is a dark shadow. When she emerges she crawls, clicking as lamplight touches her shell. When the light finds her, her eyes retreat into their nooks.

'My husband is a fisherman,' I whisper, fingertips brushing her back. I want her to know I am soft. Safe. Small, imperfect barnacles cling to her body. I wonder if she wants to be smooth like me. 'But he doesn't love me any more. When we first met, his pupils were large and dark. He wanted me in every way a person could. But now I am old. And boring. And drab. I am easy to throw away. Do you know what it's like to be easy to throw away?'

The creature moves closer, her claw nipping my bottom lip. But I don't flinch. Blood trickles into my mouth. Salty. Metallic. I swallow it.

'I think I still love him,' I say, but my voice breaks as I whisper my confession. A lump forms in my throat, expanding until it puts a stopper in my lungs. I recognise the sensation, like a dense stone pushing against my atlas bone. I bite my tongue, hard. The sharpened edges of my teeth press deep. 'He was so repulsed when he found my first silver hair. We were lying together in these sheets. His hackles went up as he fished the hair out from my locks and plucked it free. He opened the window and let it blow away.'

She edges closer again, until her shell rests hard beneath my chin. For a moment, I pull back, watching the black eyes twitch.

'If you were my wife, would you throw me away?' I whisper softly, pulling my wedding ring from my finger and placing it before her. 'Do you want to share a body with me, creature?'

We gaze at one another.

I rest my chin on the edge of the mattress, but she does not retreat from me. She is eager to come inside.

I open my mouth. The plump of my bottom lip drops as the crab's leg presses deep and punctures its softness. She tastes the blood. Slipping between my lips, the creature reaches down my throat.

She's too big to swallow. My eyes bulge from their sockets as I gasp for air. My hands stay on my throat as I try to cough her up, but she burrows down my gullet. I can't breathe. The creature slips deeper, landing in the pit of my belly. A weight lifts as her legs potter inside my gut, gentle and light on her feet as she explores.

This is how it feels to be loved.

*

When I wake, the world is black. There is an ocean in my stomach, splashing against the lining of my gut. Churning beneath like riptides. Vomit tunnels through my intestines, reaching for my throat.

I try to swallow, lapping up spit from beneath my tongue to push it all back down. My saliva is thick and warm, drying up fast until it's sticky. As my stomach rolls, sweat beads on my brow. I swallow again. The crab shifts inside me, lurching.

I wonder if she has already changed her mind. Maybe she has decided that I am to be thrown away. My midriff is still as the creature settles. When I press my finger deep into my stomach pouch, my flesh wobbles like jelly. I wait for it to still.

My stomach warps.

Rolling.

Shifting.

Swelling.

The creature is calm in my belly, nesting as she sheds her hard shell. But something is happening to my organs. I swallow my saltwater tears. And hers.

My stomach lurches again.

I peel away from my sheets, but they are mired to my skin by sweat. They come away as I tumble from my bed. Stumbling through the door, I collapse. My kneecaps hit the hard tiles.

Inside, something tears.

Thick and scratching, something burrows through my intestines; I can already taste vomit in my mouth. Sour and salty. It splutters between my teeth and splashes across the tiles. Warm ichor and sinew. Purulence and blood. Fragments of the creature's shell hit the floor with a clatter.

A thread of silver drool falls from my lips. In the vomit below, a crab's leg lies still, slender with fine hairs. Its foot has a needle-sharp point at the end.

There is no grief, because my creature-wife is not gone – only her shell. I don't feel burning hot anymore. My body isn't humid. It's cool as I take a deep breath. My body is changing. And I like the way it feels.

*

A hermit crab crawls across the pregnant curve of the giant stone. Its tiny legs are pale and creamy. Beady black eyes poke out from beneath the rim of the twisted conch upon its back. Barnacles, no bigger than pinpricks, have grown in the deep creases of the shell.

I take a deep breath. I smell the salt in the air and the cigarette smoke from my husband's mouth. I smell the fishy scent every fisherman carries with him. By the shore, sitting on a soft bed of washed-up seaweed, the fisherman reads his newspaper. A cigarette hangs from his lips as he breathes in a dark twist of smoke. Trying to escape his fingers, pages flap with the gale. When the sea birds call, the fisherman looks up. He spares me a glance, but his head is back between the pages quick.

'This spot, by the rocky crags and the pelting sea spray, has always been our place. The fisherman's and mine. No one comes here but us,' I whisper to the hermit crab. On the crest of this rock, the tide will never reach us. This cove is hidden between the flat-faced, monolithic crags and the large stones pulled into shore by the lick of the waves. Rock pools are scattered, water warmed by the low sun. The tidal tongue of the ocean washes over the pebbles.

The fisherman likes it here – away from the sandcastles and fuss. Far from the ringing of the 2p machines in the arcades. Here, we cower beneath the mud and rocks and the high bluffs.

The hermit crab stills beneath my shadow. I press my ear to the flat of the stone and hear the gentle patter of its feet moving over the slow curve.

'Look at me,' the fisherman says.

But I'm looking at the hermit crab scaling the rock. I wonder if it can sense the creature-wife I'm keeping locked in my body. If it can feel how much she's changing me.

'Wife of mine.' Heavy and hard, the fisherman's boot comes down. The conch on the hermit crab's back cracks and splinters.

'We should leave. There is work to be done,' the fisherman says, the cigarette perching on his bottom lip. He takes another deep breath of smoke and lets it free. When his boot comes away from the rock, the remains of the hermit crab are stuck to the sole. Its body is broken. A stray leg lies bare on the crest of the rock, ready for the hungry beaks of the sea birds.

*

My eyes are blacker than they used to be. And my skin is losing its colour, growing harder. I wonder if I am moulting. When I look in the mirror, I see creature-wife's eyes in my sockets. I know I am more beautiful now I've absorbed her.

190

My head cocks to one side. Creature-wife wants to speak. 'Husband of mine,' we whisper.

*

From the bedroom window, we can see the fisherman's boat leaving the bay. His boat tips on the waves. White horses turn the water opaque. Sea birds with white feathers graze the surface. The world is sickly and warped. It is moving and we are floating. *'She was round in the counter and bluff in the bow. Way aye blow the man down. So, I took in all sail and cried, way enough now. Give me some time to blow the man down.'* We mutter the shanties beneath our breath as sweat leaks from our pores. Our skin is almost translucent and it's turning as hard as shell. More calloused than his ever was. We twiddle our hair, which is starting to come out. One strand at a time. Not just the silver hairs, but the brown ones, too.

Creature-wife only likes hair to grow on our legs.

Our skin sparkles with sweat. It sounds like the ocean when our insides grumble. We wonder if the fisherman is thinking of us and this body we share.

*

The fisherman puts two crabs inside the boiling pot. Their shells whistle. They are screaming. But the fisherman closes his eyes, taking a deep breath. His shoulders drop. To him, the sound is like music.

'You hungry?' the fisherman asks, listening to the shriek of the trapped crabs.

We are silent. We don't look at the fisherman. We can't look at the fisherman. It hurts too much. 'No food.' The words sound alien in our mouth. Like they do not belong there on our tongue. Like language isn't ours to speak.

'I work hard to fill our bellies,' the fisherman whispers softly, tapping the side of the pot with his tongs. The crabs within still cry out as they are boiled alive.

'No food,' we snap.

The fisherman is quiet, standing at the stove. His eyes are like stones, still on us, heavy and unmoving. We wonder if he thinks we are beautiful.

'Do you know what happens to blood when it boils?' we ask. 'It bloats the beating heart. Blood vessels burst. Eyes bleed.'

'You're too soft, wife of mine.'

'No.' For the first time, we feel hard.

'You've always been too soft.' The pot boils over, lid clattering against the rim. The shrieking crabs fall silent. 'You got away with it more when you were younger. It was endearing.' He leans over the table, his mouth brushing our forehead. His breath is warm. We want to swallow it. 'But you aren't young anymore. Your hair is turning grey. And you sag,' he whispers, fingers combing through our hair. A few strands come free from our scalp.

We close our eyes when he speaks. All we hear is the boiling pot. The bubbling. The popping. The cracking. The crash of the churning waves beyond. The sea birds' cries as they nest in the cliffs. The hardened shells of the crabs as their bodies whistle and wheeze.

We imagine boils and blisters blowing up big on our arms. The splash of boiling water on our cheeks as we open our mouth to scream. And how the water, almost hot enough to dry up completely, eats away at our gums. Skin falling from our bones. Teeth falling from their sockets. Creamy eyes popping, wet but burned.

Our fingers curl around the edges of our chair. The fisherman comes closer. His skin is warm. But ours is warmer – especially when we're angry. Hot to the touch. Blood rushes to our cheeks. We open our mouth, and we shriek.

The fisherman stumbles back.

'In here,' we say, beating our sternum with our fist. 'The feelings are the same. They've always been the same. Since the day you married us.' We heave a deep breath. 'Why do you make a monster of our body?'

The fisherman's eyes are wide.

'Maybe it is you. All these silver hairs. Maybe they're because of you.' We point to the boiling pot. The crabs inside are dead now. Silent. The water bubbles.

'We do it slowly,' the fisherman whispers. His eyes are wide. 'They don't notice. Beasts don't feel pain.'

'Do you think we are a beast, husband of ours?'

The fisherman cocks his head and fastens a tight knot upon his brow.

Our earliest memories of him are fading, lost and buried in the far deep of the below. We watch the boiling pot.

Stepping back towards the stove, the fisherman turns up the heat. He looks back over his shoulder. He keeps his eyes on us. We think he is afraid.

We stay sunken deep into our chair. And he stays over there.

*

The fisherman is sleeping in the spare room. He has even locked the door. But we are used to being alone.

The bed feels less like an expanse now creature-wife is here. We stretch out our jaw. Something is happening in our mouth. A canine is wobbling. Loose. Our fingers find their way up into our mouth and nip at the tooth. We close our eyes and we pull down hard.

When the tooth comes free, a smile appears on our mouth. Blood tastes like seawater. Metallic. Salty. *Home.* We feel it dribble down our chin and all we want to do is laugh as our fingers snare another tooth free.

'This is fun,' we laugh, dropping the tooth into the bedding. Blood spreads through the white of the linens. Later, we can suck the blood away from the sheets if we are hungry.

Our stomach grumbles.

*

In the kitchen, the crabs are still in the pot. They would understand if they knew how hungry we are.

We reach for the lid and dip our hands inside. The water has cooled off. The crab corpses are floating, bobbing around on the water's surface. They do not fight us. Cradling their bodies in our hands, we pull their legs free and crunch them between the remains of our teeth.

Creature-wife is crying. We can feel tears on our skin as we tear into the body of the first crab. Something churns in our belly, but we are not afraid.

These clothes feel too tight. Our hands move down, nipping at the buttons on our shirt until it's come free of our body. The skin binding our stomach is pitched like a tent, sharply ridged. Something is trying to breach through the surface and pierce its way to air.

'Husband of ours,' we shriek, but creature-wife wants us to hush. The fisherman stays behind his locked door.

The sharpened point from inside our belly sinks back into our body. Another tooth comes loose. When it falls to the floor it lands with a clatter. Creature-wife lets us cry. She lets the tears flow. All the tears we have held back. Our bones splinter, ribs opening out, tearing our skin. Sharpened legs armoured in hard shell emerge from within, cutting through our flesh.

We don't remember our name anymore.

*

Light feels strange. It's warm on our shell. But we're not all shell. Nor all skin. I don't know what we are.

We sit at the table, waiting for the fisherman to come to us. We wonder if we are beautiful enough for him now, but we're too scared to look in the mirror. We stay wrapped up warm in our dressing gown. Parts of it have torn. Our limbs needed somewhere to go, so they cut holes through the cotton. Our shell stretched out the back, tearing the seams. We can taste the ocean in our mouth.

There's an unsettling quiet, but we can hear the roar of seawater in the distance. And the call of a sea bird's harking silence.

'Wife of mine?' the fisherman whispers, escaping from his room. For the first time, we feel the gentleness in his voice. Even if he's not perfect, we've never been more in love. Even if he doesn't love us the same back.

But the fisherman will grow to love us.

'What have you done, wife of mine?' the fisherman whispers, standing beneath the frame of the door.

We gaze at him and smile. We hope there are still teeth left inside our mouth. 'Hus—' The word snags on our spiny tongue. The word dislodges. 'Husband.'

The fisherman stumbles back.

'Where are you going?' we ask. He looks afraid. 'We have no more silver hair. And we've taken away all our crooked teeth. And our skin will not wobble.' We collapse to our knees. These human legs are hard to walk on now. Tendons snap. The muscles are wearing away. We use our other legs instead.

The silence between us is horrid. The fisherman takes a cautious step forward. He kneels down to tame the beast. We feel the edge of his nose tickle our shell as he looks over us. The warmth of his breath spills. We open our mouth and taste it. 'Do you want to share a body with us, husband of ours?'

Stumbling back, the fisherman shakes his head, but creature-wife reaches for him. She grasps his wrist. He shrieks, cheeks turning red and hot as the strength of our claw breaks his bone. Human men are so fragile. Brittle bodied. Easy to break.

'Look at us,' we say.

But the fisherman will not look. We smell the blood spilling from his arteries. Our mouth waters. We are hungry, but we are saving the fisherman. He is not a meal for us to pick at.

We love the fisherman.

His skin is turning pale as his eyes roll back inside his head.

'It's okay, husband of mine,' we whisper into his ear. 'It stops hurting after a while.'

As our ribs part, newly formed limbs take him into an embrace. We feel him come into our body. His flesh is soft and he is quiet as he melts into us. We swallow his screams. Now we never have to part.

Be still husband of mine. We love you. And you will grow to love us too.

*

We go to our place. The fisherman's and ours. The tide brushes up against our feet as we leave behind our human legs and fall into a crawl.

We don't remember the human songs. The shanties. But we hear them in the far distance. Sailors are calling to us, hungry for their catch.

The fierce ocean crashes up against the rocks. It churns, snaring its way to meet the land. Above, the sea birds sing to us. And for the first time, we understand what they are saying.

Behind us, stones bear the bloody footprints of needle-point legs. We walk to the ocean, shedding the remains of our human clothes. The water welcomes us.

Together, we float. Our body jerks as the remains of human bone and skin slither away from us, reaching down for the seabed. Blood fills the water and we breathe it in until it is blue again. Beholden to the darkness, we sink into the black. We take the weight of the below.

Above, where the light touches, the outline of a fishing boat bobs upon the waves. We are quiet in this emptiness, patient for the next hungry fisherman.

Going Large

by Lionel Shriver

At first, Evelyn was solely focused on the one remaining empty
space in the overhead bins just behind row 46, cursing her luck
at having been assigned to board with Group 5. She'd been
consigned to Group 5 on the flight over to Lisbon, too, which
in that case had meant the bins were already chocka. Checking
her carry-on had entailed travelling the whole two and a half
hours with her precious red fedora in her lap. The feather would
have got crushed under the seat, and she hadn't been about to
tempt those thieving baggage handlers with headgear in which
she looked terribly jaunty, even rakish, if she didn't say so
herself. Maybe it was time to capitulate to the airline's larcenous
early boarding add-on. It wasn't fair, you know. They'd all
bought airline tickets, not lottery tickets. Granting some passengers but not others the right to a carry-on amounted to
commercial fraud.

It therefore took a moment for Evelyn's gaze to lower and
her stomach to fist in dread. *Oh, my fucking lord.* This holiday
owed to a last-minute impulse, and she'd had no choice but to
accept one of those detestable middle seats on the homeward
journey. But the woman in the aisle seat had to have been
wider than she was tall. She was kitted out in a puffy yellow
blouse that any stylist would have counselled against; the tiered
flounces made her look even fatter, and the saturated buttercup
colour drew the eye, whereas any sane person that size would
pray to fade into the backdrop. More to the point, this passenger

197

was spilling halfway across Evelyn's seat. The woman didn't appear to be sweating yet, but just wait; they always did.

Evelyn crammed her nacreous hardcase roller bag into the overhead space that in fact contained someone's duty free at the back and left it to a flight attendant to deal with the extruding bulge.

'You in this seat? Hold on a sec, honey, okay?' So, 46C was American: even worse.

As the enormity struggled to a stand and squeezed between the seat and seatback to stumble backwards down the aisle, Evelyn tried mightily to wear an expression of patience, but her smile must still have looked pained. After slipping to her seat, she hammered down the raised armrest between C and B the way castle guards must have once clanged shut the metal gates to Lisbon's Belém Tower – although this light-blue plastic rectangle looked conspicuously less effective at repelling barbarians. Sure enough, once Buttercup Blouse resumed her seat with much huffing and puffing, the armrest was occupied (and then some) by a pale forearm that could have passed for a normal person's thigh. The woman's actual thigh spread well over the crease between the seats, and to keep from being intimately pressed against the gargantuan passenger's rhinestone-spangled leggings Evelyn was forced to scrunch to the opposite armrest – also occupied by a slim young man in noise-cancelling headphones poking intently at his mobile. She shot him a look of apology and shared exasperation, but he wasn't having any of it. Evelyn glanced forlornly at the green indicator lights ten rows ahead. Getting seated had involved so much folderol – so much, if you will, *mass migration* – that ever escaping to the loo would be out of the question.

Evelyn was furious. Yes, our new era of 'body positivity' sponsored Dove adverts with 'plus-sized' models exploding from their smalls – not the optimum expression in this case – who we were all meant to pretend were every bit as fetching as the svelte ones. But technology hadn't quite advanced to the point where the Beauty Police could censor what went on in her head. Wide loads like that should have to buy two seats. Failing that, a passenger weighing in at barely eight stone should be offered a discount. As it was, Evelyn's fare subsidised this capacious woman's ticket and pretty much every other passenger's on this plane, while she was also expected to abdicate half the mingy square centimetres allotted to 46B. Buried in a romance paperback, Buttercup wore the fixed well-meaning expression of people who were always apologising – and for good reason. Occupying that much space was a territorial incursion on everyone else's. Evelyn had no idea why designating obesity a 'disease' made fat people any less responsible for their dimensions. You can't create something from nothing, so you don't get that big without food. If she herself were that ginormous – perish the thought – Evelyn wouldn't fly to Lisbon, or London, or anywhere else. *Travellers of size* were unjust impositions on people who exercised more restraint.

Sure enough, when the refreshment cart came round, Buttercup ordered a hot ham-and-cheese, soda, and two bags of crisps. Evelyn herself yearned for a glass of white wine, if only to soothe her disposition, but that would be at least 130 empty calories she'd be obliged to subtract from her modest dinner that night. She settled for a Diet Coke and declined the free pretzels.

Evelyn thus felt still more deprived, even if she had deprived herself. She was getting a crick in her neck from veering so far left for a solid hour. Her bladder nagged. Running through the sales figures on her iPad as planned was out of the question; she was too annoyed to concentrate. Once Buttercup had finally gnawed through her considerable snack and restored the tray table to its upright position, Evelyn had had enough. She would take a stand for all the tiny people, what few they were.

'Sorry,' Evelyn announced, looking straight ahead. 'I believe that according to an article by a flight attendant I read in *The Times*, both armrests belong to the middle seat.'

Noise Cancellation was oblivious. But Buttercup was flustered and blushed with embarrassment. 'Sure thing, sweetie, you go right ahead,' she said, withdrawing the arm-cum-thigh with a look of dismay as to where else to put it. She pulled her elbows together in her lap, looking miserable. Evelyn perched her own arm gingerly on the inside edge of the rest, and now she'd no choice but to keep it there all the way through to touchdown.

When Evelyn rose to deplane, the waist of her skinny jeans pinched. She'd gathered that the style was now out of fashion, but she was reluctant to relinquish a cut that so flattered her narrow hips. Nevertheless, after locating an airport loo at last, she tugged her shirt down and left the waistband unbuttoned. Air travel caused water retention. Everybody knew that.

At a Tesco Metro on the way home from the Tube, Evelyn picked up a 70g package of smoked salmon, a packet of rice crackers, half-fat crème fraîche, and a prepared mixed salad with a sachet of Caesar dressing. Back in the flat, the singleton treated herself to that glass of white wine while catching up on the new season of *Bridgerton*. Yet as she stirred little enough of the dressing into her salad that she might as well have left it unadorned, that bloated sensation persisted. When she brushed her teeth before bed, her face in the mirror displayed an oddly rounded contour that made her look less intelligent.

Dressing for work the next morning, she opted for a form-fitting black pencil skirt, boots, a white blouse, and a beloved rust-coloured waistcoat with antique brass buttons that would give the ensemble its panache. But once fastened, the buttons pulled at their threads. The top one threatened to pop off, while her diminutive breasts pushed into a decolletage unsuitable for the office. Irked, she threw on a boring blazer instead, acting on an uneasiness by barely skimming her toast with butter. The following morning, after another standard sartorial backstop felt inexplicably tight across her back, she gave the toast a miss.

Across the following weeks, the pattern continued. One item of clothing after another simply ceased to fit. Of necessity, the pencil skirt was soon exiled to the nether regions of her wardrobe, carelessly folded over a wire hanger. She was forced to resort to fabrics with springy elastic sizing, to notch out her belts, and to disguise straining seams and unlatched hooks with shawls or coatigans. In exasperation, she'd taken to skipping lunch. After only black coffee for breakfast, gnawing hunger the whole day through made her cross and irritable when in sales you were expected to be perky and optimistic. After her acidic stomach had been yowling for ten hours, too, once she arrived back home it took stupendous discipline to not overdo the rice crackers.

Meanwhile, obeying an instinct she'd no interest in examining, Evelyn found herself brushing her teeth with her head bowed to the sink and glancing in the opposite direction whenever she crossed in front of her bedroom's full-length standing mirror, whereas previously she'd have paused to strike an admiring pose.

She wasn't given to eavesdropping – she had respect for others' privacy and wasn't, ordinarily, paranoid – but she pulled up short one afternoon at the office when she could only conclude that the two female colleagues making tea in the canteen were speaking sotto voce about her.

'. . . I know. Double-quick, too. Do you reckon something happened on that holiday to Lisbon? Like, some mad romantic fling she had high hopes for which didn't pan out? There's almost always some emotional reason, some unhappiness behind it.'

'But she's always been, like, a functional anorexic. Neurotic, actually. And super vain. To be honest, it's almost satisfying.'

'Oh, don't! It is not.'

'Come on. Admit it. Another one bites the dust. Less competition for the rest of us.'

'More like doom for the rest of us, sunshine. If that fox can't keep it together, what chance do we have?'

'You know, the weird thing is I almost never see her eat anything.'

The co-conspirator sighed. 'It's not weird. It's a red flag. Abstinence as display. Most serious pig-out is in secret.'

At length, Evelyn had to confide in someone. Thus, when negotiating with her main London running buddy Dana to arrange another of their regular hangs, she suggested a quiet Lebanese restaurant as an alternative to the club scene, whose clamorous nightspots were deliberately contrived to spare their customers the odious obligation to talk.

'Dinner, really?' Dana said sceptically. 'You wouldn't rather, like, I don't know, go for a long walk?'

The last thing Evelyn needed after practically fainting through a long Friday workday was a long walk. '*No*. If you're worried about the money, it's my treat.'

'I'm not worried about the money.' Dana left the corollary unstated: *I'm worried about you.*

The long menu was a torture. Evelyn craved everything it listed – aside, perhaps, from the Greek salad, which was all she ordered. As she picked at the free pickles, she looked longingly at Dana's hummus starter, glistening with olive oil and studded with nuggets of fried lamb. The aroma from the freshly baked pillows of pita was making her high.

'Go ahead, have some,' Dana urged. 'There's enough for us both.'

The single corner of pita, dab of chickpea, and lone titbit of lamb were worse than nothing. The sample ruined her purity – *I only had a salad* – and merely whetted her appetite for more.

Dana was a solidly good-looking woman – with corkscrew black hair and a knowing grin whose chronic tendency to rise higher on the left than on the right made her look sarcastic even when she was being sincere. She had the kind of figure most people would describe as 'healthy', meaning there was nothing wrong with it but she didn't turn heads. Until recently, the friendship had evidenced a subtle hierarchy that Evelyn had never thought about in those terms – or hadn't until the sneaky power disparity reversed, at which point it was glaringly apparent that she was suddenly playing second fiddle after three-plus years of first chair.

What had hitherto drawn the two together was collusion. Another aspect of the relationship Evelyn had never given much thought: they spent much of their time together mocking other twentysomethings, whispering in each other's ears about some slag's exposed bum crack or awful hair. It was a default spectator sport that had never failed to entertain, but Evelyn's interest in taking pot shots at strangers had waned.

'Dana, I'm gaining weight,' Evelyn said to the sliced tomato once her salad had arrived. She could pick out the cheese and avoid the olives.

'Um – yeah. I wasn't sure if I should say anything.'

'No one ever does. Or not to your face.'

'You're not that far gone. Maybe you've got into some bad habits without really noticing. Easy to do. Just start paying a little more attention, and cut back.'

'I can't,' Evelyn despaired. 'If I ate any less I'd cease to consume food altogether.'

Dana's eyes narrowed. 'Seriously? You know, it's a doddle to go through two thousand calories just idly munching on crisps and peanuts in the pub.'

'I am not "idly munching"! I haven't touched a crisp or a peanut in months. Honestly, it seems as if the less I eat, the fatter I get!'

'Which is impossible,' Dana said flatly. 'Sure you're not snacking? A lot of the problem is self-deceit. When I'm honest with myself and tally up *everything* I hoover in a given day, it's a whole lot more than I thought.'

'I'm telling you, I eat practically nothing!'

'Evelyn. That's what they all say.'

That dinner soon became a rarity, because Evelyn was growing less sociable. She'd probably have resigned from her job for that matter, if it weren't for the rent. She could have lived without an attentive audience tracking the relentless expansion of her circumference with horrified but addictive fascination, a pastime that now clearly constituted her workmates' in-house Netflix. She'd become a sort of anti-mascot, a walking cautionary tale.

Getting around had grown effortful; the six streets to the Tube station were exhausting, and she had sometimes to stop and catch her breath. Her neat, natty outfits of yore were replaced by kaftans, waistless housedresses, pyjama-like athleisure wear, and the odd tented confabulation with which a family of four could have comfortably gone glamping – all of which led to the unpleasant discovery that the larger the size, the more garish the fabric. Hardest to accommodate were the breasts, which pre-Lisbon were close and firm and about the size of half an orange. Were she in the mood for commando, she could once have got away with not wearing a bra at all. These monsters required the kind of tack that rigged ships, without which they sat in her lap, as if she were bouncing babies after giving birth to twins.

Evelyn had long been accustomed to the pleasures of being seen, and nights of clubbing with Dana were organised primarily around parading a new ensemble that made a clever use of scarves, or sashaying in a skirt skimpy enough that she had to be careful about bending over. In this confoundingly corpulent manifestation unfairly foisted upon her without so much as a single chocolate digestive biscuit in compensation, she was loath to call attention to herself, hulking the pavements with a downcast gaze, as if neglecting to see anyone else would ensure they didn't see her, either. One lonely evening, she tried to brighten her mood by trying on the red felt fedora. But she didn't look jaunty, much less rakish. She looked ridiculous.

After a long hiatus during which she seemed to have successfully clad herself in a cloak of invisibility in public, Evelyn detected that she was turning heads once more. But during her arduous shamble to the Jubilee line, she no longer drew the flatteringly salacious leers she'd garnered when launching off in heels with Dana. These glances were furtive, and if she ever stared back they looked away, shamefaced.

Moreover, Evelyn had been blithely habituated to other people being nice to her in shops. Sales assistants smiled, made small talk. She'd not been so egotistical as to have imagined that this ceaseless conviviality was exclusive to her or to her especial personal credit. She'd simply assumed that people in shops were nice – or even that people in general were nice. But it turned out they were not nice! Hardly anyone was nice!

They certainly weren't nice to Evelyn. Assistants never smiled or beguiled her into dallying at the till with laments about the weather. They were eager to be rid of her.

Although nothing had changed aside from the, ah, minor matter of her perimeter, Evelyn was fundamentally becoming a different person. Formerly confident – some would say over-confident – witty (if not a bit catty), upbeat, and extroverted, she'd become ingrown, wary, and timid; the only jokes she told were at her own expense. Meanwhile she kept being plagued by an unfocused guilt, but over what? Existing at all, really. That's right, she felt *guilty for living*. Her physical presence seemed to be regarded by the world at large as making an unjust claim on other people's space, as if she were illegally squatting in some wealthy stranger's lavish house and leaving stains in the toilets. In truth, she tried to make herself as unobtrusive as possible. She'd grown mortified by asking the smallest favour, even help getting a packet of Canderel down from a high shelf. In the office, she washed up other people's coffee mugs. She put in longer hours with no expectation that her diligence would ever earn her an appreciative acknow-ledgement. Which it didn't. Her diet was only more joylessly spartan. She'd come to detest nibbling rice cakes, which was like gnawing on flatpack furniture, and lettuce was more trouble to chew than it was worth. Since giving up on such grim fare entailed little enough sacrifice, in desperation she tried a whole week of fasting. After seven solid days of nothing but bottled water – she even boycotted coffee, its surface shimmering with a suspiciously unctuous swirl – suddenly her voluminous blue kaftan was straining across her bum.

Then there was the sweating. It started as a mere glisten at first, a shininess across her brow. Even when she wasn't exerting herself, her forearms caught the sun. She'd often dart into the office loo to hastily powder her face, hoping that if any of her colleagues noticed they'd write it off sympathetically to early onset menopause. But in no time the beige powder from her compact began to clump and muck up the brush; on her face, it formed uneven patches of paste. There was too much moisture for the makeup to absorb. During her ministrations in the mirror, drips would form at her hairline, trickling down her temples and drizzling salt in her eyes until they stung. The dark circles of damp under her arms did nothing but grow greater in circumference, while her clothing striped with wet horizontal streaks where the fabric had got caught in the rolls of her torso. She soon kept a towel at her desk to discreetly mop the seat of her chair before leaving the cubicle, lest passers-by witheringly conclude that the pools on the plastic were wee. There was one morning when she arrived at the office already so soaked from head to toe that someone asked if she'd got caught in a cloudburst.

It was bad enough that Evelyn had started to leave a trail across the carpet, like some dim-witted Hansel planning to retrace his steps by dribbling a gallon of water instead of crumbs. But one evening, as ever, she draped her sail-sized dress over the bedstead to dry, only to discover the next morning that none of the dark swaths had evaporated. As she shambled to the Tube, the liquid beading and trickling down her arms evidenced a curious viscosity, and when she wiped the sweat away from her eyes it wouldn't flick off but smeared. At the end of her workday, there must have been a cup of liquid left behind on her chair. Yet the feel of the towel on the orange plastic was newly slithery, and once she'd finished the seat gleamed, as if it hadn't been dried but polished. Uneasily, she tested a drop tickling down her neck and rubbed it between her fingers. *Oh, my fucking lord.* She was no longer merely perspiring. She was sweating oil.

There is no stain more diabolical than grease. Every garment Evelyn donned she destroyed. Worse, the trail she left behind on the office carpet didn't disappear overnight any more, but deepened and gathered dirt, as if she'd been sloshing a brimming chip pan. The trail left no one in doubt, either, as to the habitué of which cubicle had soiled the premises. Eternally exuding some sort of unguent also matted her hair to her scalp, while a comb left track marks; Evelyn had always been meticulous about hygiene, but now no one would believe that she showered more than once a month. Dana had warned her about the dangers of investing in an off-white sofa, and now Evelyn was suffering the consequences of not heeding her friend's advice – though Dana had been more alert to the perils of dribbled red wine than to the likelihood of pouring a litre of cooking oil over the cushions on a nightly basis.

Evelyn was sitting miserably on this once-ivory upholstery, which made a squishy, bubbling sound whenever she shifted her weight, and picking dully at the usual undressed mixed greens, when she reached behind her ear to scratch a persistent itch, only to find this weird *thing* hanging at the back of her jaw. It was ragged and rubbery with no sensation, but it wouldn't pull away; it was attached. With foreboding, and stepping with great care because the floorboards were slick from her secretions, she ventured to the loo mirror to examine the growth. Dangling like an ugly earring slightly behind the lobe, it was flesh-coloured and spongy, like a skin tag, only this one was three inches long with pointy bits shagging off. It was blobbier by far than the vegetal version, but when she spread the droopy excrescence on her fingers, it was still shaped uncannily like a leaf of rocket.

By the time it registered that each time she swallowed a single scrap of greenery it would bloop from her body as a fleshy extrusion, these itchy vegetal skin tags had proliferated everywhere – catching in her collars, tangling between her thighs, and forming a semblance of a beard along her chin. Evelyn was wearing her salad on her sleeve.

Well, that was the limit. If she was going to be fat, and sweat lard, and spontaneously sprout puffy, pendulous fronds as if trying to camouflage herself in Tesco's fruit and veg aisle, she was not going to go hungry. The sole consolation of having become a pariah should at least be a proper meal. As she'd been spending practically nothing on food, her bank account was bursting, and she could more than afford a night out. Accordingly, she lunged onto a bus one evening to return to that Lebanese restaurant. A minute later, the man she'd sat next to quietly stood and filtered off to another seat. She didn't care. She would embrace her new status as an untouchable and its marginal advantages. This time when she left behind an oleaginous pool for the next unsuspecting passenger to sit in, she didn't feel abashed, but vengefully satisfied. As she lumbered down the bus steps, one foot, then the other, one foot, then the other, she could tell that the expression of patience on the driver's face was fake. Fine. She would take fake patience any day over honest irritation.

This time the menu spread before her in all its glory. She ordered the hummus with lamb. She finished off the entire basket of fresh pita and asked for a second. She went for the smoky baba ghanoush swimming in tahini, polished off an order of stuffed grape leaves, and went on to devour the mixed grill for two. She was drawing the usual furtive stares tinged with pity, but she could tell she was making onlookers happy. She was playing to type. The more she ordered, the more they felt superior and the less they felt they'd eaten themselves in comparison. After finishing the sides of roast potatoes and rice pilaf she was in truth much too full for pudding, but she ordered the baklava out of spite. She deliberately left a glisten of honey around her mouth, because that's what the other patrons expected: greed, carelessness, shamelessness, and a paucity of self-respect.

Evelyn enjoyed the first sound, serene sleep she'd experienced since her Portuguese holiday and woke to find that her blue kaftan was no longer too tight around the bum.

That very day after work, Evelyn took her remaining package of rice cakes out to the front of her building and stomped them into crumbs on the pavement, though it was dubious whether even the birds would be enticed. She imploded the last unopened bag of red lettuce, rocket, and watercress in her vegetable drawer with a festive *pop* before chucking the tangle in the bin, where the greenery garnished a crenulated mound of discarded spandex shapewear.

She continued to experiment. She restored the toast with her coffee and soon slathered the slices with butter. Before that

Lebanese extravaganza, the waistbands of her XL leggings had bitten deeply enough to leave a mark for hours. Yet the more butter she went through, the further the leggings began to sag, until she had continually to tug them up, lest they slump to her knees. Best, then, to add two fried eggs to that breakfast, along with a banana muffin – at which point the oil diluted, then eased at last to ordinary perspiration. Once she resumed eating lunch as religiously as she had previously skipped it, she dropped another dress size, and one by one the botanical skin tags shrivelled and fell off. After she mastered the consumption of an entire roast chicken for dinner, the splayed extra-wide slippers in which she'd taken to shuffling the flat evenings grew so loose that they were a tripping hazard. She went back to trainers, which would now tie in bows without knotted-on lace extensions. In the face of whole pans of lasagne that didn't stint on the béchamel, the breasts retreated somewhat – and that is how she had come to think of them, *the* breasts rather than her own – less the size of jackfruits than of honeydews. Cantaloupes were within sight, though it would take a mighty mound of glacé-cherry-dotted ham to return to citrus.

Evelyn was unembarrassedly public about her new regime, asking colleagues to join her for lunch, at which she was cheerfully immune to their stifled mortification as she ordered bacon double cheese burgers, extra chips, and chocolate fudge cake with Chantilly cream. Her desk was strewn with Pringles tubes and KitKat wrappers. She was getting fitter and her gait was growing brisker, which was fortunate, as she was forever hauling heavy bags from the supermarket.

'You know, lately you've seemed a little more like . . . yourself,' commented the colleague who'd been certain Evelyn was stuffing her face in secret.

'You mean I'm not as fat,' Evelyn said.

'Well, no, like, sorry, it's more, you know, your whole *vibe* . . .'

'You mean I'm not as fat.'

'Okay, okay! You're not, you know . . .'

'*Fat.*'

This perverse form of dieting, if you could call it that, took a surprising amount of work – all that shopping and hauling home of joints and frozen raspberry cheesecakes and bags of brioche. Constantly cooking meals large enough for six people was the equivalent of staging a dinner party every night, involving the same overkill of prep and clean-up. Even the eating part was burdensome once the novelty of immoderation had worn off, and some nights before bed her jaw ached. The excess in her current account was dwindling, too. Those super-market bills and restaurant lunches added up.

Nevertheless, so long as she was disciplined about gorging, the gluttony seemed to be achieving her objective. The flapping housedresses and tented frocks were off to the charity shops. Salesgirls were nice to her again, which was strangely depressing. She didn't avoid her full-length mirror any more, and gradually the face that stared back when she brushed her teeth was chis-elled down to the slyer, cannier contour of yesteryear – though a subtle softening remained behind that was new.

When at long last she could slip on the form-fitting pencil skirt, her supple black leather boots, a starchy white blouse, and her beloved rust-coloured waistcoat, whose antique brass buttons didn't pull against their threads in the slightest, Evelyn decided it was time for a celebration of sorts. It had been eons since she'd gone on holiday, and that current account would still stretch to an off-season airline offer. Berlin, perhaps. She was too superstitious to return to Lisbon.

For the outgoing flight she was stuck in Group 5 again, but it had been so long since she'd got out of London that she wasn't fussed. At the worst, a flight attendant would insist that she check her carry-on, and if some baggage handler was infatuated enough with that red fedora to steal it, the underpaid minion could have the hat. Glancing down the plane, Evelyn noticed that a very large woman in a pink and grey tracksuit was seated in her row in the middle seat, confined by armrests the way cattle were boxed in before slaughter. Evelyn had the aisle.

'Sorry,' Evelyn said, leaning down towards her seatmate, who immediately looked terrified that she'd done something wrong. 'This is my seat, but I was wondering – would you be more comfortable on the aisle? I know lots of people just hate middle seats, but they don't bother me in the least. I've a touch of fear of flying, and, if anything, having other passengers on either side makes me feel safe.'

'Well, now that you mention it,' the woman said, 'I would fancy the aisle, if it's all the same to you. This is a full flight—'

'I know!' Evelyn said. 'It's that Lufthansa winter-break offer! None of us can resist a bargain.'

'When I checked in, all the aisles were gone. And with me, well, a window seat – I'd never get to the loo, would I?'

Evelyn waited while her seatmate slowly disconnected her seatbelt extension, then laboured into the aisle. The while, Evelyn didn't merely 'wear' an expression of patience; she felt patient and so persuasively looked that way.

When the refreshment cart came round, Evelyn ordered three hot ham-and-cheese heroes. At the flight attendant's quietly raised eyebrow, she explained, 'A girl has to keep up her strength!' Although Pink and Grey Tracksuit ordered only one microwaved sub, they devoured them side by side with a detectable sense of solidarity that onlookers would have found mysterious.

Bob-a-Job

by James Smythe

Richard knew that he was being taken before it happened: because the shop started to clear, the security guards softly ushering people out. He was good at observation, that was his job: watching other people on the city's cameras and reporting them when they did something wrong. So he didn't miss that he was the only one not being quietly spoken to by the shop's members of staff. A glance outside and he saw the identical deep blue vans parked up, the windows tinted to pitch dark, the sliding doors opening, the soldiers getting out. They were coming for him, and there was nowhere to run. They sent *force* for situations like this, four men in each van – or women; they were in non-gendered armour, faces hidden – which made twelve of them, just for him. Nightsticks and rubber bullets, he knew: the internet was full of videos of desperate people running as the dark round balls whacked them on the back of the head. Those videos where you were never quite sure if they were real or some sort of advert from the requisition companies.

Then he was the last person in the shop, sweating over by a display wall. He could see the security guards holding the doors open for the requisition team, hear the scuffle of their boots on the marble flooring as they entered the shop.

'There must be some mistake,' he said, but he was already putting his hands up.

*

The lawyer for the companies he owed money to read out all the numbers one by one, the actual items where they were big ticket, or the experiences he had paid for. His mother had said to him, the last Christmas, that she didn't understand it. How he had these nice things, and his job wasn't all that, a junior surveillance officer, what could they earn? Fifty? Sixty? Not enough for that car, and these presents. He said, 'Money was different back in the old country,' and she replied, 'I've been here thirty years, you think I don't know what things cost?'

After that, the final number was read out, and then the fees and the associated legal costs that were being brought against him, which nearly doubled it to an amount that he found incomprehensible. What he paid in rent, the cards he had borrowed on to and not paid back: they priced his life up – this is what we can get back by selling everything – and it barely scratched the surface. They had a solution: he would work for the requisition companies until the debt was paid off.

He sobbed; he knew what it meant. It meant going to Barrow.

Barrow and its twin town, Gilt, were formed and named by the requisition companies a decade ago. They bought up hundreds of new-build homes after a development company collapsed, and made it their base of operations. They split the area in two, one half for the men, one for the women – they didn't want them mixing, it would be a distraction – and they adapted them. In the Asian markets, places like this already existed: in Kowloon, in Sihanoukville. They were smaller scale, maybe, run out of abandoned hotel complexes, places that could house hundreds. Each inhabitant with their own room, each of them with a telephone, so that they could make calls. The requisition companies who formed Barrow and Gilt knew that they could use the model their own way. A modern-day labour camp. The press reported on it, but then the stories were quashed, because the investors were on both sides of the story. Barrow and Gilt existed regardless; nobody lived in them apart from the thousands of people who were forced to.

The bus was an old double-decker, driving along the motorway as though on a day trip. Richard sat on the top deck, next to an old man in the window seat. He wasn't looking out, he was working a rosary through his fingers, which were thin, his knuckles barely larger than the rosary beads themselves.

As they approached Barrow it looked just like any other new town, all sandstone-brick houses and clipped green lawns and quiet streets that seemed to wind around each other. The difference was the hoarding, which had been originally erected around Barrow's outskirts to show pre-vis images of the houses, of happy families playing and laughing and cooking. That had been changed, co-opted, mounted with solar panelling, which had the advantage of stopping anybody from looking in or getting too close, but which also, unfortunately, meant the sun was directly reflected back on the grass around the fence, scarring the ground into desolate soil. When they reached the gate – the fence giving way to high towers, manned by soldiers, bollards that rose from and sunk into the ground to prevent anybody ramming their way through – everybody stood up. Their first look at where they would be spending the next however many years. And it looked nice, or fine, but then: there were no children playing, no people walking the streets, no cars, no bikes, no flowers, and the grass inside wasn't grass at all, it was astroturf. Every curtain at every window was pulled to.

The soldiers got them off the bus, made them line up. A woman sat on a chair, watching. She was older than Richard, although he was bad at telling. But she was dressed like a boss would dress. She watched as the soldiers went down the line, as they told the new arrivals to strip down to their underwear. It was warm, and they all did as they were told, except for one younger man, just out of school, who refused.

'I'm not taking anything off,' he said, 'these are mine, get me?' So the soldiers forced him to the ground. One of them pulled out a device that hummed, and ran it along the young man's back, his clothes sizzling and burning as he screamed, his shirt and trousers flopping to the side like wrapping when a bow had been pulled, leaving a burn-mark on the skin beneath the clothes; and then, as Richard watched, embarrassed for the man, the skin parted like lips moving to speak. They left him there, twitching on the ground; a distraction, and, Richard knew, a warning.

The soldiers handed each of them a parcel wrapped in what seemed to be butcher's paper.

'This is your uniform,' the woman said. 'My name is Alison, I'm the director here. Every couple of days, we'll deliver a clean uniform to you, and you'll send this back in the laundry bag provided. You won't be required to do your own washing.' She stared down the line. 'You will live here, and you will work here. You'll be paid for your work, of course, at the government-specified minimum hourly rate. We will provide food and services for you, such as the laundry, and your accommodation; the cost of these will be deducted from your pay packet. The remainder will be used to recoup funds owed from your outstanding debt. By the time you leave here, we'll have ensured that your debt is managed, and that you're in a position to finally progress financially.' She looked behind them and they followed her gaze, to see men coming towards them, all identically dressed: duck-egg blue shirt, pleated trousers, suit shoes. Sweat patches under their arms, or across their chests, the cheap material sticking to their skin. 'You've each been assigned a buddy.' Richard stared as his buddy approached him: a man who was clearly once heavyset but had lost it, taller than Richard, with less hair. His eyes this curious off-yellow colour. Not brown, somehow weaker than that. He held out his hand to shake Richard's.

'I'm Len,' he said.

Len told Richard that, prior to Barrow, he had been an estate agent. 'This is different, but then it's also sort of the same, I suppose,' he said. He led them to a house, where the hallway had been hammered apart, plywood walls constructed to split it off. 'Two others live down here, you and me, we're upstairs,' he said, and they trucked up the stairs, which had been stripped of carpet, or had never had it installed. At the top, two doors faced them. 'I'm left, you're right,' he said. There were no locks, Richard noticed as he grabbed the door handle and went inside, followed by Len.

The room was magnolia, and there was a bed, and a kitchenette, and a desk with a monitor on it, and a webcam. Another door led to a stark white bathroom. A gap on the wall where there had been a mirror once; marks where it had been wrenched away, chunks of paint missing, taking it back down to the plaster.

'What do we do here?' Richard asked.

Len patted the back of the desk chair and waited for Richard to lower himself onto it. 'The screen comes on at nine every morning, and it'll auto-connect for you. You don't need to worry about anything. You wear the little headset, you talk to the person on the other end.'

'About what?'

'Well, it's sort of like dating. Did you date? In the real world?'

'A little bit,' Richard said. He liked to meet women, and he liked to take them out. When the prosecution was reading out his charges, a lot came from those nights: expensive dinners, bottles of Patrón, spontaneous gifts. The relationships never lasted, which was a shame. But still. 'I know the way that it goes.'

'Then you're already ahead. You'll be playing a part, mind you. These are men you'll be talking to, and you'll be playing the part of a woman, for them. The computer changes what they see and hear. Fancy system.'

'That'll be strange,' Richard said.

'You'd think,' Len replied, 'but it's not, you really get used to it. Some of the men here, they get quite into it. Whatever floats your boat, eh?'

'So what do we say to them?'

'The screen'll give you prompts. Follow them, you'll be golden. You're trying to get information *out* of them. Took me a while to cotton on to that. Don't go in hard, they'll get scared, this is more softly softly. Think about what *you* would like. Somebody just being interested, taking an interest in you.'

'But what's the endgame?'

Len was about to reply when a bell rang. 'That's lunch,' he said, and he turned and moved, nearly running out of the door and down the stairs. Richard followed him, watching the doors at the foot of the stairs open. Two men came out: they glanced at him, but then immediately away. They seemed sickly, Richard thought: their skin so sweaty that it looked almost wet, deep purple sagging bags beneath their eyes. Skin both bloated and loose, with this almost translucent glaze to it, like one of those fish where you could see right through to the little spine, the little fish organs. One of them grunted – some men made that sort of noise, Richard supposed, instead of saying hello – but then they turned away as Len opened the front door.

There was a cardboard box on the doorstep with four bags inside it. Len grabbed two, and then stepped back inside, hands raised. 'Whoops,' he said, trying to move out of the way of the other two. They descended on the box, their hands pulling at the cardboard, grabbing a bag each, tearing it open before they had even lifted it.

'They're like animals,' Richard said.

'You haven't tasted it yet,' Len said, 'it's incredible.' He handed Richard one of the bags, but he eyed it for a moment, as if wondering whether he could have them both.

'What is it?' Richard smelled the contents: a waft of something meaty.

'Not got a clue,' Len said, 'they make it here. One of those new impossible meats, but oh my God, you won't believe it. It's injected with stuff, vitamins, I think. Keep us healthy.'

Richard unwrapped the small parcel inside it. Greaseproof paper giving way to a puck of something pink, the size of a large enough burger. There was a single thick vein running down the middle of it. He thought of the man's back, his clothes stripped from him. 'I don't like the look of it,' he said.

'Taste it,' Len said, 'or don't, I'll have it.' He was already eating his, his mouth full of the substance. 'It's fucking incredible. If they sold this, they'd make more money than any of us could hope to earn back for them, honestly.'

Richard lifted it to his mouth. It was dry, which surprised him, and the texture was like an oatcake or something, not unpleasant; as soon as he had swallowed his mouthful, he went in for another.

'You see?' Len said.

Richard looked at the other two. They had already finished, and were sucking on the greaseproof paper, to get whatever they could out of it.

Later, when the dinner arrived, another puck of the meat, he said to Len, 'It's not human flesh, is it?'

'What, you think they're feeding us people?' Len asked, and he laughed, as if he hadn't wondered that at one time himself. 'This isn't some telly programme, this is all above board. It's pork. It's got to be, hasn't it?' He lowered his voice, as if he might be heard. 'Sometimes, in the night, you hear the pigs. There's a farm here; it's that, I reckon. *Squealing.*'

The next morning, an alarm went out, a crowing of noise that seemed to come from every surface. Richard staggered to his bathroom. Strange, with no mirror to see himself in. He brushed his teeth, and spat blood; more than usual, but then, he ground his teeth when he was anxious, and he *was* quite anxious. He was in the shower as the food alarm sounded, so he rushed out, dried himself. Through the window he could see the houses opposite, their front doors open, the men standing there in various states of undress, just *feasting*. Biting into the pucks, not making eye contact with each other. All Richard wanted in that moment was a coffee, but heading out to the little kitchenette, he couldn't see the apparatus for it. So he opened the door, and smelled the waft of the bag. There was one solitary puck left; presumably, the other three had already taken theirs. When he was finished – he ate it in the stairwell, suddenly ravenous – he went back to his room; and then there was another buzz, which he took to be an alarm for work starting. He went inside and upstairs, and he sat at his desk, put the headset on. There was a button on the screen: *Press to begin*.

He pressed on the screen. It flickered, and suddenly there was a man's face. Behind him there were pictures on the wall, of family and friends, Richard supposed. Pictures of the man on holiday; a picture of him standing near a boat. The man was in his fifties, gaunt – but in a healthy way – and he had put some sort of product in his hair, combed it. He smiled, shiny new white teeth like Tic Tacs standing to attention.

'Hello,' he said.

'Hello,' Richard replied. He heard another voice echoing through the camera system: a woman's voice, soft and high.

'This is new to me,' the man said, 'I don't know how to start these things. It's all very, very new, isn't it.'

'Yes,' Richard said.

'There's a guide here,' the man said. 'It says to start with introductions. Okay! Yes. My name's Bob. What's your name?'

Richard's screen flashed. A message on the top of it: *Your name is Paula*.

'Paula,' he said.

'Paula, that's a beautiful name. Where are you, Paula?'

Kazakhstan, the prompt read. 'I'm in Kazakhstan,' Richard read.

'Oh! Is it nice there?'

'Yes,' Richard said, 'very.' He couldn't remember if it was or not, if he had ever actually seen pictures of it. He imagined it was maybe war-torn, once, or had he seen it in a film?

'I holiday a lot,' Bob said, 'but I've never been there. I would love to visit, one day. I'm in England, actually, maybe you knew that. Probably you could tell from my voice! Could you?'

'Yes,' Richard said, 'I can tell.' The prompt blared at him: *Talk more.* 'You sound very nice,' Richard said. That echo of the girlish voice again, coming through; and he realised it was him, his voice altered, to be this woman's voice. To be Paula. 'Where in England are you?' Richard asked. An accent running through this new voice, the English being broken up somehow, making it disjointed. Jumbling his words for him. It was nice, though, he thought; it was a nice voice.

'Dewsbury,' Bob said, 'it's a small place. Not a village, though, it's very welcoming, you know. Not like some places; we're accepting, here. If you ever wanted to visit.' He smiled, laughed at himself. 'I'm getting ahead of things, of course.'

'It's fine,' Richard said. Another, more direct, prompt: *Why don't you tell me about yourself?*

Richard repeated the words. 'Yes, yes,' Bob said, 'absolutely. Well, where to start? I work for a marketing company, I won't say the name, but you've heard of them, or maybe they're not in Kazakhstan, I forget. It's a good job, though. My gosh, you're very lovely,' he said. He smiled – beamed – and Richard stared at him. *Smile*, the screen prompted, so he did, the biggest smile he could manage.

'Thank you,' Richard said, and he heard the female voice echo through the speakers.

Over lunch, Len asked him how it had gone.

'Fine,' Richard said. 'It's strange, isn't it. Being somebody else.'

'Yeah, but it's also, you know. It's work. Is it any different to what you used to do? I used to have to smile and sell some nice young couple a total shithole for more than they could afford. In some ways, this is better.'

The puck tasted so good that lunchtime. There was an even thicker vein running right through it this time, twice the thickness of the previous puck's. Inside it was something cool and warm at the same time, like a spicy heat that tickled the back of Richard's throat and made his brain buzz.

'So is this catfishing?' he asked Len. 'I've seen that on the news.'

'I dunno. Catfishing is more like, you get specific information off them, right? And they've never pushed me for that. All it is, right, is getting to know them, learning everything about them.' He was staring at Richard's greaseproof paper. 'Are you going to?'

'No,' Richard said, although he wanted to. Len grabbed it, started licking it, sucking on it. Tucking it into his mouth, ripping it so that a little chunk went into the pockets of his cheeks, like tobacco.

'You can still taste it,' Len said, his mouth stuffed, 'get the most of it. My first few guys, they didn't stick, but this one I'm talking to now, he's all in. He loves me! He's a widower, bit sad, but, you know, I'm doing my best. Cheer him up a bit.' He yelped, then, and reached his finger into his mouth, to pull out one of the bits of paper. Felt around in there a moment, his fingers probing. And then it came out: a tooth, in the crook of his finger. 'Fucking hell,' he said, 'ow, bloody Nora.'

Richard recoiled. 'Is there a dentist here?'

'Yeah. I lost one last week, as well. A dentist, and a doctor.' He stared at the tooth a moment, and then pocketed it. 'Never mind. I've got others.'

Richard blinked. He had never seen anybody quite that nonchalant about losing a bit of themselves before. He noticed one of the bags still in the box outside the front door. The inhabitant of room one had taken his – Richard hadn't seen him, but heard his door opening and closing, and could hear the sounds of consumption happening through it – but room two's door had stayed closed.

'Is he alright in there?' Richard asked.

'Maybe he's gone,' Len said, picking up the bag, taking the spare puck as if it was his by default. 'Maybe he's fulfilled his debt. It happens.'

That night, Richard heard the pigs for the first time. The snuffling of them, and then the squealing, almost like wolves howling against the moon. He shivered in his bed, as if he had a fever; and he wondered when it would be time for breakfast.

The next few weeks went easily enough. Richard spoke to Bob every day, always first thing. They got into a routine of saying good morning to each other: sometimes it was clear that whatever Bob was seeing of Paula had her in pyjamas; sometimes in a dressing gown; once in only a towel, and Bob fake-recoiled, barely covered his eyes – 'Oh, I feel as though I'm intruding!' – and then occasionally that lasted all day, otherwise it was more checking in. As if Paula was being kept for Bob, waiting there until he called. Richard never had another call, the screen stayed dark when it wasn't on; he sat there and waited for Bob to come back online, zoned out. There were no books, no televisions. Nothing to look at, besides the room and then the street, but nothing ever happened in the street. They weren't allowed to go out for a wander unless they requested it, but he hadn't been told to request it. So he sat there and didn't think of anything, really. He tried to think of the past, but it was more vague than he would have liked. Like it was sort of gone. Sometimes, memories of things Bob had told him intruded, or things he had said to Bob as Paula. So he tried to not think that much instead. He stared: at that blank screen, and what he would say when he had the chance to speak again. Sometimes he caught a glimpse of his reflection in the screen, even though it was matte, just a flash. With no mirror and nothing else reflective in the room, he had started to forget what he even looked like. Still: in that glimpse he could see that he was thinner, perhaps. Maybe he wasn't getting quite enough vitamins in the pucks. Maybe he needed more? He could raise something, perhaps. Go and speak to Alison.

He didn't see the man who lived in room two again, and then somebody else moved in. Richard was assigned as that man's buddy – that was the system, last in does the next one – and the man, who was called Ian, was terrified, jittery. Richard tried to reassure him. He was there for Ian's first meal, and eating that softened him, a little.

'It does taste nice,' Ian said, a little more calm than he had been.

Len, however, was looking worse. He was sick, Richard thought. Len said he was fine, but he spoke less. At mealtimes, he moved quicker down the stairs and had a wild-eyed look on him as he ate. Huddled over, afraid somebody would take the food from him. His eyes were sunken; and Richard thought, as he ate, that he could almost lean over and pull on the bag beneath one of them, pull that loose skin out and out further, peer down inside it and see right to the bone of Len's skull.

Alison welcomed visitors, she said, but Richard didn't know how to request a meeting. He went to the front door to leave the house; as soon as he reached the edge of the little path, a guard appeared. 'Can I talk to Alison?' Richard asked, but the guard didn't reply, they just stared at Richard until he went back inside. So in his room he said it, a few times, to himself, or to the computer. If they were always listening, like Len said, maybe this was how you made contact.

The next morning, there was a knock on his door. He wasn't feeling himself: the night before, he had been off, like the start of a cold, and he thought he had a wobbly tooth, maybe, but it could have just been his gums being sensitive. His sinuses, the way that they got. The knock woke him up, and he staggered to the door. Alison was in the hallway, smiling at him. He thought how professional she looked. 'I heard that you wanted to see me?' she asked.

'I do,' Richard replied. 'I wanted to check we were getting our vitamins.'

'Do you feel poorly?'

'I think so,' he said, 'and also my friend, Len, across from me. He's worse than me.'

'There's something going round,' she said. 'Do you want a booster? I can get some bonus vits put into your meal, if you like.' The way she said it was so casual. The thought of food was a salve; he pictured it, as if it was all that he could see. A carrot on a stick, but more delicious, shaped like a disc, that thick thrombic tube running through it.

'That would be great,' he said.

That lunchtime, as he was eating his puck, wondering if the tang in it was the taste of the extra nutrients, he lost his first tooth. During his session with Bob in the afternoon, he lost two more. But they came out easily, and he remembered how gently Len had taken it when his came out, and that helped. Maybe this was normal, here. This was what happened. As it made him lisp in his room, he could hear the echo of Paula's voice, lovely and clear, tripping over her words just enough as she told Bob exactly what it was that he wanted to hear.

Bob told him – Paula – *everything*. He stopped short of bank details, of course – this wasn't about that – but everything else. There were no stories he hadn't recounted to Paula, no details spared. Bob wondered about a possible future together, perhaps; he asked, again, when they could meet in person. *When we know each other better*, the prompt said.

'Of course,' Bob replied, 'you can't take any risks these days.' So as they spoke, Bob laid his soul bare. Richard took it all in, because that was all there was to do, and Bob did have a tendency to repeat himself. 'Did I ever tell you about the time' – but of course, he invariably had; still, Richard said he wanted to hear the story, because that's what the prompt told him to say, and sometimes he actually *did* want to hear it. Sometimes, it filled the silence, because what else was he going to do?

One night, after he had lost his eighth tooth, Richard was woken again by the squealing. It sounded close, this time, so very close. He went to his door and reached for the handle – he noticed a fingernail peeling away from his index finger, he must have snagged it, but it didn't hurt, not even a little – and he turned it. He had to know. Maybe a pig was loose? Maybe he could herd it back? He opened the door, slowly, and he saw it: bloated, bulbous, pink, lumpen on the floor, heaving in deep breaths, wheezing with each one. The motion-activated light out in the hallway was off, so he couldn't see much, but he could tell well enough which end was which. He expected a curly tail, like a little pink spring. He reached for it, and that made the lights come on. It wasn't a pig, he realised: it was Len, curled up, almost, knees and arms tucked close to his body as if he was trying to stop somebody kicking him.

Richard bent down to see his face. But it was loose, like a skin sac with Len's features printed onto it. Len's forehead, his scalp, his thin baldness, had slipped forward, like a hat that was too heavy to wear; through the translucence of the skin, Richard could see those urine-yellow eyes, darting left to right, looking for something. There were seams all along the skin sac Len was now wearing – they reminded him of something, he couldn't quite think what – where the skin was thin, splitting, tearing, bursting. He could see brand-new flesh, new skin, beneath it. Richard could see hair, blonde hair – Len had been nearly bald. A fissure of some sort ran down what had been Len's leg, and there was something inside it, something plain and white and featureless. It was a new body, Richard thought. A new body, grown inside of Len's old one.

Len, or the thing that had been Len, squealed again. A mouth, glimpsed past the skin, nubs of teeth set into raw pink gum. The eyes of it so wild! And then it started to move. Richard stepped back, away from it, to his door. It was shifting, changing. Dragging itself down the stairs, then sort of standing, a whole body's worth of skin hanging from it like some godawful cloak, feet trailing on the floor behind it. It squealed again – it's a scream, Richard realised – and then it ran outside, across the Astroturfed lawn, to the street. Richard ran upstairs, to the window, to watch: the armoured soldiers appeared, keeping their distance, poking at it. The old skin – the whole Len of it – fell to the ground, flat, like some cartoon character run down by a steamroller, and the new person beneath it stood tall.

'We're turning into something,' Richard said, quietly.

The person standing in the street reared back, squealed again, and looked right at him. It was humanoid, it was the expected shape, but featureless, or the features were still growing. Something nascent to it.

The soldiers descended, and barrelled the thing that had grown inside Len away.

The next morning, Richard wasn't hungry, but the food alarm went, and he went downstairs to get his puck. He couldn't help it: he tore the bag apart and ate it there on the doorstep as if it was about to be snatched away from him. Ian, the new man in number two, said, 'Are you okay? You look a bit sickly.' Richard ate, and he stared at Ian's greaseproof paper, and he *lusted*.

Bob was declaring his love for Richard daily, now. His plans, for their meeting, their marriage, their honeymoon. 'My friends say that I'm a fool, but they don't know what we have,' he said, 'they don't have what we have.'

Say you will meet him soon, the prompt read. *Tell him a few days' time.*

Richard said as he was told. Bob looked so happy. Maybe we turn into the wives for them, Richard thought. Maybe that's it. We pretend to be them, and then we become them. Maybe I am becoming Paula. He wanted his lunch. He spoke to Bob, and he heard Paula's voice coming back, so unlike his, so high and squealy; when he laughed, it sounded almost like the whine of a stuck pig.

One day, Bob said he needed to arrange something, so he wouldn't be around. Richard could feel that he was losing himself: his skin was soft and wet to the touch, and his fingernails had nearly all peeled away. His feet had altered, he thought, to a point of strange softness; as if all his toes had become one, his nails like some – ha! – some awful trotter.

Richard sloughed his way across his room to the hall. Nobody was in Len's place yet; he wanted to see what Len's end had been like. It was the same room, mirrored: the same walls, curtains, desk, bedsheets, monitor. He made his way to the desk and sat down – feeling his back shifting, as if that movement might make it burst; he had very few memories now, but he remembered walking on a beach as a child, poking a fish sac with a short stick and watching the eggs tumble out of it – and the screen had a new prompt on it. He sat down and pressed the button, because why not.

A man appeared. He looked like he had been crying. This thin, wan little man, white-blond hair, five foot nothing, and his eyes lit up as he saw Richard, and he said, 'Betsy! Betsy! You're back!' Richard liked that this man was happy. 'I didn't know where you'd gone. I missed you! I love you so!' He rifled in his pocket and brought out a little box. 'I got this!' A nice ring sparkled against the velvet of the box's interior. 'Would you . . .' He stopped himself. 'Betsy, I can see you, why aren't you moving? Why aren't you replying to me? Betsy?' Richard didn't move. He didn't want to. He wanted to stay very still; he could feel something shifting inside him. Like he might be sick if he so much as twinged. He sat very still for a while, until the thin man got tired, and he said, 'Betsy, what's going on? Should I call somebody? The police? Betsy, what's wrong?'

Suddenly there was a banging coming through the speakers. Coming from the man's house. 'Wait,' the thin man said, 'don't go anywhere, Betsy!' and he stood up and went to his door, and opened it.

The armoured soldiers piled in. They grabbed the little man, held him, trussed him. He screamed, but he was silenced as they carried him out of his house.

There was nothing in the room for a moment, just silence. 'Hello?' Richard slurred; a female voice came through on the other side, another echo. His voice changed by the computer program.

Then the door opened again, and the soldiers came back. They were escorting somebody, a naked man, they shoved him forward—

Richard watched as this other man sat in the chair. It seemed to be the same little man who had been there before, but this one was naked, and his eyes were different. As the man reached over and turned off the webcam, Richard could see Len's dull yellow-brown eyes, staring out of the facsimile of a head.

Richard's final transformation took him by surprise. He was thinking how much he would like his breakfast now, even though his teeth were gone, and he couldn't really use his hands any more – they were loose, like gloves come most of the way off – and then he thought, *or maybe I actually want to be sick?* And he rolled to the edge of the bed, to try and crawl to the bathroom. His flesh squelched as he landed on the carpet, and then he tried to move, and he realised, it's here, it's happening. He felt it: like something pushing out from inside him, some force. He thought of urges, of bodily functions, of being drunk and trying to hold them back, of nights out in expensive restaurants and eating too much and drinking too much and not knowing how the night would end, except with expulsion, with sick and piss and shit, and that was the feeling he had right then, that it all needed to come out. That was the last true thought he had as his body split itself apart, and his skin shed itself, and he was born again, new, as the glistening purity of another Bob.

He watched as the first Bob, the original Bob, was dragged away, but it didn't really register. Some intruder in my house, he thought. He was escorted in and sat in Bob's chair and he thought, *This is perfectly nice.* He knew how to answer the phone when Bob did, what tone to take on a call, he knew what Bob did – what *he* did, he reminded himself, silly old Bob, you would forget your own head if it wasn't strapped on – and he knew that, every month, a big old chunk of Bob's salary, *his* salary, went to pay off his debts. He couldn't quite remember what those debts were, but they were pretty insurmountable;

when he checked his bank statement – his face, his voice, they were his password to get into his bank accounts – a big chunk of that money was gone every month. Still: it was better that than one of the alternatives. And at least he had a lot left over – he earned *really* well; he was proud of himself and his nice marketing job.

A month into being Bob, he looked at his bank statement and thought to himself, *well, I deserve a new car*. He didn't have quite enough, so he applied for a loan. 'Why *shouldn't* I have nice things?' he said, out loud, filling out the forms and ticking the little box that said he understood what could happen if he failed to repay them; and he coughed as he signed his name, *Bob*, a high-pitched little squeal coming out of him, and he wondered what on earth caused him to make a sound like that.

Fairies

by Lavie Tidhar

A gnome stood on the lawn in front of Mrs Hutchinson's house. It stared at Maya as she passed it on the way to school. The gnome wore a blue hat. It had small black eyes.

Maya wrapped her coat tighter around her.

'Stop it,' she said.

'What?' said her dad.

'There's a gnome on Mrs Hutchinson's lawn,' Maya said.

'So?' said her dad.

'It wasn't there yesterday.'

'It's just a garden gnome, Maya,' her dad said.

Maya could feel the gnome's stare against her back. She shivered. The day was grey, the pavement slippery with frost. Something with gossamer wings buzzed in the canopy of the apple tree. A row of electric cars squatted along the road, black cables like umbilical cords connecting them to the power outlets in the base of the street lamps. They looked like dead beetles and Maya had the urge to prod them to see if they would simply crumble at her touch.

'Don't touch the cars,' her dad said irritably. '*How* many times do I have to tell you?'

Maya pulled her hand away guiltily, then jumped as a large body slammed against the low fence of Mr Morris's house. The dog growled, and Maya shied away from the fence in fear.

'I hate that dog!' she said.

'Hate is a strong word,' her dad said. 'We don't hate.'

Maya didn't say anything, but she stared at the dog, which was big and rust-coloured and had drool dripping from its teeth. It wanted to hurt her.

'I hate you,' she whispered. She walked faster, reaching the main road and the crossing. Other children were walking to school with their parents and the pavement was busy with people. She looked around for anyone she knew but it was just the usual faces, already worn with the misery of the coming school day. She walked slowly to the gates, stepping on something small and dead with gossamer wings on her way.

*

'Maya? Are you listening?'

'What?' Maya said, awakening guiltily from her daydream and hiding the book she was reading on her knees under the desk. It was a book about fairies. It said fairies stole children and made milk go bad. In the book, they weren't nice at all.

'We're discussing isosceles triangles,' Miss Jessup said. Miss Jessup was young and pretty but had dead fish eyes.

'Yes?' Maya said.

'Could you tell the class what an isosceles triangle is?' Miss Jessup asked her.

'Um, no?' Maya said.

Everyone laughed. Maya felt her cheeks grow hot.

'Maya smells!' Alfie said. He sat two chairs down on her left.

'Be quiet, Alfie,' Miss Jessup said.

'Yes, Miss,' Alfie said. Miss Jessup sighed.

'Do try to pay attention, Maya,' she said. 'Now, let's get back to—'

As her voice faded to a murmur, Maya went back to her book. It said that to appease the fairies in the olden days people used to leave them little offerings, of food or trinkets. Maya didn't really like books, but you weren't allowed phones in class.

At playtime she walked around the field on her own while the boys played football. Maya tried to stay away from the boys, but then some of them ran close and Alfie had the ball. He kicked it viciously; it hit Maya in the face and she fell. Her cheek hurt where the ball hit her. Alfie laughed as he ran to get the ball.

'Sorry, Maya!' he said. 'Didn't see you there!'

Maya tried not to cry.

No one came to help her. She was all alone.

It wasn't fair, she thought. It just wasn't fair.

She stood up. She'd hurt her knee falling down, and a tiny bit of blood stayed on her finger when she touched the scratch. Trying to keep away from the boys, she picked up some tiny stones and found a little buttercup growing in the grass. Some girls were playing in the mud kitchen, but they ignored her. Maya went to the corner near the fence. She knelt in the mud, and gathered some together in her hands until she'd made a little mound. Then she put the dozen small pebbles around it, and the flower, and wiped her bloodied finger into the mud.

'I hate them,' she whispered. Something buzzed in the grass. Then it was time to go back to class.

*

'I had a bad dream again yesterday,' Maya said. It was bedtime. 'Can I sleep in the big bed with you?'

'It's okay to be worried,' her mum said, and she gave her a hug. 'But you need to sleep in your own room, darling.'

'But I'm scared,' Maya said. There had been rustles against the window in the night, as though small, vicious winged things were trying to get in. 'I'm scared of the fairies.'

'Fairies aren't real,' Maya's mum said. She stroked Maya's hair. 'And if they were, they wouldn't live in the suburbs. Now go to sleep.'

She took Maya back to her room and helped her into the bed. The room was dark.

'Will you please stay with me?' Maya said. 'Just until I fall asleep.'

Her mum sighed.

'We can't do this every night,' she said. 'I never get any time to myself.'

'I'm just scared,' Maya said. As long as her mum was there the fairies wouldn't dare come in. She didn't want them to steal her away.

'Why don't you talk to them?' her mum said. 'Make peace with them.'

Maya knew her mum wasn't talking about the fairies. She was talking about the kids at school, all the ones who didn't like her. She tried to tell her parents how unhappy she was, but it just made them angry. They were fighting a lot lately. Maya could often hear them beyond the door, talking angrily to each other in low voices. They thought she couldn't hear them, but she could.

'Maybe I'll try . . .' Maya said. She yawned. There was nothing outside the window. She closed her eyes. It felt good to have Mum sitting there beside her.

She fell asleep listening to the quiet.

*

Two gnomes stood on the lawn in front of Mrs Hutchinson's house. They stared at Maya as she passed them on the way to school. The gnomes had small black eyes. One wore a red hat and the other wore blue.

'You *see*?' Maya said. She spoke quietly, barely moving her lips. She didn't want the gnomes to hear.

'See what?' her dad said.

'There's two of them.'

'Two of what – oh, those?' Dad laughed, in that irritatingly superior way adults had. 'So Mrs Hutchinson went to the garden centre again.'

'If you say so,' Maya said.

'Look,' her dad said. 'I'll speak to the teacher again. What's her name, Miss Jessup? About that boy. And the problems with the other kids. And, well, maybe they could find you something else to do at playtime. Something indoors.'

'There's nothing else,' Maya said listlessly. 'We have to be out in the field. It's important for children to play.' It was what the company that set up the play areas kept telling everyone.

'Well, I'm sure . . .' Her dad gave up. He held her hand as they walked past Mr Morris's house. Maya jumped as the dog barked, right on the other side of the fence where it must have been hiding, just waiting for her.

'I hate you,' she whispered.

The dog growled.

*

Fairies stole children. They liked food. They made bargains and could make wishes come true. They were doing trigonometry in class again. Maya hated trigonometry.

'A ladder is placed against a wall,' Miss Jessup said. 'To be safe, it must be inclined at between seventy and eighty degrees to the ground.' She drew a ladder on the whiteboard and tapped the pen next to it.

'Is this ladder safe?' she said.

But Maya knew that nowhere was safe. She thought back to when she was small, what she could remember of it. It was fuzzy, because it was a lifetime ago. Back when she was really small, where everything was tiny, and cosy, and happy. It was a picture-book world, the sort her mum used to read to her about in bed. A world before school, before the darkness.

At playtime she went back to the mud kitchen. The small mound she had made by the fence was still there, but the stones had been moved sometime in the night and spelled a new shape in the dirt. They'd learned about runes in class. Maybe it was a rune. Or maybe one of the kids moved the stones.

The flower was there too. It hadn't wilted. Somehow it had put new roots into the dirt. It swayed slightly in the breeze, a tiny thing, beat up and bloodied but still holding on. Maya stroked it with the tip of her finger, then she carefully took out the things she'd brought: a dry tea-biscuit, two grapes and a small toffee in a plastic wrapper. She placed them reverently on the mound.

'I hope you like them,' she whispered.

She felt a little better when she went back to class. The day continued with its dreary miserableness. They did English and Geography. Alfie passed around a note with something rude about Maya in it, and everyone laughed.

Maya almost cried on the way home. She just couldn't help it. She couldn't remember a day without the misery, the heavy oppression of being in class.

'Will you just stop it?' her dad said. 'You have to stand up for yourself. You can't be a victim all the time.'

Maya didn't say anything. They got home. She watched television. Cartoon creatures did terrible things to each other on the screen. Maya laughed. Then she went up to her room.

*

There were more garden gnomes on Mrs Hutchinson's lawn the next morning. Five of them congregated under a rose bush as if busy in conversation. They only half-glanced Maya's way.

'Mrs Hutchinson really is going a bit over the top with the decorations,' Maya's dad said.

'I like them,' Maya said. Something with gossamer wings buzzed in the rose bush, where all the roses were wilted. She tensed as they passed Mr Morris's house.

But no growling, hateful sound came, no heavy body trying to reach her to do her damage. Something whimpered beyond the fence, a sound full of pain and confusion, and Mr Morris came out of the door just then.

'Hush, Rex, hush,' he said. 'You poor thing.' He picked up the dog, saw Maya and her dad.

'I must have left the garden gate open last night,' Mr Morris said. 'For the life of me I don't know how, but Rex got out and ran across the road and, well. It's all those cars.'

Maya stared. The dog looked back at her with black button eyes full of hatred and pain. One of his back legs dangled uselessly in the air, matted with blood.

'Poor doggie,' Maya's dad said.

'Poor doggie,' Maya whispered.

The dog looked at her. It tried to growl, but could only whimper instead.

*

'Maya did it,' Alfie said. He looked on the verge of tears. 'Maya threw away my pencils.' Everyone knew Alfie loved his pencils.

'I didn't!' Maya said.

'Why did you throw away Alfie's pencils?' Lily said. She was one of the girls who always had the latest mobile phones and whose mum drove a Land Rover. 'That's not nice.'

'I didn't! I didn't do it!' Maya said. She wanted to lash out, to hit Alfie. To hurt them all. Why was he lying about her? Why did they all take his side?

'I am going to have to talk to your parents, Maya,' Miss Jessup said. 'This is very disappointing.'

'But I didn't do it! Alfie's making it up!'

'We'll have to get to the bottom of this,' Miss Jessup said, in the way teachers did. Teachers didn't want to solve anything. They just wanted to get through the day so they could go home and drink wine. Alfie stuck out his middle finger at Maya when Miss Jessup had her back turned, and everyone laughed. Maya's face turned red with humiliation.

It wasn't *fair*, she thought. It wasn't fair!

At playtime she tried to avoid everyone else. They didn't want to play with her anyway. She went to the mud kitchen. Someone had been there before her. They'd kicked over the fairy fort viciously and stomped it. The flower she had planted lay dying in the mud. Maya felt hot tears of rage and wiped them angrily away. She knelt in the mud, unheedful of the mess she was making of her uniform. She gathered the mud back into a little shrine, then picked up the flower, stroked it, and reburied it in the mud on the top of the mound.

She left half a banana, with the peel, and a bar of Twix, and a fifty pence coin that had Paddington Bear on the reverse. It was from her piggy bank. Maya closed her eyes and spoke to the fairies wordlessly.

When she at last opened her eyes she realised with some surprise that she had bitten her lower lip, so hard that it was bleeding. A drop of blood fell on the fairy mound and was quickly sucked away by the mud. Something small and nasty buzzed by the dripping taps on her left.

She got up, covered in mud, and went back to class.

*

'Look at her!' Dad said. He stood with an angry helpless face in front of Miss Jessup at pickup. 'Bleeding lip, muddy clothes – this really can't go on.'

Miss Jessup pursed her lips.

'I'm afraid Maya is proving quite a disruptive influence in class,' she said.

'She's just a little girl,' Maya's dad said.

'She reads under the desk,' Miss Jessup said. 'She doesn't pay attention. She argues. She never plays with the other children.'

'That's because no one will play with me,' Maya said quietly. But no one was listening to her.

Dad didn't say anything on the way home. He had that tense set to his shoulders that meant he was angry.

'Go to your room,' he said when they got home. He had his angry face on. Maya stood on the bottom stair. She didn't want to go up to her room. She just wanted a hug. She wanted Dad to tell her everything would be all right.

'I don't *like* my room,' she said.

'Go upstairs, now!' Dad shouted. Maya burst out crying, but went up to her room. Something buzzed against the window, hitting the glass over and over as though trying to get in.

*

Maya drew a picture. She drew the playground, and the fairy mound, and she drew a heart on the mound like an offering, and she coloured it red, frowning in concentration as she inked inside the outline. The heart came out misshapen, the red bleeding onto the page. A dog lay whimpering in the corner of the page. It was quite a good drawing of a dog.

'Good doggie,' Maya said. She drew a crowd of faceless children and a pretty teacher as tall as the trees.

'It's time for bed,' her mother said, appearing in the doorway. 'Did you brush your teeth?'

'Yes,' Maya said.

'Are you lying to me?' her mother said. 'Go and brush your teeth.'

Maya hated brushing her teeth. She stared at the blood-red ink on the page.

'What is wrong with that dog?' said Maya's mum.

'He got hit by a car,' Maya said.

She went to brush her teeth and then her mother tucked her into bed.

'Bad day at school again?' she said.

'They're all bad days,' Maya said.

'You do like feeling sorry for yourself, don't you,' her mother said. She sighed. 'It's the weekend tomorrow,' she said. 'We'll go shopping. You need new shoes.'

'I hate the shoe shop . . .' Maya said. She felt sleepy. Her mother turned out the light and kissed her goodnight. Maya drifted off to sleep. She dreamed of small yellow flowers blooming in a big parched patch of dirt.

*

There was a gnome next to the water feature in Mrs Adams's house that morning, in a yellow coat just like the colour of the flowers in Maya's dream. Another gnome stood watching her with button eyes from on top of the wall of Mr Fredrikson's house.

'They're multiplying,' Maya's dad said. He sounded amused. He gave Maya a quick kiss and said, 'Well, I'd better be going,' and went off down the road. He looked happy to get away.

Maya and her mother waited at the bus stop. The strange man who always hung around there, for as long as Maya could remember, was there, smoking a roll-up cigarette and looking sorry for himself. Maya looked up at the electronic board, which said six minutes until the next bus. When she lowered her eyes she saw the strange man looking directly at her.

'You see them too, don't you?' he said.

'Don't talk to my daughter!' Maya's mum said. The man looked at the ground and mumbled around his roll-up, and then he shuffled away.

'He doesn't have anywhere to live,' her mum said. 'It's sad, really.'

When the bus came, they climbed upstairs. Maya stared out of the window. Outside the parade of shops that bordered the estate she saw Alfie and his dad. His dad looked just like Alfie, only bigger. He was shouting at Alfie, who cowered away from him.

Even from the top of the bus Maya could see Alfie was crying. She never saw him cry like that before.

She thought it would make her feel good, but it didn't.

The bus drove on. They got off over the bridge and went around the shops. As Maya was trying on school shoes, she looked out of the shop window and saw Miss Jessup in a pretty dress walking hand in hand with a man. Miss Jessup was laughing at something he said. She looked happy.

'I wish something bad happened to you,' Maya said quietly, and the shoe saleswoman looked up at her sharply, then went back to her foot. Something small with gossamer wings buzzed low against the pavement stones outside, and Miss Jessup cried out as she stumbled. The man steadied her as she rubbed her ankle.

'Something bit me,' Miss Jessup said – Maya could read her lips from where she sat. Miss Jessup had lost her smile and there was an ugly red welt on her skin.

Maya smiled.

*

She carried the new shoes in a bag from the shop. She didn't like the shoes.

They went to the market square. It was cold.

'I want to go home,' Maya said.

'Did you even say thank you for the shoes?' her mother said. 'They're expensive, you know.'

'Thank you for the shoes,' Maya said.

'Don't use that tone,' her mother said.

'What tone?' Maya said.

'That one,' her mother said.

'I'm cold,' Maya said. 'I want to go home.'

'You can't sit in front of the television all day,' her mother said.

Maya didn't bother answering. She trudged in silence behind her mother as they walked around the stalls. One stall sold all kinds of twinkly lights and fairy-themed decorations. The little crystal fairies looked so sweet and innocent. They were lovely.

'Can I have one?' Maya said.

'Aren't you a little old for fairies?' her mother said.

They looked around some more and didn't buy anything, and then they went home.

*

On Sunday they went to the park with the duck pond. There was a small wood where teenagers went to smoke, and some open grass where people walked their dogs. The duck pond was an unimpressive circular deepening in the park, filled with murky water and weeds. A crow wrestled with an empty packet of crisps in the shallows. In the middle of the pond, a tiny artificial island stood like the pupil in an eye. There was a nesting house for the birds on the island, but it was empty now. A gnome stood on the bank of the island. In the wan sunlight its lips looked stained red. It watched Maya and she shuddered. She knew what it wanted.

Mum and Dad were arguing again. They left her on her own as they went behind the blackberry bushes but she could still hear them, their voices low and angry. Maya stared at the pond and picked up a pebble to toss into the black water.

'Hey, Maya,' Alfie said. Maya jumped. He came and stood beside her. All the hate and anger and misery that Maya felt welled up inside her into a fury she didn't know how to control, and she shoved Alfie away from her.

Alfie looked surprised.

'Careful,' he said. 'I can't swim.'

'Why can't you swim?' Maya said.

'My dad doesn't have money for swimming lessons,' Alfie said.

'Oh.'

'He says I don't need to, anyway,' Alfie said.

There was a brief silence.

'Why are you always so mean to me?' Maya said.

'I don't know,' Alfie said.

'Well, I hate you!' Maya said. She ran away from Alfie, from her parents, from everyone. She hid in the small wood. Something small with gossamer wings buzzed in the undergrowth. Maya savagely stepped on it, and it stopped.

She heard screams. She heard her parents call her name. She didn't want to go to them. She didn't want to leave the wood. There were fairies in the wood, and wonderful things. She could live there, she thought. She heard sirens in the distance, growing closer.

'Maya!'

Her dad looked terrified. He held her tight. 'I was so worried,' he said.

'What happened?' Maya said.

'It's that boy from your class,' her dad said. He took her by the hand. 'I'm going to take you home. Right now.'

'I want to see,' Maya said. Something terrible had happened, she could tell. But her dad pulled her after him. She could see her mum and a lot of other people gathered on the edge of the pond, some of them in uniform, with boxes of equipment. They all stood around something on the bank, but she couldn't see what it was. As her dad kept pulling her along, calling her mum on his mobile with his other hand, Maya craned to see. The crowd parted, for just a moment, and she saw a small human figure lying in the mud. It wasn't moving.

'What happened to Alfie?' she said.

'He must have slipped and fallen in,' her dad said. 'It's best you don't look. The council should have put a fence around it.'

Maya looked back one last time. Her mum was hurrying towards them, and the gnome that had stood on the small island was gone. The fairies buzzed between the blackberry bushes. Maya ignored them. Alfie lay on the ground, not moving. Maya went home with her parents.

*

'I didn't mean it,' she said. She crumpled the drawing and tossed it in the basket. Something with gossamer wings buzzed against the window but Maya wasn't going to let it in, she was never going to let them in.

'You know it wasn't your fault,' her mum said, tucking her in that night. 'It's a terrible tragedy. You must be so upset.'

'I'm just tired,' Maya said. The weekend had felt like an eternity. She couldn't believe she had to go back to school again tomorrow. She tried to imagine how it would be. Everyone will be so sad, she thought. And Alfie won't be there anymore.

'It's all right to cry,' her mum said, stroking her hair.

'I wasn't,' Maya said.

'Shh,' her mum said. She tucked the duvet around her and kissed her on the forehead. 'Sweet dreams,' she said. 'I love you.'

'I love you, too,' Maya said.

The door closed. Maya was alone in the room. The room was dark. The blinds were shut and behind them she could hear the faint buzzing and the broken-crystal laugh of the fairies, but she was safe. She closed her eyes.

That night she slept deeply.

Ghost Kitchen

by Francine Toon

The workmen have left for the weekend and you are ravenous. It is only 5.30 p.m., yet the windows are black rectangles. Winter surprises you every year. It was a stupid idea to live in your house during the renovation, but where else were you to go? In the half-formed kitchen, you trace your finger along one of the countertops and take out your phone. Your mother has asked you to stay with her, back on the island, while the workmen are here, but no. You've only just left her.

Moving from Haar to the mainland was a means of escape. Escape from your family home, overgrown and crumbling by Lake Slauk. The Grendiths have been there for generations: everyone on the island knows you, but you don't fit in, with your weird food and mint-green hair. Here in the city the anonymity pleases you, most of the time. The family money doesn't stretch far, though. You will have to get a job soon. You bought a house by the canal, in the rundown part of town. In the next street sits a former toothbrush factory that is now an arts space. You like old buildings and your new home dates back to the 1870s. It was the big bay window that caught your eye.

The excitement from winning the auction quickly dissipated when you noticed the inky blooms of mould on the landing and the cracks in the flashing on the roof. In the living room, plaster lay in clumps around the bay window, like someone had taken an axe to the wall. When you feel overwhelmed, you look at the fireplace tiles in the master bedroom. The dark green flowers unfurl themselves towards you. It makes you feel okay.

The biggest surprise of the mainland was that you feel like an islander. The workmen squint when you speak. Apparently your accent is strong. Sometimes they smirk 'Come again?', but most of the time they just turn their backs and get on with building things the way they want them. You're an islander but you are also a woman. You're a woman who has a coughing fit as she walks about this shell of a house. The plaster from the living room has gone, but a fine layer of sawdust covers all surfaces. It blows into your hair, like sand. When the workmen first arrived, you stuck up thin plastic sheeting, a protective membrane. A few hours later you heard it being ripped away.

At least if you order food now, in the early evening, you will miss the Friday night rush. Haar does not have delivery apps (or Friday night rushes) and so, at first, ordering was overwhelming. Now it is second nature. You know the opening hours, the discount codes, which dishes look like their photos and which do not. Bratwurst is closed on Mondays but Gustosa has free tiramisu. The ramen at Shiso is homemade, Yo Mama's is watery. You avoid any fish or seafood, as you want to be a new person. On Haar you ate enough to last you a lifetime.

This afternoon, you have ordered from a so-called ghost kitchen. A ghost kitchen, you have learnt, carries the name of a well-known restaurant, but only cooks for delivery apps. There are quite a few of them out here, by the canal. When you first scrolled through the logos, you wondered how you could have missed these famous burger joints and noodle places when exploring your new neighbourhood. Then you realised they looked like the other warehouses, invisible to passers-by. You haven't ordered from this place before. It's called Heirloom and does pasta.

You cough again. The dust and dirt coat everything, you can feel your skin drying out. The workmen have left their equipment strewn downstairs. Drills, saws and a sledgehammer all lie waiting to slice your manicured hands, or smash down on your sheepskin slippers if you stumble in an ill-lit corner. You hate the rubble, the pipes, the planks everywhere. As you wait for the delivery, you try sweeping the Victorian tiles that line the hallway. Originals. Dust swirls into your eyes and the white cornicing grins down like a row of teeth.

At least they finished the bathroom today. You have been using the showers at the local gym and even the pool. You grew up swimming in Haar's great lakes and rivers, with their electrifying chill. You know you will get used to this warm, chlorinated substitute, eventually. At least it makes you feel clean.

You have a sofa in the living room, but no power, so each evening you light candles. You should really read a book. You check your app again, and see the driver as a tiny yellow scooter, on his way to the ghost kitchen. It is true that you could go out for dinner, of course you could, but you don't like walking around at night. The estate agent called this place 'up-and-coming', but it has some way to go. You wonder if the men that work here live nearby. You don't like the way they look at you, when you pick your way through the jetsam of each room. They don't like it when you ask questions. They frown at your artwork, at your hair. They talk like they are correcting a silly mistake you made: this damp, rotten house with its sloping floors and crooked walls.

There is a knock at the door. You leap up and your phone slips to the ground. Your stomach aches with hunger, so you leave it there.

A tall man in a black balaclava is standing at the door. His eyes meet yours. He's the delivery man. You can hear his bike running, somewhere behind the skip in your driveway. He holds up a phone and for a moment you think he is going to take your photo, the way men with packages do. His other hand is holding a paper bag.

'Thanks,' you say. Your lips cover your teeth when you talk, a self-conscious habit.

'Code,' he says.

It takes you a moment to understand. 'Ah, one second,' you

reply, aware of your accent. You turn your back as he stands there. If you close the door, you worry he'll drive away with your food. When you scoot to the living room, your phone slides in your hands like a wet fish.

'Seventy-one!' you say, breathlessly, back at the door. Sweat is dampening your hairline. 'Seven One.'

He punches in the number, thrusts out the bag and leaves, his black clothes melding with the night, his motorbike fading away.

There is a joy in eating privately, when the house is quiet. You open the brown box of Linguine Vegan. There are no men to witness what you have ordered or how you are consuming it. You spill tomato sauce on your T-shirt and don't clean it off.

You are about to pick up your phone again, when you notice something strange in the sauce. Small, grey blobs of flesh. You pick one out and find the menu listing. This must be the Linguine Clams. You feel angry. They could have killed someone with an allergy. Your face could have swollen up. You could be lying alone on the dirty floor, fighting for breath. You search 'anaphylactic shock' and think about phoning to complain. You're still hungry though. You grew up eating clams. With some reluctance, you finish the pasta and its unwanted reminder of home. Anyway, they gave you a more expensive order.

You go back to your phone. It is the only thing that works in this house. That and the bathroom. You look forward to singing in the privacy of your own shower. Lately, you have become fascinated by an app called Neighbourhood. It's like a social network for your area, accessed by post code. You read sad updates about missing cats. There is a long, oddly compelling thread about the bin collection. Someone is looking for work.

Your eye is caught by black and white footage from a doorbell video. A man, rummaging through recycling boxes. Time stamp: 3.45 a.m. He takes something away, or puts something down. His face is unclear. You look out the curtain-less window. The dull yellow skip sits there like a boat made to sink. It's already full: 70s kitchen cupboards, smashed plasterboard, the old toilet. Would this man want those things? On your walks around the neighbourhood you see other skips, as new people move in and gut the houses like fish.

You scroll some more. Someone has posted that they heard gun shots in the park last night. *Come off it*, another neighbour says. *Those were the fireworks for Diwali.* You look at the thumbnails of their photos. Who are these people, that surround you now? You don't have a profile picture and you don't post anything.

In bed, while the electric heater purrs, you think of Brennen Daeg, your island's winter festival. You'll miss it this year. Haar's elder residents walk through the street with burning torches. Young people throw gold coins into the river. Every year, a song, an old song, is sung about your family. The festival ends when a flaming rowing boat is pushed out on Lake Slauk.

That night, for the first time since moving to the city, you dream about drowning. Your long green hair floats in black water. You smell blood.

You wake up early and your body aches. It is Saturday. No workmen. You realise you have slept in your underwear, and put on a grey waffle dressing gown. Bleary-eyed, you walk to the bathroom in a daze. The hot water feels so good you don't want it to stop. You haven't had a bad dream like that since you left the island. Maybe it was the clams. Night terrors are common among the Grendith women. Back home, the dreams were made of island things: blind owls, cats' teeth, entrails on the pebbled beach. Your mother has them, and your grandmother. Some say they are unlucky, even harbingers of death. You hoped that the city would change you. Yet bad dreams can travel with you, as they say on Haar. They can sneak into your new home with the crockery and candle sticks. You have brought some nice things from the island: traditional blankets, stoneware, horn spoons. You still use the comb your grandmother gave you, its fine teeth made of bone.

You scurry out of the house and to the laundrette. The nearest one closed down and is being converted into a yoga studio (Neighbourhood tells you) so you have to take a bus. You sit on the top deck, a checkered bag of dirty clothes on your knee. There is a young man a few rows ahead of you, talking on his phone. His accent sounds the same as yours. Maybe you knew him as a child. When you reach your stop, he gets up and glances at you, then looks away. You follow him down the stairs, your shoes pummelling. You swear he is humming the old song about your family. '*Hoy!*' you call, the way people do on Haar. A dog barks. The man is already gone, lost in the mass of shoppers on the high street. The city makes people grow cold and ugly, you were always told this. Fake snow has started to appear in the windows.

While your clothes spin at the laundrette, you walk across the road to the pawn shop. The woman examines your antique coins and jewellery on the glass counter and gives you a low price. But this is solid gold, you tell her. She doesn't care. You know you can find a better dealer, just like you did for the bigger things. Your family won't miss them. It's your inheritance.

At lunch time, you pause mid bite and realise you're eating sushi. It's technically seafood, of course, but not your kind of seafood. On Haar, you cure fish by burying it in a shallow hole on the beach. What does it matter, nobody cares here. You click open your mood board of home interiors. You want a seagrass stair runner, stormy slate tiles and forest green walls. You are trying to source a particular type of clothes airer, like the one your mother uses.

On the bus back, the light is already waning and it is not yet three o'clock. You dread your filthy, broken house. It won't be long until it is beautiful. You tell yourself this every day. Both of you deserve to change. In the bus seats behind you, a group of friends are talking. 'Terrible. Absolutely terrible. They're searching the area.' You listen harder. Police are looking for a local man. The bus stops with a jolt and you leave the group behind.

On the walk home you buy more drinking water and snacks from the corner shop. You don't want another delivery or any more strangers. You'll eat crisps and couscous instead, with hummus, taramasalata. Gummy sweets.

When dusk falls, there is a knock at the door. You automatically expect food, then remember what you have just eaten. The packets litter the sofa. You shouldn't have eaten the taramasalata.

Standing at the door is a huge man, smiling at you. His head is shaven and his skin reminds you of cooked ham. 'Hello,' he says, uncrossing one arm to show you a battered card, some form of ID. 'Sorry to trouble you, but we're doing the rounds this evening. Just up visiting the city for the day, if you have a few minutes.' His accent *is* from the city. His tone of voice suggests this is some kind of standard procedure. One you must comply with. Something about his body, its size and proximity, scares you.

You give a close-lipped smile, expecting him to say more. He smiles tightly back at you. He is willing you to let him into the house, you can feel it. For once, you wish the workmen were here.

'Sorry,' you say. 'What is it you're . . . ?' Is he even selling anything?

'Oh, cleaning, dishcloths, stuff like that.' He steps closer towards you in the doorway. You step back, your slipper thwacking the tile. His eyes dart to the candle-lit space behind you.

'No,' you say, abruptly. 'I'm okay, thanks. No.' You close the door hard and your chest feels tight. You stand there, listening. After a pause, you hear his footsteps walk back down the drive. In the living room you blow out the candles and watch him through the window. You don't light the candles again. The orange glow from the street light lets you see the edges of things.

When you finally go to bed, you open the Neighbourhood app again and scroll its dog walking adverts and council rants, searching a door-to-door scam. This man must have visited others. You need to order a video doorbell. So many people have them, it must be needed here. In Haar, your family doesn't lock the door and no one bothers them. You can't find anything about a scam. Everyone is commenting on a recent post that links to a news story. You open it up. The missing man has been found dead. His body was in the canal. He has been named as Pete Shaw, a builder. Your neighbours are grieving. There is speculation about suicide.

That night you dream about the salesman's face. It twists. The water screams. Blood fills your mouth.

When you wake, you are standing in the pitch dark and hot water is cascading down your shoulders. You are naked and you can still smell blood. Your cheek stings. You feel around and realise you are in your own bathroom. It's still dark outside, but you find the light and a towel. You stand on the new, pink tiles and look at yourself in the brass-edged mirror. There are scratches on your face. There are some bruises on your left arm. A large one on your right leg. For comfort, you drag your grandmother's comb through your straggly green hair.

The house seems messier than before and your head feels woolly. When you eventually find your phone, it tells you it is 5 p.m. on Sunday. This has to be wrong. You dig out your watch and, to your shock, it is 5 p.m. You've lost a day. Maybe you are coming down with something. You don't feel as though you have slept for that long.

Downstairs, you notice the checkered bag on your kitchen floor, among the shiny, dead appliances. It still contains your laundered clothes. You haul the bag upstairs and absent-mindedly put them in your chest of drawers, wondering what's happened. When you pull your pyjamas out of the bag, they are blotched with dark stains. You shove them in the kitchen bin. Something went wrong at the laundrette. Maybe you should complain.

The evening closes in. The workmen will be here early tomorrow, a matter of hours. You are definitely feeling unwell. You need to avoid seafood at all costs. You open up the Neighbourhood app. A second local man has been found dead. Another suspected drowning. It takes you two attempts to read the story. The words distort, the phone slips in your hand. His remains were found in a shallow hole, by the canal. He is believed to have been a travelling salesman. More details to follow. Police say this is a complex and fast-moving investigation. Someone has posted a video, blurred out due to graphic content. They shouldn't allow this kind of thing.

You throw the phone on the floor and the screen cracks. You are an islander. You shouldn't have come here. You are a Grendith. Out of the bay window, past the skip, you see a parked police car.

When you finally pick up your phone, you feel compelled to click on the video. At first, there is nothing but an empty road. It is monochrome and wobbly like the others. The time stamp says 2.17 a.m. There is a shadow. It is a small woman, moving like a ghost across the screen. The footage renders her almost completely white, with large black eyes, slicked hair and a dark mass in her arms. As she passes, she turns her head towards the camera, with a blank expression. She dips her head. You pause the video. Your chest is tight again and you feel like you are going to throw up. The gelatinous curl of intestines is unmistakable. You recognise them on screen, the same way you recognise the white blur of your own sharp teeth, as they take a bite.

There is a knock at the door.

You sit there, frozen. The old song sung at Brennen Daeg thumps in your head, like blood.

Grendith, grendith take my coins
Grendith, grendith take my boat
Grendith, grendith take my fire
But don't take my body to the water

The Old Lion

by Evie Wyld

The train carriage had emptied out by the time it got to Home Station. When Sarah was at school the line had linked up with Ferbridge and the carriage would be full of kids eating crisps and counting out their change for the waiting-room fag machine. Once someone had a pack of fruit-flavoured condoms and they'd passed them around so everyone could have a taste. Now it was just Sarah and the guard, who stared at her as though she might suddenly discover where she was and demand to be taken elsewhere.

At Home Station the café had permanently closed and the telephone had been ripped off its moorings. The only information, an out-of-date timetable that had been papered over with MISSING posters. She stopped and looked at the girl, all yellow hair and straight teeth. They'd used a photo from a night out, she was looking at the camera with a smile, lip gloss. All the young people had those perfect teeth now. For Kerry's poster, they'd used one Sarah had taken in the Lion – you could see her snaggle tooth and too much gum. Kerry would have hated it, and it was who she was now, her lasting impression. Who had taken this one of – she squinted at the name – Anita Keys? Was there a friend of Anita's with her school skirt rolled up, locking herself in the toilets and trying to relearn how to breathe, remembering the exact moment of the photograph, the smell and the sound of it? Sarah stepped backwards into a puddle which soaked immediately through her shoe and into her sock. She swore, and at the sound of her own voice became aware of the silence. The train had turned off its engine. If she got back on it, she could be back in London by midnight. She moved along the platform towards the exit. The water got into everything – she could smell it in the wooden benches, and beyond the shutters of the old café; where it used to smell like sausage baps it now smelled like wet newsprint and burnt tyres.

She didn't know any of those kids now – though she could still taste the lime-flavoured condom if she thought about it. The train revived itself and backed slowly out of the station like someone trying not to anger a bull.

Sarah stood twenty-five minutes in the cold, shifting from foot to foot. Her nose grew pink and she hoped his car would appear, but it did not, and there was no getting signal on her phone. She should have phoned to remind him – things must be worse than she'd thought.

As a teenager she'd walk from Home Station to her house, before it started and they'd all had to be back before dark. And a few times in the middle of it all if she was honest – the pull of the Old Lion, and how they'd serve her and her friends so long as they didn't have the boys with them. The thrill of walking home in the dark, of being adrift in the black field, her parents asleep, her friends failing to keep their voices low. It was like they expanded to fill the space, the only people in the world, untouchable.

The hedgerow along the Way was just as it had been on her last visit. A year's growth, less than a quarter of an inch to its fingery thorns. The metal gate was still off its hinges and the gap patched over with the same barbed wire and blue nylon rope. The rain was still in the air but never falling. She did not have too much farther to go, her hands curled red around her phone, and it started to buzz as she walked through pockets of reception. When she saw who was messaging her she dropped it into her bag and pretended she hadn't seen. 'Can you please just sign the papers, Sarah.' If she tried to get signal now to call her father, he would be embarrassed to have forgotten her and there would be that to deal with on top of everything else. Her concern always threatened to make him cross.

She arrived at her parents' house – no, she corrected herself, her father's house. Dad's. It had never been a house that she could bring friends back to, not even for the sweet teas she got invited to when she was very small. Somehow she knew not to do that, and even pretended her birthday was deep in August when school was out so no one would expect an entertainer and French fancy on a paper plate at hers.

There was a time before secondary school, she came onto the landing in her pyjamas to see why the record player had been turned up so loud. From the top of the stairs she saw her mother and father locked together, swaying like lovers in a film. Her father spun her mother around in a tight circle. She looked into his face so they were nose to nose, then laid her head against his chest. Sarah had the feeling she would like to run and throw herself in between them, so they remembered her in that moment. And then quickly behind that thought was a voice that said *they don't want you there*. It wasn't an unkind voice. More like a voice that might hush you at the cinema when the film was starting, so no one would give you a cold look.

The car was still in the driveway and her father had left the door unlocked, even after everything.

'Dad?' Sarah called, but was met with silence. The house, exactly as it was before, the thermostat so high it brought on a flush. It used to make her feel sick when she was a child, sleeping in that tropical heat. The plastic sheet over the carpet in the hallway, wiped down at the end of every day by her mother on her hands and knees, even though all shoes were to be left at the door, neatly inserted into a cubbyhole, enough for each of them but not for visitors. Her mother's shoes, clean beige ortho-paedics, still sat in their section. They looked like nothing at all was the matter. She had been wearing those the last time Sarah saw her, just beyond two years now. Her mother had come down to London for her birthday, a rare treat. Sarah had taken her to the Wolseley for afternoon tea and her mother had worried and worried that she wasn't framed well enough for the type of person they wanted blessing their tea room.

Honestly Sarah Jane, I would've been happy with a Pret A Manger. With every new plate of finger sandwiches or fairy cakes and tiny éclairs that came out, her mother sighed and said *Oh no,* and ran the gauntlet of not seeming like a glutton while not wanting to be seen as wasteful. She packed the majority of it away in her handbag, outraged when Sarah suggested they could ask for a box to take it away in.

Sarah Jane, what would they think, we don't have food in our own home?

Next time, Sarah had thought, I will buy you a Mr Kipling and be done with it.

But there was no next time. And now these shoes rested for ever in their cubbyhole.

'Dad?' she called again, but still no answer. She had expected to see his bald head protruding from the top of his chair, which faced the garden as he liked to watch the finches. He hung a fresh coconut half out for them every other day in winter. The back door to the garden was open and the plastic sheet was curled and muddied. An unusual current of cold air whipped through the house and the boiler raged from the kitchen. In her mother's time there had always been a smell of bleach riding the back of a soda bread in the oven. The record player's lid was up and Sarah closed it gently.

'Dad?'

Close up she could see the coconut was bare, stripped of meat. It turned slowly, finchless.

Sarah surveyed the garden, which was just as empty of her father as it was of birds. When she'd seen him at the wake, he had sat motionless while people moved around him, gathering him unwanted sandwiches and half pints of stout, making sure he was looked after, just for that hour. The wake was held in the Lion. No one was invited back to the house, to honour the fact that her mother hated to have visitors call by. No funeral; he'd gone to the crematorium alone. He had taken off home when she wasn't looking, and she'd heard that voice again, *he doesn't want you there*. She went round the pub with a black bin bag instead, as her mother would have done, and swept up the sandwiches and prawn rings left behind. Her husband had paid the tab and driven them home.

Neither of them was the sort to crowd the other. She'd said he should come down for a visit on the train, but he'd said his back wouldn't stand it. He didn't say she should come and stay, and she used that as an excuse not to go. She'd rung him on Christmas and her mother's birthday. There was no one for him to hand the phone to after they'd done the first bit, and the conversation dried up quickly.

'Dad?'

This time she startled something in the bushes at the fence that backed on to the woods, and the something – a fox? – made a drama of scrabbling under the fence and through the bracken behind it. Sarah closed the garden doors. The carpet either side of the plastic sheeting was wet through. She went to the kitchen. Her father liked to keep the appliances clear of the counters, and she took the electric kettle out of the cupboard. She didn't much want a tea but she also did not know what else she should do. She left the kettle boiling, and checked the downstairs bathroom, calmly expecting to see her father face down in a pool of his own blood. But he was not there. He would hate most of all to have worried her.

The summer people started to leave plates of raw meat on their doorsteps, Sarah had found her set of girls. She and Kerry just had to look at each other in class and they would be sent into the hallway to get themselves together, heaving with laughter. Their form tutor called them in and asked them to stop behaving like telepathic morons, which they loved. They could see that he loved it too, and he one time bought them half pints in the Lion, on the condition that they sit outside. Kerry passed him at the bar later on, outrageously carrying five full pints with a lit cigarette pinched in the corner of her mouth. 'Get the door for us sir?' she'd asked and he had, and you could tell he was deeply impressed.

At first it was just pets going missing. Then they started showing back up, or parts of them did. Some people poisoned the meat they left out and the local population of hedgehogs and foxes took a nosedive, but the killings didn't stop.

'Dad?' she said senselessly to the empty bathroom. The bath gleamed. Her mother would wash it down with white vinegar, and when it was dry buff it with a chamois. She never bathed in it, preferring to use the shower upstairs. She called it the Visitors' Bathroom, as though someone might call round and need immediate washing. She remembered the sound of her father's razor rasping against his face as he stood at the mirror. How he would catch her eye as she watched, and wink at her. The kettle clicked off and the house was left in silence; even the boiler was quiet. Sarah looked up the stairs, listened for laboured breathing. The air was still. She climbed halfway up, was startled by a sound from the living room – her phone vibrating against the keys in her bag.

She came back down. She would have to check upstairs. She did not want to check upstairs. There was, every now and again, a smell which couldn't be explained away by the apples rotting in the fruit bowl because they were plastic. To delay the matter further, Sarah found her phone in her handbag and checked the messages.

'It's been a week. Please, for old times' sake, just make this part simple at least?'

The tone was almost kind if she looked at it with one eye closed. Like the voice that steered her away from her parents when they didn't want her. There were more messages from him which she didn't read; from a glance she could see they had lots of exclamation and question marks, and her eye couldn't help but snag on the phrase *vindictive bitch*. She tried not to let it settle on her.

The first to go was Marcus Pullman's dog Shep. She disappeared, and days later an almost clean spinal column and Shep's collar were in the hedgerow. Sarah's father never left out any meat.

Let 'im come, let 'im dare to walk up to my front door. He'd shouted at her mother when he found the back door locked. *I'll not be prisoner in my own home.* It was the only time Sarah heard him raise his voice at her mother.

It was hard to know who to call. Standing at the kettle again, Sarah began to think that maybe she was all there was. It would be nice to run something by someone. Kerry would have told her to walk back to the station and let someone else discover what in fuck was the matter. It would be nice to eat something. She was hungover, she realised, and that was making everything seem worse. She opened the fridge. Inside, nothing. Not even milk. It reminded her she should put the kettle away. There were tea bags in the right place in the cupboard at least, and she drank it black and weak anyway. Her husband, in the good days, would say she liked her tea like she liked her men.

Her phone vibrated and a news banner popped up:

STILL MISSING – Anita Keys.

Sarah sat on the sofa.

Blonde from a bottle, her mother would have pointed out.

ANITA KEYS, 17, WAS LAST SEEN ON FRIDAY EVENING LEAVING THE OLD LION PUB IN FERBRIDGE.

Just the same as the last time she saw Kerry.

Sarah didn't recognise the name Keys, they must be new to Home Station.

The third since April to disappear from the surrounding area.

Another message from her husband: 'Are you really this small?' it asked.

He doesn't want you, said the old voice, *he won't be driving you home from this one.* The first time he'd reached out and touched her face she had known that in that moment he found her beautiful and clever and funny. But maybe, she thought, he had done the reaching out with one eye closed.

Either I have to address these messages, thought Sarah, or I have to check upstairs.

She stood. *If he's up there dead at least I'll be able to send that back and he will feel bad for calling me small, vindictive and a bitch,* she thought, *just like a small vindictive bitch would.* Before leaving the kitchen she put the kettle away, still warm. There'd been a home help who'd come round for a few weeks, just to do a bit of cleaning, make the odd meal. But that hadn't worked out. *She keeps leaving the kettle out,* was all he'd say on the phone.

The first had been Katrina. Katrina wore a jean jacket over her uniform in a way that had someone else done it they would have been told off, but she did have to wear a plaster over the ring in her eyebrow. Katrina's mum worked in the Tesco's at Ferbridge and Sarah and Kerry had seen her not long afterwards in her blue bib, sat on the wall in the car park, smoking. She looked just the same. *Rough as arseholes,* Kerry had said.

Upstairs all doors were kept closed apart from her parents' room. *My father's room,* Sarah said to herself, though it was unchanged since her mother died. It was decorated like a quilted housecoat, tiny dog roses on the walls, an almost matching bedspread and scalloped valance. The curtains were neatly tied back, the bed made, the pillows plump. In the centre of the bed was a four-foot black stain. Sarah stood and waited for her eyes and her brain to communicate and then to present something helpful to her. It wasn't a stain really, not what you would commonly call a stain – a stain was what would be there afterwards. This blackness you could scrape up with a butter knife. *Is this blood?* she thought. Had her father simply melted into the bed? She sniffed: the smell of mulch; the water got in everywhere. Rotten apples and something deeper, the parts of soil made from animal bones. Sarah took a tissue from the quilted cosy and wiped at the very edge of the blackness. She looked at the residue. At best it was very dark brown. Carefully she sniffed it. It smelled like rotted potatoes, made her throat leap, and she dropped the tissue in the waste paper bin.

'Dad?' she called yet again, for something to say.

Once in the middle of the night Sarah had come down for a glass of water. On the floor of the kitchen her mother knelt, cradling her father's head. It was her father's bare feet that had scared her, the soles dark with mud. She had backed up the stairs and if her mother had noticed her there in the dark, she never said anything.

In her bedroom, nothing much was different other than the giant PC her mother had found in the charity shop. Sarah had explained she could get a laptop which did all the same things but didn't take up so much space. *But Sarah Jane, how would I listen to my CDs?* she'd said, patting the tower. And Sarah hadn't wanted to make a show of her mum, so she dropped it. Now the grey eye of the monitor followed her around the room. In her drawers her parents had kept all of her clothes, neatly folded. Her books on the shelves, a cuddly toy panda, threadbare on the foot she used to suckle as a child. The bed still held the memory of her young body. She lay down and felt the head-board and the foot of the bed contain her, just. There was a poster of Tank Girl on the ceiling. She remembered her horror of her jeans arriving ironed in the washing basket. The only clue her mother had not been in the room recently was a small settling of dust at the corners of the window. It had been so long since she'd had a proper sleep. Outside the sky had begun to descend, night so much faster and more complete out here. And still she hadn't found her father or figured out what she ought to do, and her phone buzzed, but this time it was telling her that she was nearly out of battery. She hadn't remembered a charger. Perhaps in one of her mother's saved bags of wires and cords she might find one, but she doubted it – unless she had come across one in the charity shop. A swift movement in the grey eye of the computer. Sarah waited but there was nothing more. She kept very still. From time to time at night she had heard banging in the Visitors' Bathroom, had that same feeling of stillness, had looked at Tank Girl's teeth and the grain of her shaved head in the dark. There had been four more after Katrina, all in the hedgerow like Shep. *Flensed*, was the word her mother used.

Sarah came to and it was dark. Somebody hammered at the back door. She hadn't, she remembered, locked the front door after she came in. In her little bed she felt the soles of her feet strain against the footboard. She knew she'd left it too long to spring up and do something.

When it had all stopped was when they caught Karl Pullman, his pockets full of Stanley knife blades and duct tape and a claw hammer that he wore through a hoop on his belt. But no one thought that he was anything other than a boy who hated his father and his father's dog. It made Karl happier to look his father in the eye and say he'd done all of that just to show him.

*

In the dark Sarah could see the glowing stars on her ceiling. She counted them until the hammering stopped. She should check. She would check because she was not a child leaving saucers of meat on her windowsill anymore. She stood, tried not to fear the creak of her bed, and turned on the light in the hallway. The house reminded her of how an animal will freeze if you point a light at it. One time when she was very small her father had taken her into the field, got her to hold the lamp. She'd been excited to be invited along. Watched him walk up to rabbits and pluck them by the ears, their eyes large and round and red. He'd whispered to them gently.

'Dad?' she called, softly.

The only sound was the boiler. It was a young house and not given to creaking, but even so. Her breath was loud; she tried to soften it. All is well under a roof with four solid walls and the doors locked tight and the windows sealed. The front door stood open. Outside, black. She closed and locked it.

'Dad?'

There was no answer.

Sarah took out the kettle again. This time she would leave it out. It wasn't as though her father was likely to show up and try and make tea – he had no milk anyway. She tried to make carefree noise in the house. Her ears popped. They didn't catch Karl before Kerry. Taken from under their noses as the five of them walked back over the field on a Friday night. They hadn't even known she was gone until they came out on to the road at the street lamp, waited in the orange glow with the mayflies dancing in and out of the light.

Kerry's teeth identified her, the gap in the front, the fillings in the back because she was one of those that had been given Ribena in a bottle – it was a scandal at the time. At a time when a scandal could be juice in a baby's bottle.

*

There was a sound like sand being poured through fingers. In the reflection of the oven, there was movement behind her. Sarah moved only her eyes, kept her hands on the electric kettle. She watched as a shadow, low to the ground, moved slowly across the floor. Just at the edge of her hearing, the sound of muttering. She turned to see dirty yellow hair as it was dragged slowly around the corner into the hallway.

Blonde from a bottle.

Sarah put the kettle back in the cupboard.

Mouse

by Louisa Young

She didn't think mice came up this high. High-rise flats have problems of their own: the black mould, the fine views of all the shit going on in the neighbourhood, windows you could hardly open more than an inch because they expected us all to be so miserable we'd just jump out given the chance. Which we might. But mice? How would they climb the stairs? What, would they take the lift?

She thinks about the lift for a bit. Back when she'd wanted to be a writer, back when she wrote things in notebooks, she'd had a five-point checklist for how to be observant. It was in the Top Tips of a successful writer who clearly wasn't that successful because if they were how come they were doing this kind of thing?

Always think about what you can See Hear Taste Smell Feel.

See: Dirt

Hear: Yells

Taste: No thank you. Even breathing this shit air is bad enough

Smell: Piss

Feel: Sticky

A mouse would just stay down in the basement, with the wheelie bins. Why wouldn't they?

The other five-point list for writers: never forget to make clear who, what, where, why and when.

Who: Me

What: Mouse
Where: Here
Why: I don't know yet
When: Now

So: there's a mouse in the flat. That tiny shadow in the corner where the floor meets the wall, darting along like a medieval assassin under the gloomy arches of Borgia Rome. Furtive. From the Latin *furtum*, which means both stealthy and stolen; the thief and his spoils.

If he hadn't seen it too, she'd have thought she was imagining things: shadows in the corners of her eyes, lack of sleep probably. She could very easily have denied it to herself, or ignored it, or not minded – she was practised at all that. But he saw it, from his position of power in the squalid brown easy chair from which he couldn't rise without her help. So it was deemed real, and therefore she had to deal with it.

If it had been just her, she'd have started by just telling them to leave. It can work. But he thinks she's insane when she does things like that.

She's been to the doctor. Not about the mouse. Not even about him. About her*self*!

'Are you not coping?' the doctor had asked, kindly. Then: 'Oh! I see. Worse than that. You *are* coping.' Pills had been provided. She didn't look at what they were. She didn't take them. She has responsibilities, see. Can't go round sleeping, for God's sake.

She helps him. Brings him things; takes things away. Moves things around. Gets him up in the morning. Helps him to bed at night. Shuffles him to the chair from the couch so she can fold it out into his bed. Makes it up. It's been a long time since they slept together. Helps him wash, wipes his arse. Takes his clothes off him. Puts them on him. Washes them, hangs them, folds them, puts them away. Gets them out. Brings his breakfast. Brings his lunch. Brings his tea. Brings him a little snack. Brings his meds.

She goes to the shop and gets some humane traps: little boxes to catch the mouse, then you take it somewhere, somewhere else, and let the mouse go. Shame she couldn't let other things go, she thinks. Bills, responsibilities, habits. Him! Or, herself!

She has visions of letting herself go: stuffing her face till she's full up, Dairy Milk with the hazelnuts in it, big bar, the whole thing, one sitting.

Or, not getting up. Just staying in bed. All day.

Or – *where* would she go, if she let herself go somewhere? Rome! And when she got there she'd *completely* let herself go: thick white plates piled high with puttanesca and escalopes of veal, five Negronis and the nearest clean man.

Or, to a green meadow. A nice little B&B with a cooked breakfast. A walk, not too long, an old stone bridge over a tumbling river, a coffee shop with big umbrellas, carrot cake with the cream-cheese icing. A bus stop. Ding ding, let me off, let me go.

*

How long do mice live if you don't kill them? She looks it up:

> **A house mouse that you will typically see around your home:** the average amount of time they live is six months, but if they have food, water, and no predators, they can survive up to two years. Homeowners likely won't want to just sit around for them to die to solve their pest problem. Click here to find out more about the lifecycle of the mouse and its life expectancy, so you can understand better the infestation in your own home.

No, she won't do that.

She remembers in New York, decades ago, the ads they had on the subway there for the Roach Motel: *Roaches check in, but they never check out!* She'd been too young even to know what checking in was. Or out. There was a little cartoon of a sleazy-looking

cockroach in dark glasses, leering, and an innocent little pink
lady roach on his arm. Clearly, he'd brought her across the state
line and married her at thirteen for nefarious purposes. That
roach was Jerry Lee Lewis and deserved what it got, the *deus ex
machina* of the janitor, the terminator, the pheromone trap . . .
She remembers the guy knocking on the door of her fifth-floor
walkup on East Eleventh, knock knock knocking and when she
leaned against the frame and said, 'Who is it?', nervous as you
like, he'd called out 'TERMINATOR!' like a street cry.

Like the mouse gave a damn about any humane trap. They
weren't born yesterday. Though actually they might have been
born yesterday. Baby mice look like baked beans, somebody said.
Maybe there's whole happy families of mice tucked away. Maybe
this is their flat, not hers. *I'd be the last to know*, she thinks.

He says, if there's one mouse that means there's at least
three. Or five. Or seven. He's read it somewhere, and it has to
be acted on. It's her fault, of course. Because he can do nothing
apart from ask her to do things, everything is her fault. He tried
to go to the kitchen to get a drink, while she was out getting
poison, and he fell and couldn't get up. Her fault. She shouldn't
have gone out without leaving him something to drink. She
had, she'd left water. They both knew he'd wanted beer. So
there he was, spread out on the floor of the kitchenette like
he'd been squashed. He clung to her when she tried to lift him.
'Remember how we used to dance?' he said, wrapping his arms
heavily around her, smiling. He moved his lardy hips: suggestive.
He smelt milky and malty. She was going to have to bathe him.
There was vomit in her mouth; she swallowed and aimed her
gaze at the window.

There's no way past this or out of this, she thinks, she knows,
other than to wait until he dies. She'll be old, but she'll be free.
And fifty, she thinks. Sixty, maybe. Seventy. Eighty. She looks
after him well, physically. The food is good and she helps him
with his physio even when he doesn't want to do it. She always
loved him. It's not that.

*

Before they started sharing a bed, she used to sleep on the right. When they got together, he slept on the right and she didn't sleep, on the left. She counted her breaths: for self-soothing, for relaxation, for getting to sleep, for trying. Long and slow and deep: In for four, Hold for four, Out for eight. Full breath; total emptying. Repeat. In the time that it took her to do that one full breath, he breathed a rapid, shallow sixteen – inout inout inout inout. Dehydrated little breaths; thickening saliva. Think of the stagnant air that must squat at the bottom of his lungs, undisturbed for years, dank and disgusting. Bad breath! She pictures creatures nesting down there: fetid webs, piles of droppings, frass silting up.

She's read somewhere that we're all born with a certain number of breaths to breathe, so the slower and deeper we breathe them, the longer we live. And vice versa. She once attempted to apply maths to this, and worked out only that he should have died years ago.

She watches him on the sofa. His mouth hangs open. She holds her breath; counting up the extra days she's earning for later on. Across the room the French windows are open: all the world spread out below. He prefers them shut. Snug, he says. Stuffy, she says.

Mice must breathe fast. She looks it up: sixty breaths a minute. She tries it. Remembers it'll kill her. Slows down.

Life Cycle of a Mouse

Baby mice: Mouse pups are small, roughly the size of a small coin. They weigh about the same as a kleenex. They can't see, are hairless, and are sometimes referred to as 'pinkies' due to the pink color of their skin. Unless you find a mouse nest, likely you'll never see a mouse baby.

Juvenile mice: By age two weeks their eyes and ears open, and they have grown hair.

When do they leave the nest? By age three weeks, mice are weaned from their mother. They are able to come and go from the nest, finding food. The mouse diet varies based on their surroundings. They can eat practically anything, from dry foods, fresh or rotting produce, other insects, cushions, and more.

The nest, she thinks. There are so many smells in the flat, living ones that you can't just clean away. The smegma smell of him, the places she can't clean because either he's sitting there or his stuff is, the piles of medical equipment, the jars of Nurishment and Jevaty; the smells of bleach and lotions and the sweet claggy air fresheners he likes. Fresheners! 'Get the vanilla and cranberry one,' he says. 'Get the Christmas one.'

She can think of a lot of places where a mouse might nest. Perhaps one of the nice cushions on the couch has been nibbled into, underneath. Little pellets. Mice piss wherever they go. Dribbling all the time. Shitting in the muesli. Ruining things.

Adult mice: A mouse reaches maturity by age six weeks. Male mice attract a mate by ultrasonic songs (people cannot hear them) and with scents only other mice can detect called pheronomes. When a mouse becomes pregnant, it will only take 18–21 days for the litter to be born. On average five–six babies. When you do the math, assuming half of each litter is female and will start reproducing six weeks later, these pests can multiply at an astonishing rate! As you can see, it does not take long for one of these critters to become many. They can survive for months without water, from food and/or licking pipes.

Preventing unwanted infestations: Beyond property damage, there's also health issues to keep in mind if you have a mouse problem in your home. Don't risk of exposing your family! They may look cute, but rodents spread 35 infectious diseases to humans through contact direct or indirect.

Here are some of the diseases mice carry: Lyme Disease, Colorado Tick Fever, Babesiosis, Salmonella, Rat-Bite Fever, Lymphocytic Choriomeningitis, Hantavirus.

He is gurgling a little. He gets sleep apnoea. She thinks it's because he's got so big. He calls it 'malaise'.

Lyme Disease is transmitted through the bite of infected black-legged ticks, carried by rodents.
Symptoms: fever, rash, facial paralysis, arthritis.

Colorado Tick Fever is spread through bites of infected ticks, carried by mice.
Symptoms: fever, chills, headache, body aches, tired, sore throat, vomiting, abdominal pain, skin rash. There's no medications to treat Colorado Tick Fever.

Some nights she dreams he's really, really small; she could just put him in a little cage with some hay and a blue plastic thing for water.

Babesiosis is caused by microscopic parasites that infect red blood cells, spread by ticks carried by rodents.
Symptoms: fever, chills, sweats, headache, body aches, loss of appetite, nausea, fatigue; or, no symptoms. For the elderly or people with weakened immune systems, severe and life-threatening. Please consult a medical professional.

Salmonella makes people sick. Spread by eating or drinking foods that have been contaminated by rodent feces.
Symptoms include diarrhea, fever, abdominal cramps.

It's warm outside, almost like summer. She stands on the balcony and breathes in as best she can, the closest she can get to freshness. He notices. He wants the fresh air, too. She helps him from the chair to the couch, moves the chair so it's next to the French windows, moves him back from the couch to the chair. Heaven forbid she have anything he can't have. There's nothing he won't make her get for him. Because doesn't she have enough already, that he can never have? Doesn't she have the freedom of her own body and her life, to go up and down, and in and out? Doesn't he tell her, every day?

Once he's by the window he's cold; he wants a sweatshirt.

Rat Bite Fever occurs in humans who have been bitten by an infected rat, mouse, cat, squirrel or weasel.

Symptoms: fever, chills, headaches, skin rash, vomiting, other complications.

Oh lord I am sooooo cross and angry, she thinks. She has a little tune to go with the phrase. Kind of gospel. She sings it in her head. Often. She read somewhere this could be a thing called stimming where a person self-soothes by repetitive movements or actions which relieve stress for them.

Maybe the mouse came up the outside somehow. Up the side of the building from the street, the crowds of people down there, the rubbish. She returns often to the balcony, admires the view of the motorway heading into the west.

The mouse turns up his little nose at the poison. *Seriously? You think I'd fall for that? Try harder, dummy!*

Lymphocytic Choriomeningitis, primary host: the common house mouse.

Symptoms: fever, malaise, lack of appetite, muscle aches, headache, nausea, and vomiting. Less frequently: sore throat, cough, joint pain, chest pain, testicular pain, salivary gland pain. Second phase: meningitis (fever, head-ache, stiff neck); encephalitis (drowsiness, confusion, sensory disturbances, and/or motor abnormalities, paralysis), or both. Acute hydrocephalus (increased fluid on the brain), which often requires surgical shunting; myelitis (inflammation of the spinal cord), muscle weakness, paralysis, changes in body sensation. Myocarditis. Temporary or permanent neurological damage. Nerve deafness, arthritis. Pregnancy-related infection: congenital hydrocephalus, chorioretinitis, and mental retardation.

She creaks to her knees to search in places she doesn't often look. Behind the old cat food (it died) on the bottom shelf of the cupboard under the failing boiler, there are a great many little black pellets and a nasty sweet smell. She vacuums, wipes, sprays everything with disinfectant, gently stuffs wire wool into the corners. Latex gloves and a mask, as experts recommend.

'It's nice how you do whatever I want,' he says, looking at the telly. He's dropped the remote. She picks it up for him.

Hantaviruses infect the lining of blood vessels in the lungs, causing them to leak. Fluid then fills the lungs. Hantavirus Pulmonary Syndrome is a severe, sometimes fatal airborne disease spread by rodent saliva, urine or feces. Inhalation is the most common way to become infected; other contamination routes include bites, touching, touching your mouth or eating food. Also known as Sin Nombre Virus, Convict Creek Virus, Muerto Canyon Virus, Four Corners Virus and, colloquially, Navajo Flu. European/Asiatic Hantaviruses cause hemorrhagic fever with renal syndrome (HFRS). The virus infects the heart, reducing its ability to pump blood rapidly and leading to total or partial organ failure and death.

Symptoms: abrupt onset of fever, chills, weakness, nausea, vomiting and abdominal pain followed by difficulty breathing, illness, death.

Who Is at Risk?

I am at risk, she thinks. All the symptoms are how she feels anyway. She laughs.

'What are you laughing at?' he calls from the couch.

'Nothing,' she says. He doesn't like it when she says that.

They used to have that conversation often. 'Must be something. Why do you say "nothing"? If it was nothing you wouldn't be laughing.'

Then they would have the same fight.

*

Now he wants the chair *on* the balcony. She helps him from the chair to the couch, moves the chair onto the balcony, and moves him back across from the couch to the chair. She can see pellets in the crease at the back of the couch. The mouse is sleeping with him now. There are seams of black greasy dirt in the creases of his neck. *I could peel them off,* she thinks. *Squeeze those fat blackheads.* Lately he hasn't wanted her to wash him. He can be quite bad-tempered about it.

The draining water from the washing machine floods back up through the sink. She bails out the disgusting water and clears up the flood and pokes down the drain and takes the heavy wet things to the launderette and lets him moan about her being gone too long. Brings his breakfast. Brings his lunch. Brings his tea. Brings him a nice snack. Brings his meds.

She gets a proper trap. A trap is the only thing that works. One horrid little snap in the night and they're done for. Only then you still have to deal with the actual mouse; you have to lift the stiff little guillotine off its neck; be careful it doesn't snap back down on your soft pink finger – and then the mouse is too soft and warm, limp and somehow damp. Or too cold and stiff, nasty, glaring at you with its miniature death snarl . . . One time there was one just caught by a leg. And another time, one caught by its nose, a single tiny bead of dark blood.

Well! She'd told them. If she'd told them once she'd told them a thousand times. She wasn't their mum. Years ago, she

273

used to put the whole thing in the compost bin: trap, mouse, tra-la, gone! Try finding a compost bin round here, though. Maybe she'd just throw it from the balcony. Same impulse, after all: *get away from me*. She laughs again. It might hit someone. They'd complain to the council. Nobody would know which flat it came from. There'd be no fingerprints. She snaps her latex gloves.

'What are you laughing about?' he calls.

She puts the trap down, minding her fingers, with a little bit of his peanut butter on the spike. It's the best bait: squidgy so the mouse can't knock it off; firm enough to keep its hold. Before she goes to bed she takes a slurp of his Oromorph and drinks half the bottle of whisky he'd sneaked onto the online food order. He's not so fucking incapable when he doesn't want to be.

*

The health visitor comes round, to take blood from him for a test. She's masked up. She adds a drop of something to her little vial; shakes it.

'Oh,' she says.

That afternoon, there's a phone call.

Is he there?

Yes.

Can he come to the phone?

No.

Why not?

He's asleep.

Is he conscious?

I don't know, he's asleep.

Is he breathing?

Very fast, she says.

Does he have a rash?

Oh, yes.

Does it look infected?

Yes, it does.

Is it spreading?

Sure is.

Does it smell?

Yes, disgusting.

She half expects them to ask what it tastes like.

Do you have any idea of the cause?

Not a bloody clue, mate.

Don't leave the flat, they say. Don't let him leave the flat. *As if.*

By the way, she says, he's been throwing up.

Ah, okay, they say. Anything else?

Fever, chills, weakness, nausea, she says. Lack of appetite, muscle aches, headache, joint pain. Fatigue, sore throat, cramps, testicular pain. Diarrhoea.

Silence.

Malaise, she adds.

She hears the sound of a very quiet gulp. Then:

Don't go near him, they say. We'll send a team. It may take a couple of hours.

He has a tiny drop of blood on the end of his nose, she says.

Don't go near him.

She goes over and stares at him very closely. 'You can't kill me,' she says. He snores and gurgles very far back in his throat.

Snap goes the trap, in the dark of night. In her dream she hears a cry.

She drags herself in to him, wearily.

He's not on the couch. *Has he got himself to the bathroom?* she thinks. Sometimes he manages it. *His digestion, interminable –*

But he isn't there. Back in the room, the French windows are open; the easy chair still empty on the balcony.

She calls his name.

No answer. The silence of absence.

Oh, look, he's on the balcony, leaning, in the shadow of the corner. Snivelling and leaking, pissing and dribbling wherever he goes. She can smell him from here. Literally, there's a puddle at his feet.

He turns. 'Why do you hate me?' he says. 'I never hurt you. It's like there's something wrong with you—'

With her!

Excuse me.

I am a fucking saint.

I am Florence fucking Nightingale.

So she goes for him. She stops her breath against the smell, puts the back of her head to the disgusting belly, grabs the legs. One intense flick and heave of fury and it's done. Over the edge.

Oh dear! Poor man! How he must've been suffering to do such a thing.

She hears the shriek. The great yet muffled splat. Something wet about it. She sits on the chair and gazes out.

After a while, she hears a siren below.

She stands, turns back inside, and nearly trips –

For a moment, she sees his body right there in the trap, soft, splayed and broken. It's tiny, as if she were looking from a great distance, as if he had fallen from a great height.

But it's only the mouse.

ABOUT THE AUTHORS

SUSAN BARKER is a British novelist of English and Chinese-Malaysian descent. She is the author of four novels, including *The Incarnations*, a *New York Times* Notable Book and Kirkus Prize finalist. Her fourth novel, the literary horror *Old Soul*, is due to be published by Penguin in the UK and US in early 2025.

J K CHUKWU is a writer and visual artist from the Midwest. Her work has appeared in *Black Warrior Review*, *DIAGRAM*, and *TAYO*. Her debut novel is *The Unfortunates*.

BRIDGET COLLINS is the No. 1 bestselling author of *The Binding*, *The Betrayals* and *The Silence Factory*. Her short fiction has been published in *The Haunting Season* and *The Winter Spirits*.

MARIANA ENRÍQUEZ is an Argentine writer and editor. Her books include the novel *Our Share of Night* and story collections *A Sunny Place for Shady People*, *Things We Lost in the Fire* and *The Dangers of Smoking in Bed*, which was shortlisted for the International Booker Prize.

MICHEL FABER is an award-winning novelist and short fiction writer based in Kent, best known for his highly acclaimed novels *Under the Skin* and *The Crimson Petal and the White*.

LEWIS HANCOX is an influencer, filmmaker and illustrator from the North West of the UK. He is the author of *Welcome to St Hell: My Trans Teen Misadventure* (shortlisted for the Waterstones Children's Book Prize) and its sequel, *Escape from St Hell: My Trans Life Levels Up.*

EMILIA HART is a British-Australian writer. Her first novel, *Weyward*, was a *New York Times* bestseller and Richard and Judy Book Club pick. Her second novel, *The Sirens*, will be published in 2025.

AINSLIE HOGARTH is the author of four novels including *Normal Women* and *Motherthing*. You can find her short fiction in *Hazlitt*, *Black Static* and more.

ROBERT LAUTNER lives on the Pembrokeshire coast in a wooden cabin with his wife and children. He is the author of *The Road to Reckoning*, *The Draughtsman* and *Quint*.

ADORAH NWORAH is an Igbo writer from South-East Nigeria. Her work has been shortlisted for the Commonwealth Short Story Prize and longlisted for the Short Story Day Africa Prize. Her first novel, *House Woman*, came out in 2024.

IRENOSEN OKOJIE was born in Nigeria and moved to England aged eight. Her prize-winning novels and collections include *Butterfly Fish*, *Nudibranch* and *Curandera*. In 2021 she was awarded an MBE For Services to Literature.

LUCY ROSE is an author and award-winning filmmaker. Her short fiction and nonfiction have been published in *Dread Central*, *Mslexia*, and more. Lucy's debut novel, *The Lamb*, will be published in 2025.

LIONEL SHRIVER has written seventeen books including the international bestseller *We Need to Talk About Kevin*. Her journalism has appeared in the *Guardian* and the *New York Times*, the *Wall Street Journal* and many other publications.

JAMES SMYTHE is an award-winning novelist and screenwriter from London. He is best known for *The Machine*, *I Still Dream*, and *The Anomaly Quartet*.

LAVIE TIDHAR is a former columnist for the *Washington Post* and a current honorary Visiting Professor and Writer in Residence at the American International University in London. His books include *A Man Lies Dreaming*, *Osama* and *Central Station*. His next novel is called *Six Lives*.

FRANCINE TOON's debut novel *Pine* was a *Sunday Times* bestseller, won the 2020 McIlvanney Prize, was shortlisted for the Bloody Scotland Debut Prize and longlisted for the Highland Book Prize. She grew up in Scotland and lives in London, where she is working on her second novel.

EVIE WYLD's award-winning novels include *The Echoes*, *The Bass Rock* and *All the Birds, Singing*. In 2013 she was included on *Granta* magazine's once-a-decade Best of Young British Novelists list.

LOUISA YOUNG has written fifteen books of fiction and non-fiction, including the bestselling *My Dear I Wanted to Tell You*, which was shortlisted for the Costa Novel Award, and the *Lionboy* series (with her daughter). Her work is published in 32 languages.